Fire Bell in the Night

Fire Bell in the Night

A Western Story

TIM CHAMPLIN

SAGEBRUSH
Large Print Westerns

First published in Great Britain by ISIS Publishing Ltd.
First published in the United States by Five Star Westerns

Published in Large Print 2006 by ISIS Publishing Ltd.,
7 Centremead, Osney Mead, Oxford OX2 0ES,
United Kingdom,
by arrangement with
Golden West Literary Agency

British Library Cataloguing in Publication Data
Champlin, Tim, 1937–
    Fire bell in the night. – Large print ed. –
    (Sagebrush Western series)
    1. Kipling, Rudyard, 1865–1936 – Fiction
    2. Attempted assassination – Fiction
    3. Western stories
    4. Large type books
    I. Title
    813.5'4 [F]

ISBN 0–7531–7545–2 (hb)

Printed and bound in Great Britain by
T. J. International Ltd., Padstow, Cornwall

DEDICATION

To my brother-in-law, Ken Bundy

CHAPTER
ONE

May, 1889
Northern Pacific

Alex Thorne had to get some air. He staggered uphill through the haze in the smoking salon, levered the door handle, and thrust against the roll of the ship. Slipping through the narrow opening, he let the heavy door slam behind him.

Roaring blackness engulfed him. He groped blindly for a steel stanchion as the wet deck heaved up beneath his feet and the vessel began its roll to port. He clung to the stanchion that supported the deck above, oblivious to the salt spray that was soaking his white shirt. At least the air was cool and clean and he gratefully sucked it in.

The *City of Peking* paused at the bottom of her forty-five-degree roll. Then, with a twisting motion, she heaved herself upright. Continuing the slow, regular rhythm she had been dancing for the past twenty hours, the ship's bow fell off to starboard, the rest of the 421-foot vessel following, sliding down into the next trough.

Thorne's stomach rolled with it, and he had to swallow hard to keep from retching up what little supper he'd eaten. Crashing crockery sounded from within as stacks of dishes broke loose in the galley. The stern rose from the sea and the deck vibrated as the screws beat against empty air. A fitful moon popped out from scudding clouds long enough to reveal a smooth wave pouring solidly over the bow. The ship trembled and settled under the great weight of ocean. Would she come up? Thorne held his breath. Had she plunged too deep to rise again? Or would the next wave take the Pacific Mail steamer to the bottom? He hoped the succession of huge waves, rolling under her starboard bow, wouldn't eventually twist the long, four-masted steamer in half.

Yesterday, when no storm was raging, several of the ladies had questioned the captain about the reason for the rough seas.

"Heavy weather blowing somewhere south of us," he'd told them.

Nine hours ago, at noon, Thorne and several of the male passengers had begun to wager on the time of arrival of the next rogue wave that smote the ship every so often. After several hours, bets stopped when it became apparent chance was not a factor. A huge wave broke over the ship at exactly twenty-eight-minute intervals. They'd now come to anticipate it, to expect the electric lights to dim and flicker, and to brace themselves for the shock as the ship faltered and shuddered, heaving down, spilling food, beer, trunks, and furniture against the bulkheads.

Such a wave now struck the ship, forcing her ponderous hull far over. But she brought her bow up once more and continued at a reduced speed, tilting the mass of water back along the main deck, washing through the scuppers, pouring outboard through the clanging ports in the bulwarks.

Thorne clutched the metal pole, his pants wet to the knees from the rushing water.

A steward dodged past him and went into the smoking salon. Light from the open door gleamed briefly on the wet deck. Judging the wind gusts by the shrieking chorus in the overhead wire rigging, Thorne estimated them at fifty knots.

Earlier experience had taught him if he could fix his eyes on something that didn't appear to be moving, such as the horizon or a cloud, his inner ear would stabilize and his stomach calm down. But that wasn't possible at night. Maybe he should go to his cabin and lie down. He usually felt better flat on his back with the porthole open to the outside air.

He was ready to give the idea a try when the nearby door swung open and a smaller man emerged. "Whoa!" The man's foot slipped on the wet deck, and he grabbed for Thorne to steady himself.

"Wild night," Thorne greeted him, recognizing Rudyard Kipling, the young journalist from India he'd met the week before.

"Yes, but isn't it glorious!"

"Nature in all her splendor," Thorne returned, "if your stomach is immune to it."

There was no accounting for this seasickness, he thought. Passengers he expected to be convulsing sat calmly smoking and drinking while the steamer did its best to stand on its beam ends — fat, bald men, wiping pork grease from their double chins, bracing their bulk against the rolling as if nothing untoward was occurring. The very thought of this made him feel even worse.

He caught the odor of cigar smoke on Kipling's clothing as the two men held onto a pole across from each other.

"Twenty days from Japan to San Francisco, and the captain assured us a smooth passage," Kipling said, raising his voice above the steady roar of wind and sea.

"He may be a good captain, but he might as well be a stoker when it comes to predicting the weather," Thorne said. He and Kipling, each traveling alone, had met at dinner the second week out from Yokohama, and had taken an instant liking to each other. Thorne, whose reading was usually novels or short stories at bedtime, was surprised that he'd actually heard of this Britisher, a man already establishing himself as a rising literary light at the age of twenty-four. Thorne had even read some of the author's stories he'd picked up in pirated paper editions in the railway station before he'd left for the Far East.

"I had to get out of there," Kipling was saying. "No offense, but some of your countrymen make my ears tired with their bragging about America being the greatest this and the most wonderful that." He chuckled. "I came through the ladies salon and some

4

matron cornered me. She wanted to talk, and she was losing her audience as most of her friends were retiring to their cabins. I wanted to be polite and listen, but it quickly became obvious she only wanted to distract herself from this weather. Now I know what the picture of fear looks like. She thought as long as she was awake and running her mouth on inane subjects, the ship would stay afloat. But she was frightened half to death."

"How could you tell?" Thorne asked, shifting his weight as the deck tilted.

"The way she was gripping the tablecloth, her heaving bust, and her senseless giggling. Her gaze was jumping back and forth to the flickering lights, the stairway, and to any crewman who happened to pass through."

"With powers of observation like that, you'd make a good lawman or detective."

Kipling laughed. "No, thank you. I'll stick to writing verse and fictional tales."

"I'll have to say, you have a real talent for it."

"For composition, maybe, but not for diplomacy. I have to learn to hold my peace around blowhards spouting off on every subject about which they have a solid opinion, but little knowledge."

"Hard to do sometimes," Thorne said, beginning to feel considerably better. This man was a good conversationalist, seemingly mature beyond his years. But he was an even better writer, already famous beyond his native India. Thorne especially liked several of the so-called "Railroad Series" — tales such as "Soldiers Three", and "The Phantom Rickshaw", which had been originally published in India for distribution in cheap editions in railroad depots for people to read as they traveled. But, instead of being read, discarded, and forgotten, they had proven so well-written and interesting, they'd been reprinted and distributed in England and most of the British colonies. Kipling was already a name to be reckoned with in the English-language literary world, thanks, in part, to pirated American editions, on which no royalty was paid.

The prolific young journalist had not said so directly, but Thorne gathered from veiled hints that Kipling had been sent to report on America because the editors of his newspaper, the *Allahabad Pioneer*, were disturbed that he was making enemies by being too outspoken and brash. A few months abroad would do everyone some good.

Two wandering single men adrift on the vast Pacific Ocean, one nearly double the age of the other, but Thorne was nevertheless an admirer of the younger man's work. And the younger man, in turn, was an admirer of Thorne's experience and adventurous life. Why were people never satisfied with their lot? It was the nature of the beast, he supposed, or the nature of the universe.

"My spectacles are becoming coated with salt spray," Kipling said after a short silence.

"Too dark to see much out here anyway," Thorne returned.

"You said you were retired from the American Secret Service," Kipling said. "I find that fascinating. I envy your repertoire of knowledge. You probably have enough material in your background for a thousand stories."

"Probably so."

"With your permission, I'd like to use some of your tales in my verse or stories."

"Sure. I was in Tombstone in 'Eighty-One —"

"Did you witness the famous gunfight at the OK Corral?" Kipling interrupted. "Did you know the Earps?" The emerging author sounded like a hero-worshipping schoolboy.

"I knew the Earps, but I didn't get involved in their feuds. I didn't see the shoot-out. A friend from Wells Fargo and I worked undercover to expose a gang of robbers and killers. They were led by a former Confederate officer who was bitter about losing his home and family in the war. He was out to avenge himself on northern industrialists and to get rich at their expense."

"I must have the details . . . uh!" Both men were flung to the starboard side of the pole as the ship rolled. Kipling braced his feet while the wind whipped his black hair straight out. "We're scheduled to dock in California in three days. What are your plans from there?"

"Nothing specific or pressing. Going to stop and visit my sister and her family in Kentucky."

"So you'll be traveling east by train."

"Easier than horseback and carriage." At age forty-seven he'd had his fill of the wild places he could reach only by horseback. "The calluses on my backside are just beginning to go away," Thorne added. His trip to the Far East had been only a diversion to put off the decision of what to do with the rest of his life. Before that, he'd gone briefly to British Columbia to inquire about enlisting in the Canadian Mounted Police, but found he was well beyond the age of most recruits, and his experience as a lawman far outstripped that of the red-coated force, including the officers. Sadly he'd returned to the States and taken passage for the Orient to see more of the world.

"I'd say it's a bit unruly out here for civilized conversation!" Kipling cried above the gale of wind. "Why don't we retire to my cabin for a nightcap?"

"A little nip of brandy might be just what I need to settle my stomach," Thorne agreed.

Kipling picked a moment when the ship was on nearly an even keel, let go of the pole, and staggered aft, his coat-tails flying. Forty feet aft, along the walkway, no portholes leaked light outside; they were moving in blackness. The solid bulwarks had given way to a life line composed of three parallel strands of cable, attached to waist-high posts twelve feet apart. The two men hugged the inside of the narrow walkway against the bulkhead, maintaining a precarious balance on the wet, heaving deck.

Near the smokestack, they came to a break where a crosswalk passed through the superstructure to the opposite side of the ship. Thorne started to yell for Kipling to duck into this passage and take a door to the inside of the vessel. Suddenly a hooded figure came running out of the murk, collided with Kipling, and sent the writer sliding down the slanted deck on his back.

"Hey, you!" Thorne yelled, the wind whisking his voice away. But the phantom figure, cape flying, was disappearing down the deck at a run.

A strangled cry reached Thorne's ears above the roar as he saw a flash of white shirt on the deck. Kipling had slid under the bottom strand of cable and was caught only by his legs, the upper half of his body hanging out over the sea. The ship was at the bottom of its portside roll and the water washed up to deck level, cutting off Kipling's yell.

Thorne dove and slid sideways against the life lines, grabbing desperately for Kipling's feet. He got a shin with one hand and the toe of a shoe with the other. The smaller man was dead weight and the rushing water tore at him like some beast, trying to rip him away. But Thorne was a lean, muscular 175 pounds. Even if it broke the man's leg, he gritted his teeth and swore the sea would not get him.

For several agonizing moments, the issue was in doubt as he felt the writer's wet legs sliding from his grasp. Then the ship began to right herself and the rushing water dropped away from deck level. The ship leveled, then began a slow slant to starboard. Now Thorne had gravity on his side. Grasping the soggy clothing, then the belt, he kept a steady pressure on Kipling, reeling in the flailing man, hand over hand, like some half-drowned fish. When he was safely back on deck, Thorne dragged him into the crosswalk.

"Ruddy! Ruddy! You all right?" He turned the limp form over on his back and began ripping open the tie and collar. "Ruddy! My God, man, say something!" Thorne yelled, pounding Kipling's chest and praying the man hadn't inhaled any water.

Kipling's body jerked with a weak spasm, and he coughed. "*Ahhhgh!* You're crushing me!" He gurgled. "And what's this 'Ruddy'?" he managed to rasp hoarsely. "The name is 'Rudyard', or just plain 'Kipling'."

CHAPTER
TWO

Thorne went limp with relief. "Whew! You scared me. Thought you'd drowned. Stay right here. I'll go fetch the ship's doctor."

"I don't need a doctor," Kipling said, pushing himself to a sitting position. "Lost my glasses and I can't see a thing without them." He coughed and snorted, blowing water out of his nose. "Swallowed a good bit of the Pacific before I managed to shut my mouth and hold my breath."

Thorne helped him to his feet. "What's your cabin number?"

"Forty-Seven. Two thirds of the way aft on the port side."

Thorne half lifted and dragged his companion down the deck, staggering from side to side.

"Give me a chance. I can walk!" Kipling protested.

But the former Secret Service agent could feel the smaller man trembling with cold and the delayed shock of the near disaster, and kept a firm hold. "We're almost there."

Several minutes later, they were in the small cabin, the electric light on and the metal bolt slid on the door. Kipling stripped off his sopping clothing as Thorne found a bottle of brandy and two shot glasses in a bedside rack and poured them each a drink.

The writer pulled on a dry, collarless white shirt and a pair of nankeen trousers and sat down on the edge of the bunk. His face was pale and his lips nearly blue with cold. Black hair was plastered down on his forehead. "I'm a little weaker than I thought," he admitted, wiping the moisture from his face and hair with the hand towel Thorne had handed him. "Look in that trunk. There's a spare pair of spectacles in a brown leather case."

Thorne found the glasses, wiped the lenses clean, and handed them to Kipling.

"Much better," the writer said, adjusting the bows behind his ears. "Unfortunately I've had defective vision from birth. I never travel anywhere without two extra pairs of spectacles." He threw back the shot of brandy Thorne handed him. "Another," he gasped, handing back the small glass. Thorne refilled it, and Kipling took a more tentative sip.

"Feeling better?" Thorne eyed him anxiously.

The writer nodded. "Yes, and I have you to thank for saving my life. I'd have been feeding the sharks by now, except for your quick action. Who ran into me, anyway?"

"Didn't get a good look at him. He didn't bother to stop. Must've been in one helluva hurry."

"A crewman, you think? Some emergency? If so, I'll report the incident to the captain, first thing."

"Not sure," Thorne said. "Big man wearing a hooded cape. Crewmen don't wear such garb, even in foul weather. Yellow oilskins and southwesters are what they've got on when they're topside."

Kipling pulled out a pocket comb and began combing his damp hair in front of a tiny mirror fastened to the bulkhead near the bunk. "Well, I'll be damned sure to look among the passengers tomorrow for a hooded cape. Very rude and dangerous behavior. I could easily have been killed."

Thorne sipped his brandy, thankful for the warmth it was spreading through his chilled torso. He was soaked to the skin. "Do you have any enemies aboard?" he asked thoughtfully.

The writer turned back from the mirror and gave him a curious look. "Alex, I have a propensity for making enemies. It's my nature. When one speaks the truth, he makes enemies. If I haven't already told you, I was sent on this trip because I'd offended several high Indian officials . . . one in particular."

"Then I think you may have to face the possibility that someone just tried to kill you and make it look like an accident. Even if I'd seen who it was, or been able to stop him, he could have claimed it was just a tragic accident . . . the dark, the wet deck, the rolling ship. Men are lost overboard all the time in such weather." Thorne pulled out the only chair in the tiny cabin and sat down, bracing both feet on the edge of the bunk and the chair back against the bulkhead as the ship continued to roll and plunge. "Was it a hard blow, or did he just brush against you and knock you off balance?"

"Felt like I'd been bowled over," Kipling said firmly. "My neck's even sore where my head was whipped to one side. Never saw him coming."

"I'll be glad to have the ship's doctor check you up. Or are you feeling all right now?"

"Never better," the small man assured him. "If I have any problems come morning, I'll go to him."

"I forgot you have youth on your side." Thorne grinned, feeling gingerly of a bruise on his own thigh where he'd slid into one of the life-line stanchions.

"Although I'm in your debt for saving my life, I'm perfectly fine now," Kipling said when Thorne continued to regard him with an anxious look. "And frankly I'll have to put this incident down as nothing more than an accident. I didn't see who hit me, but I think you're making too much of it. Your years in the Secret Service have made you see something sinister lurking behind every coincidence. Mishaps *do* occur in life, you know. And the ship was rolling. No doubt he just staggered into me and didn't have the courtesy to say he was sorry."

"Maybe." Thorne let the matter drop, even though experience whispered that this was a deliberate attempt to harm the brash young writer.

"Besides," Kipling went on, "I haven't made anyone so angry that he'd want to feed me to the fishes. Even Americans couldn't be that touchy."

"Just be cautious from here on, in case you're wrong," Thorne said. He was wet through and growing weary. His stomach was under control now, so he got up and slid back the bolt on the door. "I'll say good night then." He paused with the door ajar. "See you at breakfast about seven-thirty?"

"Right you are."

As Thorne went out, he heard the ship's bell clanging erratically — a sound he'd been hearing for hours since the heavy rolling began. It was probably causing some confusion for the changes of the watch. The scudding clouds had blown away and the half moon was evidently out to stay, its light glistening on the ridges of water that continued to roll under the ship.

On a hunch, he took one last turn around the deck before retiring. Feet spread to steady himself, he circled the ship. But everything was quiet. By the light of a porthole, he saw a black-faced stoker conferring with one of the engineers. Because of the water being taken over the bow, the look-out had been removed from the eyes of the ship and stationed somewhere aloft. Thorne made a turn through the lighted salons, where several diehards were still playing cards and smoking cigars. But the rest of the passengers had left to spend the remainder of the night holding to the sides of their bunks.

Thorne finally went to his own cabin amidships on the port side. He stripped off his wet clothes and shoes and hung them on the back of the door to dry. Then he pulled on a pair of dry shorts. With a key he opened his steamer trunk and realized, with a slight pang, that nearly all his worldly possessions were contained within. Except for much experience and many memories, what had he to show for all those years? More than half his life was gone. But gone where?

Spent how? Did he have any regrets? Fortunately there were few. If he had it to do over — but he didn't, so there was an end to it. Thoughts like this came to him only in the night when he was fatigued or sick. No man could see the whole picture of his life; it was too close to him. But he had to assume that his accomplishments far outweighed the errors or the deliberate wrongdoings.

His hand, probing under the clean clothing, encountered his gun belt. He pulled it out. The worn, stained leather was still supple. Even though the .44 cartridges filling the belt loops had not been used in months, his constant cleaning had kept verdigris from forming where the brass lay against the leather. He pulled out the revolver. A blue-black 1875 model Remington with stag grips. Just after he'd purchased it fourteen years ago, he'd paid a gunsmith to take an inch off the standard seven-and-a-half inch barrel. He'd discovered that he was not a good shot with the longer barrel, and an even worse shot with a much shorter one. This length suited him perfectly, and he was surprisingly good with it. The weapon had saved his life on more than one occasion. He flipped open the loading gate and turned the cylinder, hearing the oily clicking as he dropped the cartridges into his hand, one by one. He wiped them off and reloaded, then shoved the long, slender weapon back into its holster. Why did he still tote this thing around? It was only a memento of his former life now. Although many men in the West still went armed, he saw little need to do so since his retirement. After all, this *was* 1889. The country was settling down and becoming civilized. All the major Indian tribes had been subdued and confined to reservations. Some of the cavalry units had been pulled to patrol Yellowstone National Park against poachers and destructive tourists. A few scattered outlaw gangs still ran loose, but they were being hunted down and were fast disappearing from the West. Not that there wasn't still danger from robbers and murderers in society, but the edge of excitement and danger he'd been used to was gone. Except where people were crowded together in the major cities, fat, bald policemen with pocket revolvers could handle most of the crime these days.

A year of retirement had not yet dulled the survival instincts he'd honed during all those dangerous assignments.

He rocked back on his heels and held the gun belt in his hands for several moments. He'd learned to trust his instincts, and his instincts now told him that Rudyard Kipling was in some kind of danger. He laid the gun belt atop the shirt, canvas pants, and vest he'd set aside to wear in the morning.

CHAPTER
THREE

Thorne was late for breakfast. Normally an early riser, he had been tossed and thrown during the night until he'd been forced to wedge himself into his bunk with a pillow and a bedroll from his trunk. Just when he was on the verge of sleep, the violent motion of the ship had flung him sideways and awakened him. The last time he'd reached into his shoe under the bunk and pulled out his watch, it was just after three. Finally exhaustion took him and he slept until eight o'clock.

He'd dressed hurriedly, strapping on his gun belt. He was a careful, conscientious man who hated to miss appointments. And even though his promise to meet Kipling for a seven-thirty breakfast was an informal commitment, it went against his nature to be late.

When he entered the salon, breakfast was in full swing. Kipling had finished eating and was savoring a cup of coffee while in animated discussion with several men at his table. He caught Thorne's eye and motioned him over.

Thorne sidled up to the group, but didn't interrupt the flow of conversation as he helped himself to some ham and toast. The sea had calmed somewhat and, consequently, so had his stomach. His balky appetite had returned in full force.

"They call us a republic. We may be, but I don't think so," a middle-aged American in shirt sleeves was saying. "You Britishers have got the only republic worth the name. You run your ship of state with a gilt figurehead, but the Queen doesn't cost you half of what our system of pure democracy costs us. Politics in America? It's a spoils system. We fight over gas contracts, tram contracts, road contracts . . . any darned thing that can turn a dishonest dollar, and they call that politics!" He rose from his chair as he became more agitated. "Only a low-down man would run for Congress or the Senate. The Senate of the freest people on earth is bound by monopolies. If I had money enough, I could buy the whole blessed Senate, the eagle, and the star-spangled banner to boot." He threw up his hands in impotent frustration.

"I've been around the world three times," another man chimed in, "and I've never yet seen a people who can govern themselves. You give the rabble the vote and they're as strong as the intelligent, decent citizen. You can't persuade the mobs of any country to become decent citizens."

"You're right," a fat man agreed. "We're bound hand and foot by the Irish vote. There's no damned good in an Irishman, except as a fighter. He doesn't understand work, he has a natural gift of gab, and he can drink a man blind. These three qualifications make him a first-class politician."

Kipling kept silent and looked sideways at Thorne. The Englishman's eyes were magnified by the lenses in the wire-rimmed frames. Thorne himself was rather amazed by the condemnations these Americans were heaping upon their own country in front of a British subject.

One after another, the men tried to outdo themselves, usually prefacing their remarks with — "I'm an American by birth from 'way back," or "My people have been in this country for more than a hundred years, so I know ..." And then they proceeded to pile abuse on the Irish as the most recent immigrants, or on the masses of Germans or Poles or Italians they lumped together as "common rabble".

Wiping his mustache with a napkin, Kipling leaned over to Thorne and whispered: "It must be an awful thing to live in a country where you have to explain that you really belong there."

"We made the mistake of giving every scalawag who comes across the water the same privileges we've made for ourselves," a heavy-set man said, looking at Kipling. "You Britishers will have the same thing to go through. You're beginning to rot now, because you're putting power into the hands of untrained people. When you reach our level . . . every man with a vote and the right to sell it, the right to nominate men like himself to swamp out better men . . . you'll be what we are now . . . rotten, rotten!"

"You'll never catch me contradicting a man who slams his own country," Kipling remarked *sotto voce* to Thorne.

20

"The more power you give the people, the more trouble they give," the heavy-set American continued, growing somewhat red in the face. Thorne wondered if he'd been nipping at a bottle this early in the morning. "With us, our better classes are corrupt, and our lower classes are lawless. We execute our justice in the streets. The law courts are no use. There are millions of decent, law-abiding citizens, and they're very sick of this whole business."

Another man brought up the Haymarket Square riots in Chicago three years before.

"Hell, I was there when the bomb went off," a lean man stated, and they began comparing notes. Several others started conversing with two Japanese business-men who were listening from the next table.

Kipling was gradually ignored, and he took advantage of the lull to get up and refill his coffee cup. Thorne joined him to add some fried potatoes from a chafing dish on the sideboard along the bulkhead. "Well, you've finally learned to keep your opinions to yourself," Thorne said as he moved alongside.

"It's a reporter's job to listen," Kipling replied with a mischievous grin.

"I'm sure you put in a sage word or two at the right moment to get 'em stirred up."

"Possibly. But it didn't take much to get this group going. They'd rather argue politics and world affairs than eat."

"These men are affluent and can afford to travel," Thorne said. "You'll hear an entirely different view of things in America if you take the time to listen to the poorer, working people once we get ashore."

"I can't wait," he said as the two men strolled to a far side of the room and sat down by themselves at a small table.

"Pretend you're telling me some story," Kipling said, pulling a notebook and pencil from his inside coat pocket. "That'll give me a reason to be writing. I've got to get most of this down while it's fresh in my mind."

"Still sending those letters back to your newspaper?"

"Yes. In exchange for them footing the bill for this trip."

"Are you simply reporting on what you see and hear, or are you editorializing?"

"Some are direct quotes, mixed with my impressions." He smiled. "A lot more entertaining than just dull facts. Mark Twain was practicing that same sort of journalism a quarter century ago, and look where it got him." He continued to scribble away as fast as his hand could move, pausing now and then to hold the pencil to pursed lips with a faraway look in his eyes, searching his memory, or his imagination.

If Kipling noticed Thorne wearing a gun strapped to his waist, he didn't mention the fact — which was fine with the former lawman; he didn't want to go into any long explanations for his sudden change of costume. He was the only man in the salon who carried a weapon in plain view.

Thorne fell silent to let Kipling jot down his notes for later transcription. He was glad the writer had not

22

mentioned last night's excitement. To the Englishman, it was an incident of no significance, just a close call, over and forgotten. Looking out through a nearby port, he saw the weather clearing and the sea calmer. There was no reason anyone would be wearing a hooded cape this morning. If he were to see such an outfit before they docked, he would still have no way of proving anyone had deliberately tried to harm Kipling. But it was a warning, and now Thorne was forearmed. He would have to think of a good reason — besides admiring his short stories and verse — to stay close to the smaller man for a few days, in case there was another attempt to do him harm.

"I have a working knowledge of San Francisco," Thorne ventured casually, finishing his food and putting down his fork. "Be glad to show you around when we land."

"Capital!" Kipling exclaimed, and then went on:

" 'Serene, indifferent to fate,
Thou sittest at the western gate,
Thou seeest the white seas fold their tents,
Oh warder of two continents.
Thou drawest all things small and great,
To thee beside the western gate.' "

"Did you just compose that?" Thorne asked.
"No. Your own Bret Harte did."
"He's *your* Bret Harte now. I understand he's been residing in England the past few years."

"Mostly to escape a bitchy wife than for any great love of the English, I'd say." Kipling chuckled. "But San Francisco's a fabled city. I can hardly wait to see it."

"Then I'll be your guide."

When the *City of Peking* docked at the San Francisco waterfront two days later, Thorne had his steamer trunk trundled off by a drayman and put aboard a freight wagon to be hauled to the Palace Hotel. He considered taking poorer lodgings but decided that, if a man lived only once in this world, he should do it as well as he could afford to.

In the bustle to clear the ship, he'd hoped to accompany Kipling ashore, but was surprised to see the journalist cornered by a local reporter near the gangway. The reputation of this budding English writer had already spread to America to such an extent that reporters sought him out before he'd even set foot in the country.

Thorne paused and moved back against the rail as the passengers streamed by him.

A purser stood at the head of the gangway to assist disembarking passengers as needed. Muscular stevedores were lugging boxes, bags, and trunks of all sizes through the throng of men and women who were talking and laughing and saying goodbye to shipboard friends.

"Can you give me your impression of American journalism compared to journalism in India?" the young reporter asked, pencil and pad poised.

"I can't very well do that until I've had a chance to examine the American product," Kipling replied.

"Then tell me something about journalism in India," the reporter persisted.

Over the heads of departing passengers, Thorne saw Kipling take a deep breath and start to talk. Thorne caught his eye, and the writer rolled his eyes upward in resignation as the reporter scribbled on his pad. *Pumping the gullible young newsman full of lies,* Thorne thought, motioning that he would meet him ashore. Kipling nodded, without breaking stride in his recitation.

An hour later, Thorne had checked in, had his trunk taken to a third-floor room, and was back out on the street, trying to regain his land legs. He waited another half hour in the vicinity of the hotel lobby, expecting to see Kipling. When he didn't show, Thorne assumed there'd been some delay, and decided to take a stroll to stretch his legs. He walked down to Market Street where the sidewalk was relatively level. After twenty days at sea, the solid earth seemed to be tilting under his feet.

Late afternoon shadows were filling in the spaces between the buildings when Thorne started back to the hotel. He went a block west and turned a corner into a street of small wooden houses. The gutters had collected newspapers and bottles. An empty kerosene tin clattered along the cobblestones as a group of shouting children played kick-the-can. Ahead he noticed a man in a black suit and bowler hat in animated conversation with a boy seated on a curbside dray. The mustache, the glasses, the demeanor — and then the dialect. It was Kipling.

"You want to go to the Palace Hotel?" the youth asked. "What the hell are you doing down here then? This is about the lowest place in the city. Go six blocks north to Market and Geary . . . then walk around until you strike the corner of Sutter and Sixteenth. And that brings you there."

Thorne smiled at the perplexed look on the writer's face as he struggled to absorb these rapid-fire directions. Then he looked up and saw Thorne approaching.

"Ahh, there's my guide. Never mind, son, I can make it from here."

The lad shook his head and popped the reins over the backs of his draft horses.

"I'm certainly glad to see you!" Kipling cried, greeting Thorne with a relieved smile. "I've gotten myself in a real tangle."

"Come on. I've been looking for you. I know the way to the hotel. Where's your luggage?"

"I paid the driver of the omnibus to take it on ahead for me while I talked to that ignorant reporter."

"Did you spin him some yarns?"

Kipling fell into step beside him. "It's a pity to enter a city of three hundred thousand white people with a lie on my lips. I admit, I gave him a few fabrications."

"If you plan to be famous, you'll have to put up with a lot of stupid questions from reporters."

"I'm already famous." He spoke matter-of-factly, with no hint of braggadocio.

26

Thorne made no reply, but wondered about the cockiness of this self-assured young man. Already complaining of the aggravations of fame at the age of twenty-four.

The streets were full of pedestrians, and Kipling was carefully observing them as they streamed past. "Think of it! Thousands of people gathered together on this seven-by-eight-mile peninsula, walking on real pavement in front of real plate-glass windowed shops . . . and talking something not too different from English."

"I fancy they'd think your dialect is somewhat akin to the native tongue," Thorne said, smiling to himself. A good writer this man surely was, but he was even more entertaining in person.

"We don't seem to be headed in the right direction," Kipling said, looking around, trying to get his bearings. "Where's the corner of Sixteenth and Gutter?"

"*Gutter?* The name of the street is Sutter, after John Sutter who owned the mill where gold was discovered in 'Forty-Nine."

"Well, whatever it is, are we getting close? I'm tired of walking. Been lost for over an hour. And I'm still wobbly from riding the waves for three weeks."

"Another ten or fifteen minutes and we'll be there."

"Did you ever see such beautiful, well-dressed women?" Kipling marveled. "If Americans want to brag on something, they could forget the politics and the military and start with the gorgeous women!"

"I'll have to agree with you there."

"One of the former Union officers on board ship was going on about this harbor and how well defended it is," Kipling said. " 'The finest harbor in the world, sir!' he bragged to me. Maybe so, but I could see with half an eye that the blockhouse guarding the mouth of the Bay could be silenced by two gunboats from Hong Kong with safety, comfort, and dispatch."

"Might be a good idea to keep some of those opinions to yourself," Thorne said.

"Protect me from the wrath of an outraged community if my letters to my newspaper are ever read by American eyes," Kipling said. "Before I leave this city in a few days, I'll have a batch of letters ready to post."

"Cut across the street here," Thorne said, and stepped off the curb in the middle of the block. "Look out!"

Kipling jumped forward just in time to avoid being struck in the back by a cable car. "By God, it sneaked up on me. I never heard it coming."

They gained the opposite curb, and Kipling watched the red-and-gold cable car gliding along down the street. "Some silent, invisible means of locomotion," he observed.

"A cable runs along in a slot between the tracks at a constant seven or eight miles an hour. When the car wants to go, the grip man clamps onto it . . . when he wants to stop, he lets go and applies the brakes," Thorne explained. "There's a powerhouse somewhere that constantly winds the cable."

"Amazing. Quiet, efficient, and dependable."

He started to say something else, but was interrupted by a commotion in the street a hundred yards ahead.

Three or four people appeared to be struggling. Something glittered in the last rays of sunlight. As the two men approached, a fat policeman emerged from a knot of people, holding a Chinaman who'd been stabbed in the eye and was bleeding. The blue-uniformed officer hustled the Chinaman off down the street, and the others dispersed.

Kipling and Thorne halted a few yards away to watch.

"Damnedest thing I ever saw," Kipling said, taking off his hat and wiping his face with a white handkerchief. "In India or England that would have attracted a crowd of curious spectators so thick you couldn't push your way through them."

"It's nobody else's affair," Thorne said. "So everyone just goes about his own business."

"I find that lack of interest very strange."

"Violence is a daily thing in this country, especially in the big cities and in the West," Thorne said as they resumed walking toward the hotel. "You'll soon get used to it."

"I suppose that's why you pay your constables and policemen. He was just doing his job. I wonder what happened to the man who did the stabbing?"

Thorne shrugged. "Here in San Francisco you'll find that the Chinese live and die by their own code, their own rules. The white population doesn't mix in, except to keep civil order."

The two men arrived at the hotel to find Kipling's trunk in the lobby. After some discussion with the desk clerk, he finally got two porters assigned to carry it up to his room.

"Your room is only two doors down from mine on the third floor," Thorne remarked as he and Kipling trudged up the carpeted stairway in the wake of two burly porters.

"Did you see that desk clerk?" Kipling snorted. "In India a generous tip like I gave him would buy some service. He was humming and picking his teeth and stopped to pass the time of day with some friend before he deigned to ring for these porters. I guess he was trying to impress on me that he was my equal. Hell, judging from the diamond ring he was wearing, he's probably my superior."

Thorne decided to go lightly on this newcomer. "Money in this country will buy service, but not subservience."

Kipling gave him an odd, sideways look. "If a man is paying for a service, I think he has a right to expect that the person being paid devote his whole attention to the job."

"You're still too class-conscious. You'll soon get used to American ways. They mean no offense."

"I guess it's just their superior attitude that galls me. But I'll keep my mouth shut, since I'm only a traveler in this country."

The two men stopped talking and devoted all their breath to keeping up with the porters who were a full flight ahead of them. By the time they'd reached the third-floor hallway, Kipling had caught up and had his key out to let them into his room.

The two men parted to change clothes, arranging to meet in the lobby for a drink and supper.

Thorne found Kipling leaning against a marble pillar when he arrived, the Englishman dressed in a pair of gray, striped pants, white shirt, vest, and tie. "Let's have a drink first," Kipling said, motioning toward a barroom off the lobby.

Thorne nodded, and they went into the dimly lit interior. Thorne ordered a steam beer and Kipling a gin and tonic.

"Did you see those men lounging in the lobby?" the writer asked, leaning on the polished bar and sipping his drink.

"What about them?"

"Top hats, frock coats . . . they're dressed like they're going to a ball. It's the kind of thing we'd put on for a wedding in India . . . if we even possessed such clothes. Diamond stickpins in their cravats." He shook his head and turned his back on the bar to scan the room. His foot hit a pot-sized spittoon whose flared top clattered against the brass rail. He stepped to one side with a distasteful look on his face. "And that's another thing. You'd think that men who dressed like a million dollars would have a little breeding. But they all spit in public. Everybody spits. Look . . . there are four cuspidors just along this bar. There are spittoons on the staircases, in my room, even in the privy. And, from the looks of them, they're constantly in use. Tobacco chewing is a filthy habit."

"According to some ladies I know, it's no worse than cigar smoking," Thorne returned mildly, indicating the slim cigar Kipling was trimming with his penknife.

"All this spitting makes me nauseous," he continued as if Thorne hadn't spoken.

"They have no filth in India?" Thorne chided him.

"Not among the upper classes, at least," he said.

"Different customs," Thorne said, tipping up his beer glass. He heard Kipling mutter something about making a silk purse out of a sow's ear.

Kipling nodded at some boisterous men at the other end of the bar. "And what's the big hurry?" he asked. "Men here don't take a civilized amount of time to get on the outside of their drinks. Those men have each had at least two drinks while I've been sipping on one. Does everyone here just drink to get drunk?"

"I know a good steak house," Thorne said, ignoring the question. "Let's go eat. I'm about to starve."

Ten minutes later they were seated in a cable car sliding smoothly up a very steep hill.

"Absolutely amazing!" Kipling marveled. "No need to grade down some of these hills. Cable cars level them for you. No effort, no strain. I believe these things could climb straight up a building." His enthusiasm equaled his earlier derision. "And your women!" He whistled softly under his breath as two buxom young ladies stepped aboard the car and brushed by, a delicate fragrance of lilac trailing past. "Well endowed to show off those expensive clothes."

"Well, then I sez to her . . . 'Mabel, you were mighty right to throw him out, bag and baggage . . .' "

32

"If I'd been her . . ."

Snatches of the women's conversation drifted to them.

"That ruins the effect altogether," Kipling groaned. "Great to look at, but terrible to listen to. Same kind of thing you'd hear from white servant girls the world over. Too bad they don't just parade around with their mouths shut."

"Are you always so outspoken?" Thorne asked. "I'm surprised someone hasn't challenged you to a duel by now."

"Dueling is outlawed where I come from. Only in a barbarous country such as America does it still exist."

The cable car jerked around a corner, the bell clanging. Thorne glanced about quickly to be sure the passengers seated nearby could not overhear them.

"Now that I've heard their voices," Kipling continued, "all the charm of Bret Harte is being ruined for me. I find myself, through his rhythmical prose, catching the cadence of his peculiar fatherland."

Thorne was fascinated by this viewpoint, but inclined to let the impetuous youth have his say.

"I have a good friend on my newspaper back home who is also an admirer of Bret Harte. If I could only get an American lady to read aloud to him 'How Santa Claus Came to Simpson's Bar' so he could hear how much is left under her tongue of the beauty of the original . . ." He shook his head. "A Hindu has his own language, and a Frenchman speaks French, but the Americans have no language . . . they are all dialect, slang, and provincialism. There is no proper form of English spoken here that I've heard so far."

"Including mine?"

"A man must make allowances for his guide."

They stopped at a restaurant and ate a steak dinner with baked potato and green beans. Kipling ceased his caustic comments long enough to stoke up on the food as if he'd not eaten in three days. They paid their bill and, on the way out, passed by the double doors leading into the adjacent barroom.

"By God, what is that . . . pigs at the trough?"

Thorne glanced in. "No. Free lunch. It's a standard custom in America. For the price of a drink, a man can eat all the free food he wants . . . usually pickled eggs, bread, cheese, salty pickles . . . the sort of thing guaranteed to create a thirst."

Kipling stopped and gazed, his eyes behind the spectacles wide with wonder. "For something less than a rupee, an Indian could feed himself sumptuously in San Francisco, even if he were stranded and bankrupt."

Just as they turned to leave, a man bounced out of the bar, waving a small notebook. "Mister Kipling! Mister Kipling! May I have a word with you for our readers? I'm a reporter for *The Call*." He fumbled in his shirt pocket for a pencil. He reeked of wine.

While Thorne backed away a few paces, the reporter began to pepper Kipling with the same inane questions about Indian journalism that the previous reporter had asked him. Every time Kipling tried to turn the questions toward his fiction and verse, the reporter changed the subject. Thorne could see the writer getting more and more frustrated. Yet Thorne was again amazed that this young man from India was already so famous he was recognized and accosted on sight by strangers. Even Thorne, who had read and enjoyed the young man's writing, had not identified Kipling until he was introduced to him aboard ship.

Without being outright rude, Kipling finally tore himself away from the persistent reporter, and the two men made their escape into the fog-shrouded street outside.

"Someone needs to teach these newsmen how to conduct an interview." The air was damp and cool as the mist rolled in off the Pacific. "Should have worn my jacket," Kipling said, rubbing his arms against a chill wind that blew down the street. The thickening fog created a dim halo around the gas street lamp and softened the shapes of carriages and pedestrians to ethereal figures.

"I'd like a hot toddy to warm up with after dinner," Kipling said. "But I wouldn't risk going back into the barroom and encountering that reporter again."

"I've got just the thing for you," Thorne said. "Put a spring in your step and a bloom in your cheek. You won't feel the cold at all."

"What's that?"

"Follow me." Thorne took off at a fast walk that had Kipling almost running to keep up. Into the depths of the commercial part of the city they went. Bank buildings and telegraph wires seemed to crowd out everything else. In the middle of a block Thorne paused and peered through the swirling fog until he was sure

he had found what he was looking for. "Down here."
He pointed, then led the way down five steps into a
partially subterranean room. It was a well-lighted
German saloon.

"What'll it be, gents?" The blond, raw-boned
bartender made Thorne look small.

"My friend and I will have two button punches."

The massive blond mustache stretched in a wide
grin. "It'll take ten minutes to brew, but the result is the
highest and noblest product of the age. It's worth the
wait." With that cryptic comment he went to mix the
drinks.

Shortly after, they were handed two full glasses, and
Thorne toyed with his while he watched Kipling take a
long sip. The writer put his glass down with a strange
look on his face and stared straight ahead. Then he took
another long draft, set the glass down, and licked his
lips. "My!" He took a deep breath. "What is this
composed of?"

"Only Otto Krueger knows," Thorne replied,
nodding toward the smug-looking bartender. "And he's
not telling."

"Then I have a theory," Kipling said, taking another
swallow. "It is compounded of the shavings of cherubs'
wings, the glory of a tropical dawn, the red clouds of
sunset, and fragments of lost epics by dead masters."

"Close enough," Otto Krueger concurred.

"You were right," Kipling said when they were back on
the foggy street. "I don't feel the cold at all. Yet I don't
feel the least bit drunk. Actually I feel an intoxication

with living. I want to experience more of this great city. I've heard the men in fancy dress and gold watch chains discuss theories of government over their bourbons, and I've also heard the common laborers talk the practicalities of ward politics over their beer mugs. Now I want to see the heathen Chinese in their dens and find out how they live and what they contribute."

"You want to go into Chinatown?"

"Isn't that one of the things this city is famous for?"

"Infamous maybe."

"You're the guide. Are you up for it?"

Thorne hesitated for a moment. "All right, let's go." He took off at a fast walk to stay warm. After several blocks, they began to see brick buildings with oriental signs painted on them. Thorne slowed and began looking for a particular building that he knew from past experience contained four stories below ground as well as the same number above. Finally, after cutting through a narrow alley crowded with stalls and overhead balconies, he turned a corner and stopped. "Here."

Kipling paused and pulled out a pocket handkerchief to wipe the mist from his glasses.

From all appearances the street was nearly deserted except for a shadowy figure passing quickly along the far side.

Thorne reached into his pocket for a silver dollar as they approached a brick alcove near the barred iron door. He heard Kipling gasp with surprise as a kimono-clad figure silently moved out of the dark to accept the proffered *cumshaw*. Then a claw-like hand slid back the iron bar and swung the door open for them to enter.

Down some wooden steps they went to the first landing where a small lantern gave the minimum light to see the next flight of stairs. Thorne slowed but kept going. If Kipling wanted to see all the vices and filth of a crowded Chinese quarter, here was a typical example. There was no need to hunt farther. They caught a glimpse of bunks filled with reclining, skeletal figures. The sweetish smell of burning opium smote his nose. On the third level down, painted, mask-like faces of impassive prostitutes regarded their passage. The air was thick with the smell of perfume mingled with smoldering opium and pungent tobacco. Claustrophobia reached out to smother them in the fetid atmosphere.

Finally at the bottom of the fourth flight of steps, Thorne passed into a room where four men sat, playing poker, at a small table. In this pit, the air was thick as butter, and tiny lamps were able to burn only inch-square holes in it.

No one paid the slightest heed to the two newcomers, so intent were they on their game. The slapping of pasteboard cards and whispers of silken sleeves were the only sounds in the dense atmosphere. Sweat began to trickle down Thorne's temples in the extreme heat.

As his eyes grew accustomed to the dark, Thorne could see that three of the players were Chinese, with queues tucked under their hats. The fourth man was larger and appeared to be some sort of half-breed

Mexican with a thin black mustache. All were dressed in a combination of Oriental and Western garb. If Thorne had been an imaginative illustrator, he could not have painted a more villainous-looking group. Thorne and Kipling edged back along the wall and the game continued.

After several minutes, the sweet notes of "Shenandoah" began to swell softly from a harmonica somewhere above. A shiver ran up Thorne's back at this incongruous sound. He looked but saw nothing. *Maybe an American customer in the whorehouse*, he thought. Just then an exchange of sharp words jerked his attention back to the table. The Mexican and the Chinaman opposite him were in some sort of argument. The Chinaman reached out a thin arm and raked the pile of coins and paper money toward himself. The Mexican half rose from his chair. Thorne saw it coming and instinctively yanked Kipling to the floor. The next instant the explosion of a pistol blasted their ears in the confined space. Thorne yanked his Remington and rolled to his knees. White smoke curled lazily in the lamplight. The Mexican was gone. The Chinaman was leaning over, both hands on the arms of his chair. "Ah," he said, in the tone of a man discovering a great truth. Then he collapsed to the floor, a red stain spreading over the middle of his white shirt. The two other Chinamen stooped over the fallen man, talking rapidly in Chinese.

"Go!" Thorne yelled.

Kipling needed no urging. The reedy wail of the harmonica came again as Kipling sprang for the stairs.

He caught his foot on the second step and fell face forward just as two shots thundered above. One bullet thudded into the packed earthen floor; a second dug splinters from the edge of the bottom step. Thorne yanked the smaller man backward and fired once toward the muzzle flash. They crouched in the darkness of a corner under the wooden steps, but Thorne could see nothing above them in the murk. One of the lamps on the next landing had been obliterated.

"Probably that damned Mexican, making sure he wasn't being chased," Thorne said.

Kipling crouched behind him, breathing hard, evidently on the verge of panic. "Let's get out of here before the police come!" Kipling said urgently.

"You don't have to worry about the police down here," Thorne said, gripping his Colt. "As I told you, these people settle their own differences." They waited a few seconds more.

"OK, when I give the word, we jump and run straight up those stairs and outside," Thorne told him. "Stay right on my heels. I'll shoot our way out, if need be. If anything happens to me, you keep going. And don't stop until you're out of Chinatown. Ready?"

The little man nodded, eyes wide behind his glasses. "Now!"

CHAPTER
FOUR

Thorne had never run up four flights of steps any faster. Kipling was clattering right on his heels. So close were they, one bullet could have gone through both of them. But they met no opposition. Thorne caught glimpses of Oriental faces — some startled, but most impassive — flashing by as he vaulted upward, two steps at a time. His senses were keyed to the top, but he neither saw nor heard the gunman.

Even the keeper of the iron door was absent as they flung it open and dashed into the foggy street. They ran a block toward their hotel before Thorne staggered to a stop, holstered his Colt, and bent forward, hands on knees, gasping.

Kipling leaned against a brick wall, utterly winded. It was a good two minutes before either of them spoke.

"The . . . Mexican," Thorne panted, straightening up and peering around at the deserted street.

Kipling pulled out a handkerchief, took off his glasses, and wiped the perspiration and mist from his face and glasses. "I . . . can't believe that . . . a man was just shot, maybe . . . killed, and we were shot at . . . and there's not a sign of a constable or policeman anywhere."

"No one heard it," Thorne said, drawing in a deep lungful of the cool, moist air. "We were four flights down. Besides . . . the sound of gunfire is nothing new here. Even if that Chinaman dies, nothing will be reported to the authorities."

"I . . . have little personal acquaintance with pistols as a way . . . of settling disputes," Kipling said, still breathless. "But I noticed . . . that at least half the men in saloons carry pistols."

"Used to be more than that," Thorne said, his breathing beginning to steady. He started walking, and Kipling fell in beside him.

"A barbaric country where the constabulary can't keep the peace."

"Most are private quarrels," Thorne said. "Easier, quicker, and cheaper than clogging the courts by suing each other over private grievances. And, in the end, justice is probably served just as well."

"Whoever gets off the first shot, or the most accurate shot is the one who wins the case, regardless of the right or wrong of the matter," Kipling remarked.

"It's doubtful if our judges are any better. Judges and juries and witnesses are *all* subject to bribes and threats. With a gun, the matter is decided quickly and that's the end of it."

"Are you saying you condone such practices?"

"Not in most cases. After all, I was in law enforcement for twenty years. I'm just telling you the realities of our customs and society."

"As I said, this is a barbaric country," Kipling reiterated. "Nonetheless, thank you for having the courage and presence of mind to get us out of there safely."

"Going into Chinatown was a bad idea to begin with."

"If I'm going to experience this country, I want to experience all of it."

"OK by me," Thorne said, eyes and ears automatically alert to everything around him. They were walking down the middle of the street to avoid anyone who might be lurking in alleys or doorways. An occasional pedestrian ghosted silently through the mist, dressed in quilted clothing. While Thorne's senses were alert, his mind was reviewing what had just happened. He tried to recall the details, and the only odd thing that seemed out of place in this underground world was the sound of the harmonica. Just a strange coincidence in a world of strangeness. The Mexican had been outnumbered and had fired a couple of shots down the stairwell to discourage pursuit. Surely it was nothing more than that. Two close calls in less than a week. Perhaps Kipling was one of those individuals who seemed to attract trouble. Or maybe he was always present when some kind of violence was taking place. He filed the incident away in his memory.

"San Francisco has only one drawback," Kipling proclaimed a week later while he and Thorne were preparing to board a train for Oregon.

"Only one?" Thorne said. "And what might that be?" he asked half-heartedly, expecting the usual tirade against all things American.

" 'Tis very hard to leave," he replied simply, casting his gaze on the bustle of passengers around him.

Porters had loaded their trunks, and the two men, leather grips in hand, now stepped carefully over several sets of tracks at the Oakland terminus in search of their train. The huffing and clanging of a half dozen locomotives gave warnings of their approach, and Kipling had to stop talking to dodge the slowly shunting trains. "Nothing approaching a platform in this depot," he said, catching his toe on a rail and stumbling forward out of the way of a threatening cowcatcher.

"Ah, here we go," Thorne said, spotting their waiting coaches on track eleven. They climbed aboard and found their facing seats in the Pullman, sinking down gratefully on the green velvet cushions.

"Boooooard!" the conductor's muted voice came from outside, and the train jerked into motion, proceeding out of the station into the suburbs at a stately twenty-five miles an hour.

"I'm surprised you don't have at least five fatalities a day," Kipling said, watching the pedestrians, children, and carts moving nonchalantly out of the way as the train chugged past houses and shops. "Nobody seems to pay heed to these iron monsters."

" 'Familiarity breeds contempt,' " Thorne quoted.

For the past week, while Kipling had been sought out by reporters and invited to clubs and dinners by prominent men of the city, Thorne had looked up some old acquaintances and visited the office of the western branch of the U.S. Secret Service. He'd been amazed at the changes in procedure, the new faces he saw there. Although he'd been gone only a year, time was swiftly leaving him behind. He'd worked mostly in the field, so many office personnel were not familiar with him; a few appeared to have forgotten him. He was history. Even those he'd counted as friends seemed too busy to talk when he stopped by.

He'd left there in a somber mood, wondering if he'd worked twenty-four years as a special agent only to earn a retirement pension. The human contacts he'd made and the friends he'd worked with had dissolved like the San Francisco fog in the sunlight.

". . . physical specimens are the best," Kipling was saying, as Thorne brought his attention back to the present. "Of course, it makes sense. The men who came to California in 'Forty-Nine were the pick of the lot. The weaklings died *en route*. Their children and grandchildren are superb physical specimens. They don't need a gold badge swinging from their watch chains to identify them as native sons of the Golden West. And the women . . . long-limbed beauties who can think for themselves . . . are not looking at every man as a potential husband. They've been brought up with the boys and meet them on an equal level."

The coach bumped and swayed over a switch as the train passed out onto the main line and clear of the city. They began picking up speed.

"These Californians seem to take for granted what the rest of the world would give anything to have . . . the dry air, the temperate climate, the fruit and produce that grows year round, the plums and strawberries and grapes . . . everything twice the normal size, and the food that can be bought cheaply. A paradise."

"Did you get any material for stories?" Thorne interrupted, leaning forward on the seat. He'd not had access to the places Kipling, as a celebrity, had been invited.

"A gold mine," Kipling replied. "The other night at the Owl's Club, I sat in a gathering of Americans from the far corners of this country. And they told tales, the like of which I could never have heard in India."

"Oh?"

"Tales of reata throwing in Arizona, of gambling at Army posts in Texas, or newspaper wars waged in godless Chicago, of deaths, sudden and violent, in Montana and Dakota . . . of the loves of half-breed maidens in the South . . . and of fantastic huntings for gold in mysterious Alaska. And they told stories of the building of the old San Francisco when, as they say, the water came up to the foot of Market Street. I was in awe. These men in broadcloth and linen, telling these tales over their drinks. Tales grimly humorous, some terrible . . . and knowing that they were told truthfully and matter-of-factly with no embroidery . . . episodes in which they themselves had taken part. I even heard an ex-Confederate officer comparing notes with a trooper of the Northern Horse about battles of the late war."

"I can't wait to see how you'll turn them into fiction."

"If I can get enough details, they'll more likely be in verse," Kipling said. "A man must know a subject first-hand to turn it into convincing fiction. Or, at least, he must live alongside it long enough to check his facts as he goes."

"That may not be a universal requirement," Thorne said, thinking of stories he'd read by authors who had no personal experience of their subjects.

Thorne stared at the blazing sunset out the window of the Pullman. As the sun sank into the Pacific, it swept the sky and the undersides of clouds with shades of red and purple and gold. How many people were actually enjoying this beauty? A man like Kipling certainly had an eye for it. Thorne noticed the writer staring west as well. But he suspected that most of the residents, accustomed to such displays, were going about their business as usual, with hardly a glance at the silent explosion of color.

As dusk dampened down the display, the train rolled east into the great central valley of California. The two men had eaten just before boarding the train, so didn't go to the dining car.

A burly Negro porter came to make up their berths for the night, converting seats into bunks. The two men stepped aside while he worked. Then Thorne tipped him. The man nodded, and left.

Kipling sat down on the lower bunk and began to pull off his boots. "Forgot to tell you of my experiences with a Negro servant last week," he began. "I was being served dinner by a colored gentleman who insisted on bringing me pie for dessert, when I wanted something else. Then he demanded to know something about India. I really wanted to be left alone to finish eating, but I gave him a few facts about wages. 'Oh, hell,' he said with a wide grin, 'that wouldn't keep me in cigars for a month.' But later he came back and fawned all over me for a ten-cent tip. And he ventured the opinion that the people of India were *heathens*! Can you imagine that . . . from a member of a race that's been the butt of jokes for generations?"

Thorne reserved comment as he stripped off his shirt, folded it, and placed it on the top bunk. "I'll take the upper," he volunteered.

"I've read what white Americans say about the Negro, and it's not pretty," Kipling continued. "But the whites have made their bed and they can't unmake it. They freed the slaves, but the descendants of those oppressed people will not go away. There are six million Negroes in this country, and increasing all the time."

"I don't see the problem," Thorne said, carefully pulling himself up and swinging his legs into the upper berth. "They're gradually being educated to take their place in American society."

"That's likely to be a long job. From what I've seen and heard, they throw back to their barbaric origins with annoying persistence."

"What do you mean by that?"

"Take the matter of religion. I've been told on good authority that, regardless of how neatly dressed and 'westernized' they may be, emotions take over. The links that bind them to the white man are broken one by one as the spirit begins to move the congregation. It matters not that they are professing Christianity. The people revert to shouting, moaning, and crying, shaking and dancing up the aisle to the mourners' bench."

Thorne lay back on his pillow and chuckled. "If you think that sort of thing is endemic to tribal worship, then you've never seen a Southern backwoods camp meeting."

Kipling paused, evidently taken aback. "Whites carry on like that, too?"

"Mostly the rural, less educated," Thorne said. "But wouldn't it make for a very dull world if everyone thought and acted the same?"

"Speaking of homogenous views, I had a run-in with the editor of the San Francisco *Examiner* last week," Kipling said. "Offered to write a couple of articles about the city from the perspective of a British visitor."

"I missed them."

"They never got published. I took the trouble to compose and drop them off at his office. He glanced over them and said he might buy them if I'd smooth out one or two raw spots. Then he started penciling things out and changing the wording. I told him *nobody* changed my articles or stories . . . not a line, not a word, not a comma. He claimed they weren't up to the standards of the *Examiner*."

"More likely, his readers aren't up to *your* standards," Thorne said, wondering what acerbic views had been voiced in the articles.

" 'Pearls before swine!' " Kipling scoffed. "I snatched the articles away from his grubby pencil and narrow mind. That bally ass doesn't recognize genius. I guess Bret Harte's been gone too long."

"By the way, you seemed pretty wrought up when you got home from that dinner the last night we were in town," Thorne said, intentionally baiting the small man. It didn't take much.

"The food was good," Kipling replied, then hesitated. Thorne waited for the rest. "But I had to pay for it by sitting through several speeches afterward . . . and such braggadocio! With no apologies for me sitting there, one after another of those speakers lauded the United States and, when they needed a villain to blast, picked on Britain. Being a guest, I said nothing, of course. Then, after we'd chanted 'The Star Spangled Banner' no more than eight times, we adjourned. One of the prominent merchants told me to pay no attention to the war-like sentiments of some of the old generals. 'The skyrockets are thrown in for effect,' he said, 'and whenever we get on our hind legs, we always express a desire to chaw up England. It's a sort of family affair.' Come to think of it, there's no other country for the American public speaker to trample upon. I'll admit that America is a very great country in many ways, but it's not yet heaven with electric lights and plush fittings, as some of those speakers seemed to profess."

He fell silent, and Thorne heard some grunting and scuffling. "You OK?"

"Getting undressed while lying flat on my back in this berth . . . a feat worthy of a contortionist," he gasped.

"Like being in a coffin," Thorne agreed.

"Speaking of which . . . if this train should derail, I'd have to stay right here while the kerosene lamps set the overturned car afire and burned me to death," Kipling said. "It'd be easier getting out of a full theater than leaving a Pullman in haste."

"Think pleasant thoughts," Thorne advised. "You'll sleep better."

"All this nickel-plating, plush, and damask doesn't begin to make up for the closeness and dust," Kipling said as he tugged up a window to admit some fresh air. It was barely after six the next morning and already the porter had converted their bunks back into seats. "But knowing this is Bret Harte country makes it all worth it," he added, leaning on the window sill and savoring the morning. The early daylight revealed the Sacramento River, its silvery surface dodging in and out of sight in the forest they were passing through. "There're the pine-covered hills where the miners lived and fought in his stories . . . there're the slashes of red earth where the gold was washed out . . . the dusty road where the stage traveled . . . there's the timber that was felled and sweating resin in the sunshine. The fresh smell of pine in the heat. Harte has driven all this into my dull brain with the magic of his pen!"

Thorne looked out at the passing scenery with a fresh eye. He'd read Bret Harte's stories, but, having lived and traveled in this part of the country, all this was familiar to him. Yet, seeing it again through Kipling's eyes was like seeing it for the first time. What he said about this early-morning heat was true — already he felt gummy and grimy. Once they'd left the cool coastal breeze, summertime had returned with a vengeance. Thorne stretched and yawned. Six in the morning was not his favorite time of day, especially when he had slept only lightly while being bounced and jostled in the upper berth. "Let's walk up to the diner and get some breakfast," he suggested.

Twenty minutes later they were seated at a table covered with snowy linen and putting away scrambled eggs, bacon, and toast, washed down by hot coffee with thick cream.

"It almost seems that you're on a literary pilgrimage," Thorne observed, beginning to feel more comfortable as he consumed the hot food.

"It's just good to see the country that's the setting for so many of Harte's stories," Kipling replied. "I'm sure other parts of America have their fascinations as well. And I'll report on them in due course."

Several other early diners were scattered among the tables and a low hum of conversation drifted across the aisle of the gently rocking car.

The white-coated waiter approached and set down a plate of scones, then placed a glass of juice in front of Kipling. "From fresh-squeezed California oranges, suh." The Negro waiter smiled.

"I didn't order this."

"Compliments of the Central Pacific."

"I understand, but it's too acidic for my stomach," Kipling replied. "Just bring me a glass of water. That's something we don't dare drink in an Indian restaurant."

"Yes, suh." The waiter put the orange juice back on his tray and departed.

As Thorne buttered a scone and bit into it, he became aware of the beginnings of faint music. He could barely hear the lively notes of "Sweet Betsy From Pike", sounding as if they were coming from the next car.

A minute later they heard the sudden commotion of crashing glass and a sharp exclamation. Thorne cocked his head at the noise. Some glassware broken in the shielded galley at the end of the car. Then came the distinctly unpleasant sound of someone retching. The other diners stopped talking and were staring in the direction of the disturbance.

"Something wrong. I'll be right back," Thorne said, rising and moving quickly toward the noise. He found their Negro waiter on his hands and knees in the narrow galley.

"He just took sick right sudden," a wide-eyed cook said as Thorne squatted beside the convulsing waiter.

"Yeah. He was fine just a minute ago."

The man retched until there was nothing left in his stomach. "Ohh!" He fell weakly to one side while the cook wiped the sick man's face with a wet towel.

"Are you all right now?" Thorne looked closely at the man whose color seemed to have faded from mahogany to gray.

"Yas, suh," the big man nodded.

"What happened?"

The waiter shook his head weakly as Thorne helped him to a sitting position, leaning against the counter. "I drank that glass of juice your friend didn't want. A shame to waste it, you know," he added apologetically. "It tasted kinda funny. Then I just went all clammy. Couldn't even get out da door before I started heavin'." He looked with dull eyes at the cook and another waiter who were cleaning up the mess.

Thorne reached for a broken piece of juice glass that lay on the floor nearby. He sniffed it. What was that faint odor? The smell was vaguely familiar. He sniffed again and rifled his memory bank. Ipecac. That was it! A common emetic to induce vomiting when a person had taken certain kinds of poison.

"I used to could eat or drink anything," the waiter was saying. "My stomach must be getting weak."

"No. That juice had something in it that caused you to throw up," Thorne said.

"No, suh!" the man protested vehemently. He wiped his mouth with his sleeve. "I fixed that juice myself. There weren't nothing in it."

"Was anyone else around that glass after you poured it?"

"I don't know. I set it there while I was gettin' up another order. Dey was folks passing through the car."

Thorne rocked back on his heels and sniffed the broken base of the juice glass once more. No doubt about it. Ipecac.

"Here, Rafe, you drink this soda water. It'll help settle you." The thin cook handed him a glass of cloudy liquid. The waiter began to gulp it down, and Thorne got up and returned to his table.

"Somebody sick?" Kipling asked.

54

"Yes." Thorne related what he'd encountered.

Kipling set down his coffee cup and frowned. "Could it have been accidental?"

Thorne shook his head. "It's not as if he were stirring up some fancy mixed drink and got hold of a wrong ingredient. It was just straight orange juice. Somebody did it deliberately. And the juice was meant for you."

The writer's lips compressed and he paled slightly.

The reedy notes of an Irish jig came faintly to their ears. The jaunty tune seemed to mock the somber discussion they were having. Thorne looked around, a chill going up his spine in spite of the heat. He vividly recalled the harmonica music from the opium den in Chinatown. He couldn't tell where the music was coming from. Then the sound faded and died.

CHAPTER
FIVE

"Will that waiter recover without treatment?" Kipling asked as Thorne sat down at the table.

Thorne nodded, turning to look back toward the galley. He'd seen the waiter being helped to his feet and accepting a glass of soda water from the cook. "He looked to be coming out of it. Should be OK if nothing else was in that juice."

Kipling put down a half-eaten scone. "There are some sights in India that would test the stability of a man's stomach," he said. "Now, I'm not a squeamish man by nature. But suddenly I don't feel too well. Let's go back to our car."

The writer was still pale and somewhat subdued when they again sat on the plush seats in the Pullman, facing each other. "I can't imagine anyone out to poison me."

"Whoever did it was not out to poison you . . . only to make you sick and uncomfortable for a while."

"To what purpose?"

Thorne shrugged. "Wish I knew. But I've learned to trust my instincts. And those instincts tell me the 'accident' aboard ship, the shots fired at us in

Chinatown, and now this are all connected. I hate to admit it, but someone is out to do you some damage."

"You really think these events are connected? Not just coincidental?"

"Yes. In Chinatown I heard a harmonica playing, and I heard it again this time."

"But you didn't hear it on the *City of Peking*."

"No. But we were outside. The noise of the wind and sea would have masked it."

Kipling was silent for several seconds as he absorbed this. "The sound of the harmonica is like a fire bell in the night," he mused. "The call of danger that wakes you."

"You're right," Thorne agreed. "So keep your ears open as well as your eyes."

The two men stopped talking for a minute, each entertaining his own thoughts. The train began a long, winding descent through wooded terrain, cars rocking from side to side as the grinding brakes held their speed in check.

"Did you notice the waiter didn't offer *me* any juice?" Thorne asked, his mind still sorting out events in the diner.

"Hadn't you told him earlier all you wanted to drink was coffee?"

"You're right, I did. The waiter couldn't have had anything to do with it, or he wouldn't have drunk the juice himself. He told me several passengers had passed up and down the car past the galley after he poured the juice and put the glass on the tray . . . it could have been anyone."

"It had to be someone who was watching and knew that waiter was preparing to serve our table next," Kipling said.

"Yes, that's so. Probably someone who was seated right there in the dining car with us." Thorne silently cursed himself for not being more observant. He couldn't recall the faces of even one of the other diners. And it would be fruitless to go look now. He stared with unseeing eyes at the greenery of the passing landscape. Had it not been for the sounds of music from the mouth organ, he might not have seen any connection between those three events, so far apart in space and time. The harmonica had to be an intentional sign that something was about to happen to the writer, another attempt to hurt or kill him. This was no practical joke. An enemy was dogging their steps, taking advantage of their movements to create "accidents". Thorne had recognized the threat early and appointed himself the unofficial bodyguard of the British celebrity. Yet he had not anticipated the last two events. He felt certain the music was a deliberate warning, almost as if the stalker wanted to strike paralyzing terror into Kipling's heart by making him realize danger was imminent.

Thorne's anger smoldered. Being on the defensive was not a position he favored, but there was nothing he could do about it until he identified the enemy. It was somebody on this train. And he couldn't rule out the possibility that more than one person was involved. He would work on the premise that, in all likelihood, the stalker was a man. Yet he would have to be more vigilant and observe other passengers for hints from their appearance or behavior.

Then another thought occurred to him. This could be some enemy *he'd* made in his years as an agent of the Treasury Department. Perhaps *he* was the target. Then why was Kipling struck on the deck of the ship, and served the tainted orange juice? Thorne shook his head and drew a deep breath to rid his mind of tangled thoughts. "Look at the size of that trestle coming up," he said, pointing at a spidery wooden bridge they could see as the train rolled around a curve toward a deep gorge.

If he'd hoped to distract Kipling from his morose mood, he failed. Brakes screeched as the train slowed.

"Damn!" Kipling said under his breath.

Hearing the writer's awestruck exclamation, a passenger coming down the aisle paused. "That's just the first of several we'll cross over," he remarked cheerily.

Thorne noted the man was rotund and middle-aged, wearing a checked coat and sporting a full set of gray-tinged auburn whiskers. He was going bald. There was nothing distinctive about him, but the sight of evil was not always evident.

"Looks like a collection of matchsticks," Kipling remarked.

"Over a hundred feet tall," the man continued, balancing his bulk in the swaying car when he stooped to look out the window. "I guess our timber is as much a curse as a blessing. These trestles last well for five or six years. Then they get out of repair, and a train goes down through 'em, or else a forest fire burns 'em up."

"Just what I wanted to hear," Kipling muttered.

As the locomotive crawled out onto the overpass, the trestle creaked and shivered under its weight. Two track workers stepped back on the edge to allow the cars to pass.

Kipling seemed to be holding his breath.

"This railroad doesn't waste time or money on inspectors," the big man continued. "When I was younger, I was a train engineer. Now, as back then, a lot of cattle and hogs, running loose, wander onto the track. Often the whistle doesn't scare 'em off, and getting their legs under the cowcatcher will throw an engine off the track every time. I remember when a hog wrecked an excursion train and sixty people were killed. I guess the engineer will look out, though." Then he chuckled. "We make a lot of assumptions . . . we guess a trestle will stand forever . . . we guess we can patch up a washout on the track . . . we guess the road's clear . . . sometimes we guess ourselves into the depot . . . and sometimes we guess ourselves into hell. Good day, gents!" He nodded and moved away toward the end of the car.

"Beautiful country," Thorne remarked, trying to ease the tension in his traveling companion. Kipling was sitting on the edge of his seat, fists clenched, staring fixedly out the window at the gorge below. He didn't reply. Several minutes went by and the train dipped into some shallow wooded valleys, sliding smoothly along past open fields of vineyards and wheat, alternating with an occasional orchard. Then it ground to a stop amid hissing steam at a collection of wooden crates that passed for a town.

"I have to get off and stretch my legs," Kipling said, rising and heading for the door.

"We'll probably be here only a few minutes," Thorne said.

"Just enough time."

The two men paced the platform and inhaled the fresh, pine-scented air.

"Maybe twenty or thirty houses, and I can see two church steeples from here," Kipling remarked. "Over here, boy!" he called to a youth who was hawking newspapers. He slipped him a nickel and took the journal. "Thin as a chisel and twice as keen," he remarked, holding up the four folded pages. "Doesn't appear to be much news here, but I'll bet it's full of ads and editorials."

"A settlement of two or three thousand is a big town in these parts," Thorne said. "And, as you've guessed, they all have an infinite belief in their own capabilities. You couldn't pioneer a wilderness without it."

"Boooard!" the conductor yelled, and three new male passengers hurried to get aboard with their small grips. A bag of mail had been tossed onto the baggage car, and the door slid shut.

Thorne and Kipling re-boarded and took their seats as the train pulled out. About every ten miles they passed through a small town, stopping more often than not to pick up a passenger or two, or drop one off.

"Good thing I'm not in a hurry," Kipling remarked. "It appears we're riding the local instead of the express."

Thorne nodded, folding open the paper Kipling had finished reading. It was filled with such things as the prices of livestock, ads for improved reaping and binding machines, and real estate, the travels of eminent local citizens, and ads for men to come and settle and plow, and build schools for their children. He yawned and looked out the window as the train lurched into motion again. In the distance he could see the snow-capped peak of some mountain he couldn't identify. He guessed they were close to the Oregon border. The trip from San Francisco to Portland took thirty-six hours. He could feel the train slowing as it began to labor up a grade.

"We'll be passing through a couple of tunnels before long," Thorne said.

"Don't know which I prefer . . . suffocating with a mountain over my head, or falling through a trestle into a gorge," Kipling replied, making a wry face.

"Let's hope you don't have to do either on this trip," Thorne said, standing up. "I'm going to the privy." He made his way along the swaying aisle and opened a narrow door at the rear of the car. He'd hardly slipped the latch on the inside of the door when the window above his head suddenly went black as the train entered a tunnel. Fortunately a tiny oil lamp was kept burning in a wall sconce near a vent in the ceiling, and he was able to see what he was doing.

When Thorne opened the door a minute or so later, the car was still in darkness. This Pullman was equipped with a pair of chandeliers, each containing two electric and two oil lights. The electricity was erratic at best, and the oil lamps were not presently lighted. He felt his way in almost suffocating blackness. The smell of wood smoke from the engine seeped in around the cracks and through the doors at the ends of the car.

Suddenly he bumped into a passenger moving in the opposite direction. Startled, he felt the softness of a woman, her jasmine-scented hair brushing his face. "Oh, 'scuse me, ma'am," he muttered, leaning to one side to let her pass. She said nothing as she slid by. A few seconds later, the door at the end of the car opened, then closed, cutting off the rattling noise of the undercarriage. He took a few more steps, then paused, thinking he was nearly at his seat.

Somewhere behind him he heard a harmonica wailing the plaintive notes of "Danny Boy". He stiffened, hair rising on the back of his neck. His hand went to his gun and he whirled and started back toward the rear of the coach. At that moment the train shot out the lower end of the tunnel and he was nearly blinded by the sudden sunlight flashing in the windows.

"Aaagghh!! Damn!"

Thorne whirled at Kipling's terrified yell from several feet away. The little man bounded into the aisle; other passengers stuck their heads out of their compartments at the shouting.

"Ah! Ah!" Kipling gasped, pointing, unable to speak.

Thorne was at his side. "What is it? What's wrong?" He heard a buzzing noise and instinctively knew the warning. On the floor just below the edge of the seat, a timber rattlesnake coiled, ready to strike, tongue flickering, tail erect, vibrating its dry, seed-pod rattle.

His heart began to pound. He swept Kipling behind him with one arm and yanked his Remington. *Careful, don't hurry*, he thought, thumbing back the hammer and dropping the long barrel. The gun roared in the confined space. Through the blue-white smoke, Thorne could see the snake twisting and thrashing spasmodically back under the window. Thorne cocked the pistol for another shot, then realized it wasn't necessary, since half the reptile's head was missing. He eased the hammer down.

"Did he get you?" Thorne asked, holstering the gun.

Kipling had to swallow twice before he could speak. "Here." He pointed at his right leg. In the light from the window, Thorne could see two puncture marks on the smooth black boot. The fangs had not penetrated the polished leather.

"Take a deep breath and relax. I got him."

Kipling sank weakly onto an empty seat across the aisle. Thorne became aware of the excited buzz of conversation and questions being hurled at him.

The door flew open at the end of the car and a black-coated conductor bustled in. "What's going on here? Who fired that shot?" he demanded, pushing through the knot of passengers crowding around.

Thorne felt weak and leaned against the edge of a seat. He pointed at the thick body of the rattler twisting slowly on the carpeted floor. "Evidently one of your local citizens," he said. "He's dancing to the tune of "Danny Boy".

The conductor looked at him as if he'd lost his mind.

CHAPTER
SIX

"This really isn't necessary, you know," Thorne said, his voice muffled by the bandanna covering his mouth and nose.

"Peace of mind," Kipling replied in the darkness, clinging to the rail on the open platform. "You weren't in there with a live rattlesnake. It gives me chills to think about it."

Wood smoke, deflected from the ceiling of the tunnel, billowed around them.

Each time the train approached a tunnel, the writer insisted on vacating their compartment and standing between the cars until the train was safely out the other end.

"Well, it's long gone and no harm done," Thorne said to assuage the man's fear. Thorne had dropped the dead snake into the empty burlap sack he'd found in the compartment and flung it from the train. Their fares were paid to Portland, only a few hours further, or the irate conductor would have put them both off at the next small town. Thorne had tried to placate the trainman by saying the incident was a crude practical joke, even hinting that he might know who was behind it.

66

The train rolled out into the sunlight once more, and Thorne pulled down the bandanna and took several deep breaths of fresh air. They stepped back inside, their clothes smelling as if they'd been sitting around a campfire. Better smelling of wood smoke than grimed with soot from coal smoke. Most locomotives had long since been converted to coal burners. But this line ran through country plentiful with timber, so the company had retained their wood-fired American 4-4-0 Baldwin-built engines, despite having to link two locomotives to pull some of the steeper mountain grades.

The train wound on down through the hilly country of southern Oregon, the pine forests alternating with wheat fields.

Kipling had no appetite at lunchtime, so Thorne bought them both a brandy and they sat in their compartment, sipping their drinks and watching the scenery flow by in the bright sunshine. Thorne's stomach growled with hunger, but the liquor warmed it and temporarily dulled his craving.

"Where could it have come from?" Kipling asked. Thorne's efforts had not been able to divert the writer's thoughts from the snake.

"We stopped at several small towns," Thorne said. "Easy for someone to get off and buy a snake at one of those stands selling gifts, trinkets, and souvenirs."

"But a live, poisonous snake?"

"These are not eastern towns. People out here will sell anything they think there might be a market for. And timber rattlers are common to these hills. Guess they thought someone might want one for a pet." He paused. "I don't think a passenger would have had time to catch one while we were stopped, unless he got lucky and found one in the brush near the tracks."

Kipling crossed his legs and fingered the tiny twin scuff marks halfway up his knee-high black boot. "Except for these boots, I could've been killed . . . maybe struck in an artery or vein."

"Lucky it wasn't an Indian cobra that could've spit venom into your eyes," Thorne said. "There are more species of deadly serpents in India than there are here."

"But they don't ride on railway carriages."

"I'd venture to say some snake charmers have transported their charges aboard Indian trains," Thorne said calmly.

Kipling smiled. "Reptiles don't ride unattended, with their own tickets."

Thorne chuckled. "Y'got me there." The repartee had finally loosened up Kipling a little.

Thorne was tired of rehashing the details of the recent scare. He stared out the window, and Kipling scribbled in his notebook as the wheels clicked over the rail joints, carrying them toward Portland. But the unknown stalker still loomed in his mind. How could a burlap bag with a snake have been tossed into the open compartment, and the perpetrator escape unseen in the darkness? Thorne figured the train had been in the total darkness of the tunnel for no more than ninety seconds. Time enough for anyone ready and waiting to pass down the aisle, toss the bag, and leave out the end of the car. Unless the snake tosser were a passenger in their own Pullman — a distinct possibility — he had to have walked along the aisle. But which way had he headed? When Thorne had come out of the privy at the rear of the coach and was making his way forward toward their compartment, midway along the aisle, he'd brushed past only one person. The touch and scent and hair identified the passenger as a woman. Could she have been the one? A chill went over him at the thought that he might have actually touched the stalker. He recalled only a slight bump. She had not appeared in a hurry — just feeling her way in the dark, swaying aisle as anyone would have done. He had not heard the distant harmonica music until she'd left the car.

It could be the snake tosser had gone forward in the train and Thorne had missed him altogether. He recalled only one woman with the nerve to carry out the three attempts to harm Kipling — Ann Gilcrease, alias Julie Ann Martin. Just the memory of her stirred him with attraction — and revulsion.

During the war, she'd been a Confederate spy. He'd first encountered her in Tombstone in 1881 when he was working undercover on a series of robberies. She'd struck him as a beautiful, single woman, fooling him completely for a time. In reality — if there *was* a reality in her chameleon-like existence — she was the paramour of Brady Cox Brandau, ex-Confederate captain and ringleader of a gang of border robbers. Thorne felt a thrill of fear recalling his own capture, along with another undercover operative, and imprisonment in an abandoned mine by Brandau and Ann Gilcrease. It was then he realized her mind was unbalanced because she tried to flay them alive with a straight razor while they were chained in a dungeon. Only by lucky chance had they managed to escape. Brady Brandau had later been tracked down and killed. Ann Gilcrease was captured. But she'd beguiled Morgan Earp, knocked him unconscious, and made her escape from camp, by night, before they could return her to trial in Tombstone.

That was eight years ago, and Thorne had neither seen nor heard of her since. As far as he knew, she was never apprehended. With her experience as a spy and skill at altering her appearance, he doubted he would recognize her today if he ran into her on the street. If she were even alive, she'd be in her mid-forties by now. She could be in prison for later crimes under some other identity. Or she might even be locked in an insane asylum. She was certainly not normal, and the passage of time had probably not helped her mental state. Though he shivered when he pictured the glint of her straight razor coming toward him while his arms were chained, he couldn't help but feel sorry for her. What a lonely, miserable life she must have led, never satisfied with one man — no children to love and care for — moving from place to place, assuming new rôles, new guises — the ultimate actress, a victim of some imbalance of the humors.

In order for this stalker to be a woman, she would have to be someone like Ann Gilcrease — value judgments slightly askew, but cold and calculating and completely nerveless when it came to daring.

He put this thought aside. Until proven otherwise, it made more sense to assume the stalker was a man. But

70

then he was jolted by another thought, and all his misgivings returned. The woman who'd brushed past him in the aisle had been wearing jasmine-scented perfume, Ann Gilcrease's favorite. Odors triggered strong memories: wood smoke and pipe tobacco brought back scenes of his grandfather's house; the smell of dill weed, his mother canning pickles; the sweet scent of honey clover, a South Dakota grassland. Certainly other women wore jasmine as well; he saw nothing to get excited about now.

Yet, through the rest of that day, his mind returned again and again to the face and long-vanished presence of Confederate spy and woman of multiple identities — Ann Gilcrease/Julie Ann Martin. Besides the scent of jasmine, another thing seemed to link the current attacks to that mysterious gang of robbers in the Arizona Territory of 1881. In Thorne's experience, most outlaws who performed a series of robberies or shootings were never content to remain totally anonymous. Their human nature required them to brag, to take credit for their misdeeds in some fashion. Thus, the man who murdered and disemboweled several prostitutes in London a few months before had taunted Scotland Yard with letters, signing his name as Jack the Ripper. Captain Brandau's gang had adopted a twisted symbol of the Confederate battle flag — a circle containing an X, with a star between each arm of the X. They left this symbol as a calling card at the scenes of their various crimes so the law and the public would know that their gang, the Rebel Legion, was responsible. It was a form of terror. Whoever was after

Kipling wanted him to know it was the same person or gang, and their calling card was harmonica music.

By the time the train pulled into Portland, Thorne decided they both needed a change, and he proposed they leave the train and spend a few days looking over the city of fifty thousand, then possibly taking a boat excursion up the Columbia River.

"Just what I was about to suggest," Kipling said with delight. They gathered up their leather grips and ordered a porter to place their trunks on a hotel omnibus.

Kipling's appetite had returned and they enjoyed a steak dinner on the verandah of the hotel dining room, while gazing at a long, lingering summer sunset.

Overhearing their remarks about the beautiful sky, a man at the next table said: "A rare clear day in Portland."

"Then I'm glad we arrived when we did," Kipling replied. "Are you a native?"

"Oh, no." The man waved a fork at their surroundings. "I'm on vacation . . . from California. Just came up here for the scenery and the fishing."

"If you're alone, you're welcome to join us," Kipling offered.

The gregarious gentleman promptly picked up his plate, utensils, and napkin and moved to their table. "Your accent gives you away, Englishman," he said, pulling up a chair. "My name's Rudolph Blixter."

"Rudyard Kipling."

"That's about as strange as my name," Blixter said, as the two men shook hands. "I'm not good at names. OK if I just call you John Bull or English? You can call me California," he said jovially.

Thorne introduced himself, sizing up the new acquaintance as in his mid-fifties, robust, slightly balding blond head, and ruddy complexion. He was dressed in a light wool jacket. The button was missing from the collar of his open shirt as if his massive neck had burst its restraint. His outgoing manner suggested to Thorne that he might be a drummer.

"Get a good look at those golden streaks in the sky," California said. "It won't last as long as in the desert ... shortly those pine-covered hills will obstruct the view. We're ninety miles upriver from the ocean, but the way folks around here are building and bragging about their resources, you'd think you were in a major port city."

"Every one-horse town I've seen in America thinks of itself as Imperial Rome," Kipling said dryly. "But, I'll have to say, they raise good cattle here. This is the best piece of steak I've ever eaten."

"If you gents are on vacation, too, why don't you join me tomorrow? I'm taking a boat up the Columbia for some sightseeing and to inquire about any good fishing spots hereabouts."

"California, you've got a traveling companion," Kipling answered quickly.

"Make that two," Thorne said.

★ ★ ★

The next morning dawned blue and golden as the three men stood on the deck of a stern-wheel steamboat winding its way down the Willamette.

"Can't wait to see the Columbia," Kipling said. "The river that brings the salmon that goes into the tin that is emptied into the dish when extra guests arrive in India."

"You got it right," California said. "Some of the best fishing in the world, right here . . . sport and commercial."

Thorne stood near the rail a few feet away, breathing deeply of the fresh morning air and reflecting that it was a great day to be alive and retired, with nothing but a beautiful time of sightseeing stretching ahead of him. The mysterious attempts to harm Kipling constituted a problem that rested easily in the back of his mind — more a curiosity than something to dread. For years, intrigue and violence had been part of his life. This was nothing new. Then, too, the mind rested easier when the target was someone else.

As the boat negotiated the bends toward the broad Columbia, the men climbed the steps and California introduced Kipling to the texas, the pilot house, and, pointing from the upper deck, said: "That point of land off yonder, grown up thick with willows, is a towhead. Just around the bend, there . . . that swampy area . . . is a slough."

They strode forward with a dozen other passengers to get a good view of the big river as the boat swung out of the Willamette into the Columbia. The pilot put down several spokes of the big wheel and rang the engine room for three-quarter speed. The hull slid past the top of a huge tree that was bobbing up and down in the swift current.

"Behold, the sawyer," California said. "A water-logged tree that's swinging along in the current, with only a little of it showing. Same thing as a planter, except a planter has snagged its roots on the bottom and just sets there with the other end sticking up like a trap the river's set to snatch the bottom out of a steamboat, bigger 'an hell."

"The same things Mark Twain wrote about the Mississippi River are all here," Kipling marveled. "I can recognize the very stretches where Huck and Jim drifted on their raft."

California gave him a curious, sideways glance. "This is the Columbia that forms the border between Oregon and Washington."

"Doesn't matter," Kipling replied. "As far as I'm concerned, this is the Mississippi."

Wooded islands slid by, their banks caving here and there as the river ate at them. The steamboat pilot angled the big, bluff-bowed boat back and forth across the mile-wide river, seeking the safest channel.

"Just like a Mississippi River steamer," Kipling enthused as the three men descended to the lower deck. They went forward to watch the dark water peeling away under the guards.

A half hour later, the boat gently nosed into a low spot on the north bank to discharge three passengers and take two more aboard.

"'Morning, gentlemen," California greeted the boarding passengers.

The first man merely ducked his head and went on, but the second — a long-haired young man wearing a sack coat — doffed his hat. "Beautiful mawnin' for a boat ride."

"South Carolina," California said in an aside to Kipling. Then, to the new passenger: "Where you from, stranger?"

"Up the river a piece," he replied, "but originally from South Carolina."

"Amazing," Kipling said as the man moved away with his grip. "How did you know?"

"A fella like me, who travels a good deal, develops an ear for dialects," he said. "His enunciation is a lot softer than mine. Yet it's a different softness than the speech of . . . for example . . . a Mississippian."

Thorne stayed in the background, letting California educate the young writer in the vicissitudes of the great Columbia. Thorne scrutinized everyone who came near as a possible suspect, but could detect nothing suspicious about this man who seemed as bluff and open as anyone he'd ever met. But, then, many intelligent criminals were often affable companions. He would reserve judgment on California; so far he saw nothing to concern himself with.

Thorne was not overconfident, but felt adequate to deal with any situation that might arise. His elbow bumped the holstered Remington under his corduroy jacket. He noticed that several other passengers wore sidearms as a matter of course — probably out of long habit. But California carried no visible gun. And Thorne knew Kipling had nothing that could be considered a weapon, except a clasp knife.

Several large islands in the middle of the river supported wheat fields and orchards, even white houses tucked back under the pines. From islands that bore thick stands of pine trees, they could hear the whining of sawmills — like a distant drone of bees across the water.

"I own some interests in sawmills and a few ships," California remarked at the sound. "But farming is the thing that will last. My partner is overseeing our fruit farm while I'm gone."

Unless this was an empty brag, meant to impress, California was a man of wealth, Thorne deduced, overhearing the remark. Yet, in his work shirt and canvas pants tucked into Wellington boots, California looked anything but a man of means. A disreputable floppy hat, ringed around the crown with fifteen or twenty trout flies, covered the top of his balding head. People with money often dressed as they pleased, not feeling obligated to show off.

Soon, the stern-wheeler turned out of the main channel to take a short cut up a chute between a long island and the nearby shoreline. Thorne held his breath. The current, squeezed into the narrow channel, roared along, barely covering black-toothed rocks two feet beneath the surface. Except to save time and distance, the pilot had no reason to attempt this route, Thorne thought, gripping the rail while the boat swerved to port, then to starboard, dancing, thrashing its way upstream. A sudden *thump* jarred the boat from end to end when it struck a floating log. The boat slewed around while the paddle wheel tore the water to foam.

"Look!" Kipling pointed. The white belly of a dead salmon swept past them on the current. "The canneries have no trouble snagging those big ones," he said. "That was at least a twenty-pounder."

The boat escaped the boiling, rock-strewn water of the chute, and shot into the main river once more.

"These Chinook salmon won't rise to a fly," California said. "The canneries take them by the wheel." He pointed ahead where a barge was moored in a bend. Attached to the side of the barge was a water wheel whose wire-mesh arms, turned by the current, were busily scooping up any salmon within reach as they swam upriver. Three or four men were busy emptying the bins where the silvery bodies were being deposited.

"Son-of-a-bitch!" California swore at the sight. "Think of the black and bloody murder of it! Several thousand pounds of salmon killed in one night, just to feed the insatiable hunger of people like you out yonder who insist on having tinned salmon for supper. The canneries can't live by letting down lines . . . tell that to your damned newspaper!"

Thorne stiffened at the venom in his voice. California stared at Kipling as if the writer were entirely responsible for the demand for the delicacy. It was a side of their big companion he'd not shown before.

But California's mood changed abruptly. "Ah, there it is . . . Bridal Veil Falls!" he exclaimed, springing to

78

the starboard rail and pointing at a blown thread of white vapor that broke from the crest of a hill 850 feet high and whose voice was even louder than that of the river. "But there must be a hundred bridal veil falls in America. Why didn't they call it Mechlin Lace Falls at fifty dollar a yard, while they were at it?"

Several miles farther, another falls appeared. "As the gorge deepens, you'll see some real scenery!" California said.

Thorne agreed. The river was penned between gigantic stone walls that appeared to be "crowned with the ruins of Oriental palaces", as Kipling's fertile imagination described them.

Gradually the stretch of green water widened, guarded by pine-covered hills 3,000 feet high. A wicked nail of rock stood 100 feet tall in midstream. A blinding white sandbar gave promise of flatter country to come — but it lied. Around the next bend the river ran through a triple-tiered fortification topped with lava and giant conifers. Behind and above this towered the white dome of Mount Hood, bulging 14,000 feet into the blue sky. Closer to hand, the river thrashed around the feet of some gnarled cottonwoods.

As the boat churned upstream, California jumped from side to side in his eagerness to see it all; at the same time he pumped several of the other male passengers about good trout fishing sites in the area.

The man who never met a stranger, Thorne thought. Others willingly shared their knowledge about trout streams. A few were not fishermen, but California encountered one enthusiast who told him about a stream only a few hours by buggy from Portland. "The Clackamas. That's the stream to fish!"

"I'll try it," California said, grinning. "As soon as we get back. What about it, Kipling? Thorne? You up for an afternoon of snagging some salmon?"

Both men agreed. The threat to Kipling was receding from Thorne's concerns.

"Stash that damned notebook!" California burst out. "You'll never be able to describe what you're seeing here. Unsullied nature. You put your poison pen to describing what you see in America. I defy you to say anything bad about this!"

Thorne again felt a chill at the man's words, but dismissed them as the wildly enthusiastic babble of a man carried away by admiration and pride.

California was an overpowering presence not to be denied. Kipling closed his notebook and tucked it into the side pocket of his jacket.

The steamer worked up to the foot of a long island and threw off her hawsers. The purser stood by the head of the gangway as the passengers disembarked. "The river's a trifle broken along here," he explained. "We'll go by rail to the upper end, then pick up another steamer."

They boarded open-top rail cars resembling wagons with rows of forward facing seats on each side. The small locomotive had steam up and jerked into motion. The wind blew their hair as the train whirled along in the sunshine just on the edge of the bluffs overlooking the boiling white water.

"A six-mile run to upper end," California said over the noise. They dipped into a fragrant pine forest, ablaze with wildflowers, then shot up out of the shaded woods again, the car swaying and clacking along the bluffs, the narrowed river rushing over boulders fifty feet below. Thorne was sitting just behind Kipling and California. A middle-aged woman had taken the seat beside him. He nodded to her, but didn't try to speak above the noise of the rushing wind and clattering wheels.

A log shot down the millrace, struck a rock, and split from end to end, rolling over in a lather of foam, disappearing downstream.

"Oh, my!" a woman blurted out at the sight of the violently splintered wood.

He glanced at her. The woman's frizzy salt-and-pepper hair was drawn back and tied with a ribbon at the back of her neck. Because of the wind, she'd removed her broad-brimmed straw hat and held it in her lap. She met his glance. "Powerful," she said. "Makes me feel small."

Thorne mumbled an assent and turned away, impressed by a face that had once radiated classic beauty. But make-up and the high-collared dress failed to conceal her fine facial lines and wrinkled neck. In spite of the wide hat, her face carried a bronzed, weathered look.

It seemed hardly possible they'd covered six miles, before they were grinding to a halt at the end of the island. The train eased out onto a floating trestle and the passengers debarked. Talking and laughing, they filed aboard another steamer. They cast off. The cascades were barely 200 yards below. Before the stern wheel could dig in and offset the pull of the current, the boat was swung downstream in the powerful grip of the smoothly rushing water, and drifted toward the rapids.

"We'll all be drowned!" a woman cried.

"Not likely!" shot back another. The inflection of the two words triggered a bell of recognition in Thorne's memory. His head snapped around to see who'd spoken. It was the woman who'd been his seatmate. Where had he heard that voice before? His skin tingled. Something deep in his mind had responded to that particular expression, that intonation. It was like no other. As Kipling had described the harmonica, this voice was a fire bell in the night, a warning of danger. Humans could disguise nearly everything about themselves — except their voices. Unless one deliberately affected an accent, as an actor might, the timbre and cadence of voice remained the same, regardless of aging. Even though he didn't recognize the face he stared at, he realized he'd just heard the voice of Ann Gilcrease.

CHAPTER
SEVEN

Thorne lost his usual presence of mind. He continued to stare as the woman turned away, apparently unaware of him.

The paddle wheel churned water, arresting the boat's drift, and they began to make headway upstream. But he was oblivious to it. He took a deep breath to steady his pounding heart, then thrust his way into the crowd at the rail, pushing alongside the woman. "Well, Ann, it's quite a surprise seeing you again," he said quietly, but distinctly, into her ear.

She gave a start, and he sensed her stiffen. "Who are you, sir?" she said, looking around at him.

"I know you've had a lot of men in your life," he rushed on, "but it wounds my pride to think you have no recollection of a man you made love to in Tombstone eight years ago."

She squinted at him from beneath the brim of her straw hat, and he took the opportunity to study the face he'd once known so well. She was older, but he had no doubt it was she. A pang gripped his stomach; the attraction was still there. At the same time he was revolted by his last memories of her.

"I don't know you, sir. Who is this Ann person?" she asked boldly. "You have me confused with someone else."

"Oh, no," he replied grimly. "Julie Ann Martin, also known as Ann Gilcrease, or whatever you're calling yourself now. You've changed your appearance, but you can't disguise your voice."

"Let's step over here," she said, leading the way to the port side of the boat, away from the rest of the passengers.

Thorne was careful to keep Kipling and California in sight.

She smiled demurely at him, and he recalled the young, black-haired seductress he'd known in 1881. "I'm Agnes Morgan now," she said softly. "Widowed with a small inheritance and traveling to further my general education."

He snorted a derisive laugh. "I guess that's as good a cover as any. I thought you'd be dead or in prison by now for murder or massive embezzlement."

"Really, Alex . . . *murder*? You must think I'm positively terrible."

"So you *do* remember my name. You were calculating and ruthless then. Are you telling me you've changed?"

"I recall you as being a little more gallant than to accuse a lady of theft and murder." She made a pretense of pouting. "You even kicked me in the head and knocked me unconscious the last time we were together."

"It's difficult to be gallant when a former lover is slicing my skin off with a straight razor," he said bluntly.

"You know I was just teasing," she replied, glancing away. "Besides, when you kicked me, I was working on your friend . . . what was his name?"

"Burnett. And don't pretend that you don't remember you were his lover, too."

"Ah, yes, the big Wells Fargo man with the hairy chest and the walrus mustache. My, how he could scream!"

The dim underground dungeon where their hands were chained to the wall behind them, the evening-gowned woman plying the razor with vivid intensity — all came rushing back. Until this moment, he thought he'd put that scene behind him forever. His hands were clammy where he gripped the boat's rail. He and Burnett had been very fortunate to escape that pit alive. "Have you teamed up with somebody else as crazy and determined as Brady Cox Brandau?" he asked, referring to her partner in crime, the former Confederate officer who'd formed a gang of robbers and killers to avenge himself on the wealthy Yankee mine owners.

"You think I'm *crazy*?" she asked, arching her brows.

"Crazy and murderous and a consummate liar. I don't believe you could tell the truth if your life depended on it."

"You give me too much credit. A single lady must do what she can to get by in this world."

The boat swung around a bend and the passengers at the far rail *oohed* and *aahed* at the unfolding vistas. The boat, shifting position, threw the sun full on her face when she looked up. The hazel eyes were the same as he remembered. He imagined her irises reforming into vertical feline slits. What twisted reasoning resided behind those clear orbs? What unpredictable motivation? "What will you do when you get too old and unattractive to work your will with men?" he asked.

"Conservative thinking," she replied.

If nothing else, she was certainly self-assured.

"I could arrest you on suspicion that there are still outstanding warrants for you in the Arizona Territory."

"No, you can't. You've been retired from the Secret Service for months."

"How did you know that?" She never ceased to amaze him. She was always one step ahead.

"Alex, give me credit for knowing a few things."

"Ah, yes, the master spy, seductress, the chameleon who is never what she seems. How much harm have you done, how many lives ruined, how many have you flayed alive since we last met?"

"Whatever you may think of me, you won't arrest me now."

"I could do it as a private citizen."

"But you won't. No one can identify me. I have erased my past. There is absolutely no connection between the woman I was even six months ago, and the woman I am now. I might be held for a few hours of questioning, but I would be released shortly, making you look like a fool."

He knew she was right. Her whole life had been one of deceit and hiding her identity.

"Besides, you have other things to attend to now," she stated.

How much did she know about his self-appointed rôle as Kipling's bodyguard? "By any chance do you play the harmonica?" Thorne asked.

"What an odd question." She looked puzzled. "I play several instruments, including the mouth organ," she said, giving him a last vacant smile and extending her hand. He took her hand, instantly noting how rough and callused the palm and fingers were.

She withdrew from him, gliding away to strike up a conversation with an elderly couple several feet away.

He was still stunned by her sudden appearance aboard this boat. Coincidence? Hardly. She'd been checking up on him or she wouldn't have known he was recently retired. The remark about his having other things to do besides arresting her implied she knew he was Kipling's traveling companion. She'd pretended surprise at his question about her knowledge of the harmonica. Another ruse. Was she the one who was after Kipling? He strongly suspected so. But to what purpose? He couldn't even guess. She had spied for the Confederacy during the war and later, in 1881, had allied herself with Brandau's Rebel Legion in Tombstone. What she'd been up to the past eight years he couldn't imagine. Yet, she'd never worked alone — had always sold her talents as a spy to someone or some cause. And he suspected she was doing the same now. But *who* and *why* were the questions.

At least now he could attach a face to the eerie wailing of the mouth organ, a face to the smell of jasmine. She'd been the woman in the aisle of the darkened train car. Perhaps she was traveling and working with a male partner. But were they trying to kill Kipling or just make his trip miserable? Now that Thorne had met her face to face again, he vowed to keep an even closer eye on Kipling. But the Englishman and California seemed to have disappeared. Trying not to panic, he moved quickly from one side of the boat to the other. After an anxious five minutes, he located the two men at the bow on the main deck.

"There she be!" California boomed, pointing at a settlement coming up on their starboard bow. "The Dalles. Head of navigation. Town of maybe two thousand. It's the center of a big sheep and wool district." He let go with a great laugh. "Listen to me, Johnny Bull! I sound like a tour director or something. Let's go ashore and look around. The boat will tie up here for the night and head back in the morning."

"You ever been here before?" Kipling asked.

"Only seen the place from the water once," California replied.

Thorne followed the two as the passengers filed off. No need to tell Kipling about meeting Ann Gilcrease. Since Kipling had never known her, he wouldn't understand what a threat she was. The writer would see only a harmless woman of middle years, and would think Thorne a paranoid fool. Besides, Thorne could present no actual proof she was connected to the attacks.

As he followed California and Kipling, Thorne wondered at this big, bluff man who called himself California. He was indefatigable; he never stopped talking. He seemed to have boundless energy. Whatever entered his mind came out of his mouth.

The Dalles proved to be a sleepy, comfortable town with white houses, picket fences, the townsfolk going about their business quietly and routinely. The three men put up in a two-story wooden hotel that was nothing, if not Spartan.

Next day, the trip back downriver to Portland was quick and uneventful, with Ann Gilcrease seen only fleetingly from a distance. She obviously wanted no more contact with Thorne.

The boat captain stopped and allowed the passengers to go ashore and make a quick tour of a salmon canning facility. It was a noisy factory on the south shore, the operation all bloody efficiency, the floor slick with oil and scales, the air hot with steam, the place staffed mostly with Chinese. Afterward, Kipling remarked that he'd probably never eat salmon again unless it was fresh from the river.

For the last two hours of the trip, Thorne found a deck chair and passed the time reading a paperback volume of Kipling's short stories. He was careful to keep the pirated edition out of the writer's sight to avoid setting off a tirade of invective against dishonest American publishers — especially Seaside Press.

The three men checked back into their old hotel in Portland. California got a room to himself.

"Whew!" Thorne said, as he and Kipling parted from the big man after supper. "At least my ears can get a few hours rest."

"You're just showing your age." Kipling grinned. "I find the man most interesting."

"Oh, he's a font of information about everything," Thorne agreed. "But a little silence sounds good now and then. I could do without the walking encyclopedia."

"I don't care how much he talks, as long as he knows the way to some good salmon fishing," Kipling said while the two men were climbing the stairs to their rooms.

"He mentioned it's a couple hours from here by buggy," Thorne said.

"If it's as good as we've been promised, I wouldn't care if it's twice that far."

"As you've found, to your disgust, everything is supposedly bigger and better in America," Thorne commented dryly.

"We'll see."

Next morning California rented a light buggy with a pair of spirited horses to pull it. While the team was being hitched by the livery owner, California, loud and brash as usual, drew a crowd of bystanders who began offering directions on which sawmills they would pass, which fords they'd cross, which signposts to watch for.

Thorne caught himself scanning the small crowd for sign of Ann Gilcrease. She'd disappeared the day before when the boat docked at Portland.

Thorne had never seen Kipling so happy as he was this morning. The writer was giddy as a boy on the first day of summer vacation. Thorne, although not a fisherman, wondered if he himself had ever been that happy, that carefree. Sadly he couldn't recall a time in his boyhood or youth when he'd been absolutely blissful. Perhaps he was too serious as a child, and adult responsibilities had come on all too soon. His years in the Secret Service had pounded the memories out of him. Surely there had been some time in the past — even a brief time — when he'd experienced unsullied joy.

California slapped the reins on the horses' rumps, urging the team into a dead run. A half mile out of town they struck a plank road where the buggy bounced and careened from side to side. The driver slowed the team, but still the men were thrown this way and that, as the wheels hit broken and rotting boards or gaps in the planking.

"This road would be a disgrace to an Irish village!" Kipling cried, gripping the seat as the buggy lurched sideways.

But the plank road didn't last. It gave way to six miles of macadamized road, and the horses showed what they could do. For the entire stretch, a railway ran between them and the banks of the Willamette River.

Small townships dotted the land, and they passed farmers driving wagons full of hay, sunburned urchins riding atop. Then they came upon a fair road through a pine woods, winding among fire-blackened stumps, past rail fences, and down into dusty hollows that would be hopeless marshes in winter.

Thorne had fleeting impressions of his surroundings as they flew by — billowing dust as the buggy bounded through deep dips, rank clumps of wild blackberries raking the sides of the buggy, old cemeteries where neglected wooden headboards nodded drunkenly, a yoke of oxen hauling a huge log down a skid road, an open wheat field, followed by orchards of cherry trees.

After a quick discussion, California pulled up the lathered team at a house with a sign advertising cherries for sale.

"Less than a *rupee!*" Kipling marveled as he hefted the ten-pound bag of fruit. They let the team blow for a few minutes and then graze while the men got a drink of ice cold water from a spring.

"Land of milk and honey!" California bragged. "Find a place like this in India!"

They climbed back into their buggy. Thorne marveled at California and Kipling, who talked and argued loudly and incessantly, whooping at two youngsters riding bareback, fishing creels flopping over their shoulders. The salmon were somewhere up ahead and California urged the team onward at a fast pace. All the while he gasped out disjointed stories of feuds and beautiful women; tales of fickle fortune that favored one miner over another; and a lumberman who became a millionaire many times over. The road was only a series of connected tracks. While they bowled along, California spun tales of prospecting in Nevada and deer hunting in Arizona. Paying little attention to his driving, he ran the team off the trail. Up a steep hill the team charged into a thickening clump of saplings where the track disappeared and the horses pulled up, rearing and snorting. The men could see the road below, but to backtrack would have wasted precious time and distance. Undaunted, they all alighted, appropriated a pole from a rail fence and thrust it through the spokes of the rear wheels. The big man guided the horses from one side as the others held each end of the pole, skidding the buggy down the steep grade to keep it from overrunning the plunging team.

They started off again, Kipling slinging small rocks and pieces of bark at squirrels and chipmunks that crossed their path.

Thorne laughed to himself at the sight of Kipling — mustache, pomaded black hair, eyes wide behind the lenses of the wire-rimmed glasses, his small body bouncing around gleefully on the leather seat, shouting with California at a wildcat crouching on a cut above the road.

California kept up a running commentary the entire time, but Thorne caught only snatches of his never-ending stories. Before mid-morning, the driver drew rein at a farmhouse-boarding house to which they'd been directed. They quickly arranged grain for the horses and lodging for themselves. Then, grabbing their rods from the buggy, they headed for the stream less than a quarter mile away.

Thorne had no rod, so he took charge of the gaff and the crock jug of whiskey.

The stream, seventy yards wide, was divided by a pebbly island. It ran over riffles and swirled into deep, quiet pools. Along its winding course, the Clackamas was bounded variously by chest-high crops, log-fenced meadows, and 100-foot bluffs, backed by hills of pine.

California pointed his nose into the breeze, checked upstream and downstream, waded into the current, and flicked his spoon into the tail of a riffle.

While Kipling was still assembling his rod, California's reel shrieked as three feet of living silver leaped into the air far across the water. California let out a whoop, and the salmon tore upstream, taut line cutting water, bamboo rod bowed to the breaking point.

Thorne and Kipling shouted advice to the big man while he played the fish.

"Not there!" California shouted. "Don't run, you damned shiny torpedo!" He hauled back on the rod. "Please, God, bring him to me," he added in a lower tone.

The battle lasted better than a quarter hour, but the fish, with shorter and more erratic dashes, was finally reeled in. Kipling gaffed the game salmon, and they suspended the big silver body by the hand-held spring scale. Eleven pounds, eight ounces.

"Wow!" The big man had lost his hat, and perspiration glistened on his red face. "What a beauty! I've waited twenty years to land a fish like this!" California grabbed Kipling in a bear hug, crushing the breath out of him. "Yahoo!" California danced an impromptu jig on the gravel bar. "Now it's your turn, partner."

"Supper for us and our host family at the boarding house," Thorne said.

"Yeah. Too bad I don't have any way of preserving it to stuff and mount on my wall," California lamented.

Thorne followed Kipling into knee-deep, icy water and watched the writer try to get the hang of casting. His first attempt nearly snagged a black water snake sunning on a flat rock. On his second try, he dropped the lure into a quiet pool just above the weir.

Thorne stowed the jug, the gaff, and the landing net on the bank. He'd just stretched out on the ground when the water boiled as a fish took Kipling's lure.

"*Yeeoow!*"

Thorne's heart began to pound when the big salmon jumped, flashing in the sunlight. Then it made a series of jumps, trying to shake the hook, before it submerged and ran. The drag was set on the reel, and it screeched as the fish peeled off line in its rush to escape.

Kipling burned his thumb, checking the whirling spool. He splashed after the running salmon, trying to retain the last few turns of line on his reel.

"Don't let him get away, Johnny Bull!" California shouted as the two men neared each other. "Whoops! Thar she blows!" California had himself another strike.

Thorne lounged on the grassy bank in the sun, smoking his pipe, and watching the action.

Ten minutes passed while Thorne shouted encouragement and laughed at Kipling's struggles to land his catch. "I think you've hooked Moby Dick this time!"

Kipling's hand was a blur as he cranked in line when the fish ran toward him. Then the irritated salmon stripped line from the snarling reel while Kipling staggered over the rocky bottom, giving ground to keep the big fish from snapping the eight-ounce bamboo rod. Another twenty-five minutes dragged by while the fight went on.

The two fishermen played their darting fish, scrambling to keep their lines from fouling each other as their salmon ran this way and that. Kipling braced the butt of his rod on a hip and heaved back, the tip of the rod bending like a weeping willow branch. Inch by inch the tiring salmon began to give up his life. Kipling worked him toward the shallows where sloping gravel provided a good landing area. The big fish seemed to feel the shoals under his ponderous belly, put on the brakes, and lunged back toward deep water, while the reel screeched off hard-won yards of line.

"For God's sake, get that minnow to the bank, Johnny Bull!" California yelled. "I've got a big salmon to land!"

Kipling grimaced at the insult, but was gasping too hard to respond. Finally, nearly forty minutes after hooking his fish, Kipling brought him, still struggling, to the shallows.

"Don't gaff him!" Kipling cried.

"He's too big for the landing net," Thorne said.

"I'll get him." The writer threw his rod onto the gravel, splashed forward, slipped a hand into the salmon's gill, and hoisted him aloft. The long, heavy fish battered Kipling's legs as he carried him toward the hand scales. "He just had the hook in the corner of his mouth . . . it didn't tire him at all."

Thorne produced the spring scales, and they hung the fish.

"Twelve pounds!" Kipling cried. "Ah, gentlemen of the Punjab Fishing Club . . . how you'll envy me! No, you simply won't believe me." He flopped down on his back on the grass, exhausted, soaked in sweat and spangled with scales, hands cut and bleeding, black hair awry, nose sunburned. "Now I've lived! What can I do to top this? The American continent may now sink beneath the sea. I've taken the best it can yield . . . and it's not dollars, love, or real estate."

"Some men are wordsmiths and some are poets." Thorne grinned. "You're both. Here, have a shot of whiskey to wet down your insides . . . you're already wet on the outside."

Kipling sat up and took a pull at the jug, coughed, then tried again. "Whew! I needed that."

Forty yards upstream came the voice of California, cursing in both English and Spanish.

"He'd better save his breath for the fight," Thorne commented, re-corking the jug and standing up.

"Don't worry, he's got plenty of breath for both," Kipling said, removing his glasses and wiping the lenses on his shirt-tail.

Ten minutes later, California worked his fish into the shallows and lunged for him with both hands, hoisting it above his head with a shout. Thorne held the scales while the big man suspended his salmon from it. The weight yanked the pointer to its stop at a maximum of fifteen pounds.

"Something over fifteen," California said. He dragged his first catch out of the water on the stringer and they laid the three fish out side-by-side on the grass.

"Three salmon . . . eleven and a half, twelve, and fifteen plus," Kipling said, admiring the sleek silver bodies. "Enough delectable flesh to feed a family of four for a fortnight, if they could dry it or smoke it."

"We'll give 'em to the family who runs the boarding house where we put up," California proposed.

"Good idea," Kipling agreed. "And any more we catch, we'll just weigh and throw back."

"Agreed."

Thorne slipped a cord stringer through the gills of the three big fish and swung them into the icy water for preservation.

The rest of that sunlit afternoon was more of the same. But the enthusiasm of the fishermen never waned. For the next six hours they splashed up and down the stream, hooking, fighting, and landing salmon after salmon, then releasing them. The smallest fish was a six-pounder that fought like one twice its size.

Thorne climbed to the top rail of a fence so he could see both men who had worked themselves a hundred yards apart. Kipling, playing yet another salmon, gradually waded around a bend of the stream and out of sight behind a thick stand of pines.

Thorne waited a few minutes for him to reappear. California was far upstream in the other direction. The steady rush of water, crashing over boulders, drowned all the small sounds, except for the chirping of birds in the nearby underbrush. He thought he heard a yip, like a dog barking in the distance. Then a howl. He turned his head to the slight breeze. There it came again — a distinctly human yell from downstream. He jumped off the top rail of the fence, caught his heel, and tumbled down the bank to the gravel beach, smashing the crock jug of whiskey and tangling himself in the landing net. Struggling up, he grabbed the gaff and sprinted along the pebbly shore toward the sound. Sixty yards later he rounded the bend and saw Kipling on hands and knees at the edge of a gravel bar. Panting from exertion, Thorne splashed across the shallows toward the downed man. As he got closer, he realized the shaft of a feathered arrow was protruding from Kipling's side.

CHAPTER
EIGHT

In the remaining seconds it took him to reach Kipling, Thorne's heart was in his mouth. He'd taken his eyes off his charge for less than five minutes, and someone had gotten him.

He slid to a stop at Kipling's side. "It's OK. Don't move. Let me see where it hit you."

The arrow had penetrated the creel that contained his notebook, and the sharpened metal head had only partially imbedded itself in the muscle of his right buttock. "Hold still." Thorne grasped the shaft and yanked. The two-inch barb was not in far enough to catch, and it came out easily. "Did you see where it came from?"

"No. Must be Indians," Kipling gasped through clenched teeth.

"Indians, my ass!" Thorne snapped.

"No, it's *my* ass."

"That's a factory-made hunting arrow." He had his Remington out of its holster as he scanned the thick pine trees whose branches swept low to the ground. The nearest tree line was about thirty yards away. "Here, crawl up under cover for a minute." Thorne helped Kipling to move a few feet to his right and lie down on wet gravel below the lip of a two-foot bank. Seeing the look of fear in Kipling's wide eyes, he added: "I'll be right back. You're not hurt bad."

Thorne leaped up and dashed toward the trees, praying he wouldn't feel an arrow thud into his own chest before he ducked into cover of the pines. He wove his way through the pines, revolver cocked and ready. A horse whinnied somewhere in the near distance, and he sprinted toward the sound. Before he got near, he heard hoof beats. Breathless, he burst from the grove of pines and saw a single horse and rider topping a rise a hundred yards away. But it was only a quick glimpse before they disappeared over the hill at full gallop. He came to a stop, panting and frustrated. The image locked into his mind's eye was of a sorrel horse carrying an indistinct, hatted figure, with something hanging diagonally across the rider's back. A carbine on a sling? He concentrated on the vanished impression. Instead of a rifle, it might very well have been a bow and quiver.

He stood for a long minute, catching his breath, then holstered his pistol and quickly searched the area where the attacker might have laid in wait for Kipling. He found some prints of a shod horse in the soft earth near the trees, and several places where the smooth layer of dead pine needles had been scuffed up. Slight indentations and disturbed needles showed where the archer had stood beside a tree that afforded a clear shot at anyone in the stream less than thirty yards away. With a target as big as a man, it would have been a relatively easy shot for an experienced bowman.

He hurried back to Kipling who was sitting on the grassy bank, his wet trousers down to his knees as he stretched around, trying to see the wound in his right buttock.

"It's not bad," Thorne said, coming up to him.

"Hurts like hell," Kipling said, grimacing.

"I'm sure it does. Let me take a look." The oozing puncture wound was beginning to clot. "Let me wash it off with some clean water." He made Kipling squat down and put his bottom in the cold stream.

"Ahhh!" Kipling gasped. "This water must be right off a glacier."

"Hold still. The wound is not over an inch deep. Probably could use a stitch or two, but it'll heal OK. Ought to leave the cut open and wash it out good in case there was poison on the tip of that arrow."

Kipling's face went ashen. Thorne was immediately sorry he'd mentioned the possibility. But, as long as he had, he plunged ahead. "Both the creel and the arrow fell into the water, so the tip was washed clean of any substance that might have been on it. But let that wound bleed as much as it will just in case. This nut who's after you could be capable of anything."

He helped Kipling back to the bank where the writer adjusted his clothes.

"That creel likely saved your life," Thorne said, retrieving the woven wicker basket. "It was hanging loose and took most of the force. Your notebook also helped slow it down. Let's go back and see if California's OK." Thorne picked up the arrow along with the gaff he'd dropped. "Can you walk?"

Kipling nodded as he gathered his rod, creel, and hand-held scales. He glanced apprehensively at the sheltering pines. "Did you see anyone back there? Thought I heard a horse."

"I got a quick look at a rider hightailing over the hill. Couldn't make out if it was a man or a woman."

"*Woman?*" Kipling arched his brows.

"At this point I'm not discounting any possibility." He didn't want to go into a long explanation about Ann Gilcrease. "Found some marks where the shooter probably stood to take the shot."

"Damn," Kipling breathed softly as they walked upstream. "I'll admit I didn't think at first that anyone was actually out to harm me. But you're right. This incident has made a believer of me."

They trudged in silence, Kipling favoring his right leg. Then he grinned. "Well, if this is the price I had to pay for the most glorious day of my life, so be it. I'll even have an arrow wound I can brag about to the boys at the club back home. They'll naturally assume it was put there by wild Indians. Too bad the scar is not in a location where I can display it at dinner parties."

Thorne examined the tip of the arrow. It had been washed clean. The metal had only a little wavy blue and yellow tint as might be formed by fire tempering. If they were lucky, the head of the arrow had not been dipped in a poison of some kind. He'd read that poisons used by primitive South American tribes to kill game were fast-acting. It had been almost ten minutes now, and Kipling was showing no symptoms. Thorne began to breathe easier. After all, most of the attacks, although potentially deadly, had seemed intended to injure and frighten, rather than to kill outright. Yet he had second thoughts about that conclusion. Except for the purging agent in the orange juice, the other incidents, made to appear as accidents, could easily have been fatal.

"Don't mention this to California," Thorne said as the other fisherman came into sight. "If he notices your limp, just tell him you tripped and fell on the rocks."

"Why?"

"The fewer who know about this, the better."

Kipling nodded, and, in a few seconds, said: "I didn't hear any harmonica music."

"I didn't either, but the shooter was running by the time I got there. Maybe the wind carried the sound away, or you were too concerned with your wound to hear it."

"Likely. After that arrow hit me, I wouldn't have heard a brass band for a minute or two."

"I'm going to assume it was the same person, anyway."

"Hey, partner!" California waved at them. He came sloshing forward in the knee-deep water, holding his rod to one side. "Everything OK?" He gave Kipling a searching look. "You look a mite pale."

"Couldn't be better," Kipling answered, limping to a stop.

California picked up a much smaller salmon from the edge of the water and tossed it up the gravel bank. "This one got cut up on the rocks before I could land him," he said. "A meal for a hawk or buzzard."

Thorne saw the big man's eyes go to the shredded wicker where the arrow head had been torn out of Kipling's creel. The dark bloodstains were not noticeable on the writer's black, wet pants. California's lips compressed, but he said nothing. Suddenly his face brightened. "Don't know about you gents, but I'm ready to call it a day. I'm about whipped out."

"Just watching you two all day has caused me to work up a powerful appetite," Thorne said, retrieving from the icy water the stringer containing the three big salmon they'd caught earlier. "Breakfast was a long time ago. Give me a hand and we'll clean these fish and take 'em up to the boarding house for supper."

The next morning the men returned to Portland, tired, sore, sunburned, but happy.

"Best time I've had in years," California declared after they turned in their team and buggy at the livery. "Where you off to from here, Johnny Bull?"

"Montana —"

"By way of Tacoma and Victoria, British Columbia," Thorne interrupted.

Kipling shot him a look of irritation.

"It was great meeting you, California." Thorne thrust out a hand. They shook all around.

"You going back home?" Kipling asked.

"Not right away," the big man said. "I have a little business to take care of."

Thorne and Kipling returned to the hotel to pick up their steamer trunks and send them to the depot.

Back in their room, they changed into their traveling clothes. Kipling dropped his breeches and dabbed some alcohol on his small arrow wound that was scabbing over. "Why did you tell California we were going to Tacoma?" he asked. "I have no intention of going that way, although I wouldn't mind seeing a refreshing bit of my homeland in Victoria."

"When someone's after you, it's not a good idea to go around telling strangers your itinerary."

"California wasn't a stranger."

"He was three days ago. What do you really know about Mister Rudolph Blixter?"

Kipling nodded. "You and your paranoia take the fun out of everything."

"It's my job."

"So, tell me, Mister Bodyguard, to what destination are we buying tickets today?"

"Yellowstone National Park, by way of Livingston, Montana."

"I'm glad I have someone to make out my schedule, since I'm only twenty-four years old."

Thorne shrugged. "Make up your own route, then. I thought that was the direction you planned to travel."

Kipling gave a tired smile. "It is. Sorry. Maybe when we get over the Rockies, my nemesis will leave me alone."

"What makes you think so?"

"It's what you Americans call a hunch."

"You don't know American criminals well enough to have hunches about them."

106

As they rode the hotel hack toward the depot, Thorne wondered if he himself knew enough to have hunches about this particular criminal. Was this person, among other talents, also a skilled archer? Could it have been Ann Gilcrease? Undoubtedly. She was physically strong and, from what he could see, kept herself in good condition. He recalled taking hold of her arm on the boat. Her muscles were firm enough to pull a compound bow with forty to sixty pounds of pressure. When she'd offered her hand in mock friendship as they were about to part, he'd noted the callused palm. What about the first two fingers? Most archers developed calluses on those fingers from the constant friction of drawing and releasing the string. It was another piece of circumstantial evidence to file in his mind.

Since all the Pullmans were taken, they arranged to travel in a cheaper, emigrant car. It was crowded, but clean.

Kipling tossed his grip on the floor and sat on the plank bunk that was covered with only a thin blanket. "Whew! An Indian fakir would have trouble sleeping on this."

"Immigrants are generally a tougher breed."

"A poorer breed, you mean."

The train pulled out and they were under way for a half hour when the conductor came through, punching tickets.

A muscular man in his thirties slouched on the next seat. Thorne guessed the man hadn't shaved or bathed in several weeks. An odor of whiskey mingled with the stench of his unwashed body and clothing.

"Ticket!" the blue-uniformed conductor said, stepping up to the passenger.

"Move on!" the man snapped. "This road owes me a free one." He turned back to stare out the window.

The conductor's face set at this rebuff. He took a deep breath and tried again. "If you didn't have time to buy a ticket, sir," he said in a controlled voice, "I can take your fare in cash now."

"I told you to move on. I'm not paying any damned fare for this rolling apple crate!"

The conductor was a raw-boned man at least six feet tall whose shoulders stretched the blue fabric of the uniform coat. His hand shot out, grabbed the truculent man by the jacket collar, and yanked him off the bunk. The whiskey-soaked freeloader, taken by surprise, quickly recovered and slammed a fist into the side of the conductor's head, knocking off his cap. The trainman caught him in a bear hug, and the two grappled, neither able to gain advantage as they swayed back and forth in the aisle.

The conductor chopped the edge of his big hand down on the base of the man's neck and broke his hold. In a flash, he spun the drunk around and aimed a vicious kick at the passenger's backside, booting his head and shoulders through the window. The window exploded, shards of glass flying outside. The car lurched, flinging him back inside where he fell on the floor between the bunks.

"Porter!" the conductor yelled at a wide-eyed black man who'd just entered the car. "Wrap up this man's head before he bleeds all over the floor."

The porter went for some folded towels near the privy.

The drunk sat, stunned, his head lolling, blood streaming from four or five scalp lacerations.

The conductor sent for a doctor in one of the forward cars; he arrived with his medical bag and hastily stitched up the biggest gash.

"I'll give you the address of company headquarters in Milwaukee to submit your bill," the trainman said as the doctor wiped his hands and closed his bag.

"No charge," the young doctor said, standing up.

Thorne and Kipling silently regarded the recalcitrant passenger, submitting to having his head wiped with the towel.

"Thanks, Doc. Go have yourself a free drink," the conductor said. "Our next stop's fifteen minutes," he continued, consulting his nickel-plated watch. "We'll toss this character off there," he told the porter.

"He's still leaking pretty badly," Kipling remarked to the conductor.

"These bums never learn there's no profit in monkeying with the Northern Pacific Railway."

"He might bleed to death," Kipling persisted, eyeing the stunned passenger's crimson head and shirt.

The conductor shrugged. "That's his problem."

The abusive passenger was duly ejected onto the next station platform.

"Word of this likely got around quick," Thorne said, as the train began to roll again. "You can bet anybody else on this train who doesn't have a ticket is coughing up the money or they're jumping off like cockroaches. I don't think you'd have seen anything like that back East."

"I've been hearing that everywhere in the West," Kipling said. "If there is some gruesome lynching, the editorials say . . . 'That wouldn't happen in the East.' If there's a shooting scrape between two prominent citizens, I'm told . . . 'Oh, you'll find nothing of that kind in the East.' These perfect Easterners must be a different breed altogether. More genteel, more civilized. Maybe they don't even spit constantly."

The rest of the day was dull by comparison. In late afternoon the train emerged from the forest onto a sagebrush-covered plain. Kipling watched the monotonous scenery passing in eastern Oregon for an hour or more while the sun slid down the sky behind them.

"God, this sage is never-ending," he finally said. "Depressing."

Thorne emerged from a light doze and looked out the window. "There's a lot of it, sure enough. But I never thought of it as depressing."

"It's blue-gray . . . it's stunted . . . it's dusty. And it wraps these rolling hills like a mildewed shroud wraps the body of a long-dead man," Kipling said with revulsion.

"It smells good and provides ground cover to prevent erosion," Thorne responded cheerfully.

"So does clover."

"Clover can't be used as a cooking spice."

"There's enough sage out there to fill the Grand Cañon with pork sausage." Kipling gestured at the scene outside. "Just look at this desolation. It's enough to make a person weep for sheer loneliness. It stretches for miles and miles. There's no getting away from it. When Childe Roland came to the dark tower, he traversed the sagebrush."

"Lord Byron?" Thorne asked, trying to place the poetic reference.

"Sir Walter Scott," Kipling corrected him. "You're thinking of *Childe Harold's Pilgrimage*."

"Besides salmon fishing, is there *anything* you like about Western America?" Thorne asked.

"Oh, yes . . . the women and the abundance of good food. But I am getting a little weary of spectacular scenery. When you've seen one pine forest, a bluff, a river, you've seen all the scenery of Western America. Sometimes the pine is three hundred feet tall, and sometimes the rock is, and sometimes the lake is a hundred miles long. But it's all the same. Actually I shouldn't say I'm weary of it. But that's one reason I didn't go to Alaska. I would've seen islands even more wooded, snow peaks loftier, and rivers lovelier than those around me in Oregon. If Providence could distribute all this beauty in little bits where people needed it most . . . among the people of India, for instance . . . it would be well. But *en masse*, this beauty is overwhelming . . . with few besides the tobacco-chewing captain of a river steamer to look at it."

"You haven't seen the red rock cañon country of the Southwest," Thorne said.

Kipling nodded. "Maybe next trip. I know I'll be back, since I'm probably going to eventually find a wife among the long-limbed beauties of your country."

"You seem pretty sure of that."

"Oh, I am. My only problem will be selecting one from among the multitudes."

Thirty minutes later the train stopped to drop and receive some mail and freight and to take on a passenger.

"Where the deuce are we?" Kipling asked, glancing outside.

The only boarding passenger was entering their car at that moment and took it upon himself to reply. "Pasco Junction, pardner . . . Queen City of the Prairie." A look of smug satisfaction sat on his face as he headed forward toward a day coach.

Thorne looked out the window. He counted fifteen frame houses scattered beyond the tiny depot. Showing as a tan groove in the purple sage, a road ran into the distance, snaking its way up a far hill toward the setting sun. He looked back at Kipling who inclined his head at the scene and said: "There you have it . . . Pasco Junction, Queen City of the Prairie."

The train pulled out and Kipling began scribbling in his notebook.

Late that night, one of the passengers in their car was drunk and awoke Thorne, Kipling, and several others with an uproarious and off-key rendition of "Danny Boy".

112

A red-whiskered Cornishman they'd met earlier reached from his upper berth and turned up the low-burning kerosene lamp hanging from the ceiling in the aisle. "Pipe down!"

His command was ignored in a fresh outburst of singing. The Cornishman alighted in his long johns. Three steps brought him to the drunk; one punch laid out the caterwauling man across a bunk.

As the big Cornishman crawled back into his upper berth, he commented: "Maybe when the blighter wakes up, his head will hurt too much to sing."

"I'm on my best behavior this trip," Kipling whispered. "If the train crew doesn't do for you, another passenger will."

"Bravo!" piped up a woman, peeking between the curtains of her upper berth. "That drunk is a damned hog!" She abruptly withdrew from sight.

"She may be right," Kipling said in a low voice, "but that's pretty coarse language for a lady."

"There's a big difference between a lady and a female," Thorne said, rolling over and closing his eyes.

The next morning the train began its climb on long switchbacks, to the summit of the Rockies. Following breakfast Thorne and Kipling sat in the smoking section of the Pullman and listened for hours to several men spinning yarns. Without being obtrusive, Kipling kept his small notebook in hand, now and then scribbling a few words. He said little, only occasionally pushing a story along with a question or a comment. The other men, who were mostly middle-aged, seemed to have an inexhaustible supply of bloodthirsty tales. Thorne wondered how much of it was true. He'd heard many like them before and, knew from experience, the anecdotes were likely embellished in the telling. These men loved a willing audience, especially someone from England who didn't try to top them with more terrible stories of his own.

Thorne was glad Kipling was so absorbed in these wild tales, since they distracted the writer from looking out the window at the deep cañons and snow-covered rockslides they passed as the train crept laboriously upward.

The two men broke for a late lunch, then retired to their emigrant car to rest on their hard wooden lower bunk that had been converted into two opposing seats. Kipling pulled out his grip, removed a packet of paper, and proceeded to write up his notes, stacking the finished sheets beside him. He looked up irritably a time or two at children running up and down the aisle, screaming and chasing each other. One little boy of about five pretended to shoot another. The victim fell, choking and gasping with loud histrionics. Four girls of pre-school age were playing tag, dodging in and out of their parents' bunks, under the seats, and through the doors to the platforms at either end of the car. Two of the smaller children were crying, fretful, peevish, one throwing a fit on the floor, kicking and screaming, because his mother wouldn't buy him candy. But the fit wasn't working, since the adults paid no attention to them and continued talking, some playing cards, two women knitting.

Forty minutes later, Thorne leaned over and said —
"Mind if I have a look?" — indicating the pages lying
next to Kipling.

"Help yourself. With all this commotion, I hardly
know what I've written."

"These are the letters to your newspaper?" Thorne
asked, picking up the three top sheets.

"Yes."

Without reading every word, Thorne scanned down
the sheet and read:

. . . listening to yarns in the smoking compartment
. . . and with very few exceptions, each had for its
point, violent, brutal, and ruffianly murder —
murder by fraud and the craft of the savage —
murder unavenged by the law, sometimes resulting
in an outbreak of fresh lawlessness. At the end of
each tale I was assured that the old days had
passed away, and that these were anecdotes of five
years' standing. One man in particular distinguished
himself by holding up to admiration the exploits of
some cowboys of his acquaintance, and their skill
in the use of the revolver. Each tale of horror
wound up with, "and that's the sort of man he
was," as who should say: 'Go and do likewise.'
Remember that the shootings, the cuttings, and
the stabbings were not the outcome of any species
of legitimate warfare; the heroes were not forced to
fight for their lives. Far from it. The brawls were
bred by liquor in saloons and gambling hells. They
were wont to "pull their guns" on a man, in the

vast majority of cases, without provocation. The tales sickened me, but taught one thing: A man who carries a pistol may be put down as a coward — a person to be shut out from every decent mess and club, and gathering of civilized folk. There is neither chivalry nor romance in the weapon, for all that American authors have seen fit to write. I would I could make you understand the full measure of contempt with which certain aspects of Western life have inspired me. Human life is of small account out here.

Thorne put down the pages. "It's good to see all this through the eyes of someone who is new to it," he said. "These stories in the smoking car, the carrying of a gun and all that."

Kipling gestured at two boys rolling under the seats, punching each other's bloody noses, and tearing their clothes. "These children are spoilt beyond anything I've ever seen in Anglo-India. In time they'll grow up into such men as were in the smoker, with no regard for the law."

"I was under the impression that human life was even cheaper in overcrowded India," Thorne said.

"Not in the Anglo strata of society. Only among the impoverished masses, but, there, it's due to disease more than violence. There are millions of people and the species does not care if a few hundred of them die each day. Western America does not have that many people to lose, that they can afford to be killing one another."

116

The train braked to a stop in a hiss of steam at a remote town near the summit of the Rockies. "What kind of wild Indian is that?" Kipling asked, pointing out the window at a black-haired man in a mackinaw on the depot platform.

"I believe he's a Flathead."

"Rather unlovely to look at."

"There are a few tribes who might be considered handsome by white standards," Thorne said.

"Not only do white Westerners shoot each other, but, to a man, they all want to exterminate the savages."

"I'll grant you that's probably the prevailing attitude," Thorne admitted. "Sometimes makes me ashamed of my race."

Kipling started to say something, but stopped.

"As for this gun I'm wearing, it's for protection only . . . both mine and yours. Don't lump me in with all these men you mention in your letters who drink and quarrel and fight."

"Didn't intend to accuse you of that. But, it seems to me, the presence of a revolver only beckons trouble."

"You don't wear a gun, and trouble has been stalking you. I intend to fight fire with fire. This revolver may not protect you completely, but I feel much safer with it than without it. As you know, any emergency can arise. Would the average man have gone traveling about the countryside during the Middle Ages, say, without at least a dagger in his belt? I hardly think so. Unsettled times, unsettled places. Just like the here and now."

Thorne perused more of the writer's written observations. What would the readers of Kipling's newspaper think of America after they read these? That all Americans were this way? Would they take into account that the reporter's comments were only one man's opinion? It was a good thing Americans wouldn't have a chance to see these. Then a thought crept into his mind, and he laid the papers in his lap. "Remember when California was trying to get you to look at some of that spectacular scenery in the Columbia River gorge?"

Kipling nodded.

"California was all excited and he made a remark that startled me and stuck in my mind nearly *verbatim*. He said . . . 'Unsullied nature. You put your poison pen to describing what you see in America. I defy you to say anything bad about this.' "

"Yes, I recall that now."

"Had you shown him any of your notes or letters to your paper?"

Kipling thought for a moment. "No. Mostly kept my notebook in my pocket. When I was jotting in it, I was careful that noone else could see it."

"So, at no time that we traveled with him was he able to read what you wrote?"

"Not at all. I posted two long letters from the hotel in Portland where we stayed. Left them at the front desk for the clerk to mail."

"Then how did California know you described America with a 'poison pen'?"

Kipling's Adam's apple bobbed up and down as he swallowed. "I don't know, unless he somehow

118

intercepted those letters before they arrived into the hands of the post office." His face bore a solemn look.

Thorne's mind was racing. "And do you remember how surprised he seemed to be when you returned from downstream, looking hale and hearty?"

"Yes. Almost as if he expected me to be wounded or dead," Kipling said.

"Before we get to Helena, I'm going to search this train to see if California, alias Rudolph Blixter, is aboard. You meet all kinds of characters in the West, but I had a strange feeling about that man from the beginning. He could very likely be the one who's stalking you. And I think I know who his accomplice is." Thorne went on to reveal, in detail, his meeting with Ann Gilcrease aboard the Columbia River steamer and her unsavory past.

Kipling listened, blue eyes wide behind the round-lensed wire spectacles.

"Can't we have them arrested on suspicion?" Kipling asked when Thorne finished.

"It would do no good, even if I knew where Ann Gilcrease or California presently are. As far as the law is concerned, they've done nothing wrong. We'll have to catch them in the act."

"Not a very cheery prospect."

The conductor entered the car and passed down the aisle. "Ladies and gents, we're coming up on Stampede Tunnel . . . our actual high point in crossing the Rocky Mountains. It's going to get suddenly dark. Keep your children close by."

Within five minutes, the daylight blinked off when the train entered the two-mile-long tunnel. They were barely moving. Grinding brakes echoed in the hollow space as the train slowed its momentum on the downgrade.

"Now would be a good time for fervent prayer," Kipling whispered.

Water and tiny bits of rock drummed on the roof of the car.

"I would rather have complete blackness," Kipling breathed, staring at the rough-cut rocks and timber shoring that were dimly revealed by the periodic coal-oil lamps.

"Looks just like a mine tunnel," Thorne offered.

"I know. I can't take my eyes off those old timbers for fear they'll collapse without my moral support."

"This line used to cross the summit by means of a series of switchbacks in the open air."

"I wish it still did."

"The tunnel is shorter and quicker. And it doesn't get blocked by snow slides. A watchman lives nearby and goes through the tunnel with a lantern after each train," Thorne said in an effort to reassure.

"Haphazard, at best. Someday there will be a cave in. I can just hear some enterprising reporter describing the shrieks and groans of those buried alive, and how the press was heroic in getting there first with the story . . ."

"Your imagination is overactive," Thorne said, wondering how the young man had so far escaped developing ulcers.

120

After what seemed an eon, they finally emerged into daylight again, but Kipling's nerves had no time to relax. While they descended the eastern slope of the mountains, they spent another eternity crossing an iron trestle 280 feet above a gorge. Thorne didn't want to mention that this bridge was a replacement for a wooden one that had been used long after the civil engineers condemned it.

They sat up late and talked, waiting, as Thorne said: "For all these brats to wear out and go to bed."

Finally, sometime past midnight, they slid the wooden seat tops together to form the lower berth. They bid each other good night, and Thorne climbed to the upper. But sleep was delayed a little longer since the train must have run over a skunk. The car filled with the choking stench.

"Everything that's been said about the skunk is true," Kipling gasped. "It's an awesome stink!"

CHAPTER
NINE

The crowd of loud, eager passengers debarked at Cinnabar Station south of Livingston, Montana and made a rush for five Concord stages and two mud wagons that would haul them the last eight miles to Mammoth Hot Springs Hotel just inside the northern boundary of Yellowstone Park. Another large group surged forward at the same time to compete with the train passengers for the available coach space.

"You damned hussy! Get that bustle outta my face . . . I was here first!" a woman shrilled.

"That's no bustle, honey, that's my ass!" the woman shot back, continuing to force her way first into the coach.

"Hey! There's room for everyone!" a man shouted as he got an elbow in front of his neighbor. Hats were knocked off in the crush; parasols jabbed and prodded.

"Best grab a place on this lead coach," a man at Thorne's elbow said. He turned to see a white-headed, elderly gentleman.

"Why?"

"Otherwise, you'll be eating dust all the way to Yellowstone. And this driver gets there a lot quicker than the rest. He's the best."

"Thanks, mister."

The elderly man in the tweed coat was forced away from them in the crowd.

"Who the hell are *these* people?" Kipling yelled up to the driver of the lead coach. "That bunch didn't all get off our train." He and Thorne could hardly move in the throng.

The driver chuckled as he drew on his skin-tight leather gloves and looked down from his high perch at the pushing, shoving mass. "You've struck one of Rayment's excursion parties . . . that's all . . . a crowd of Creator-condemned fools mostly," he said. "Aren't you one of 'em?"

"No. Never heard of Mister Rayment. May the two of us sit up there with you, great chief and man with the golden tongue?"

"Hoist yourselves on up here," the grinning driver said. He reached down to give them a hand.

Kipling and Thorne gratefully climbed atop the coach. The interior was already crammed with more than a dozen passengers, and two men were trying to force the door shut from the outside against a mass of bodies.

Kipling sat on the box to the left of the driver where, in more perilous times, the shotgun guard would have ridden. Thorne wedged himself in among the leather valises strapped to the roof that would not fit in the front or rear boot.

As soon as the driver whipped up the six-horse hitch and they lunged away, Thorne sensed the tall Concord coach was top-heavy, despite all the weight below.

"Yeh, Rayment runs a fair-size company that herds tourists out this way," the driver said, shifting a chaw of tobacco from one cheek to the other and letting fly with a stream of brown juice into the roadside brush. "Draws 'em from about seven Northeastern states. Well-to-do folks, mostly."

"I guess every country has its wealthy rabble," Kipling said.

"Oh, no," the driver said, his eyes on the road ahead. "I've seen the passenger list. Lots of prominent people this trip . . . bank officers, local politicos, schoolteachers, owners of businesses . . ."

"Incredible!" Kipling said. He turned around toward Thorne who was sitting cross-legged on the coach roof. "There go my dreams of a better, more perfect East."

Thorne shrugged. "People are people."

"But . . . ghastly vulgarity, oozing, rampant Bessemer steel self-sufficiency and ignorance . . . among both men and women. It revolts me."

"Don't be too quick to judge. They probably have some good qualities," Thorne said distractedly, staring off at the scenery.

Reddish dust boiled up behind them to obscure the following coaches. Thorne was glad they had grabbed the first stage as the parade moved south at a trot over the rolling hills. After about two miles, the driver cracked the lines over the backs of the horses and they broke into a gallop. The tall coach pitched and rolled like a ship in heavy seas.

"Compared to this, riding a hansom cab is like sitting in a stuffed chair!" Kipling cried above the thunder of hoofs.

Thorne merely nodded, not really sure of the comparison. He assumed a hansom cab was some sort of British city conveyance.

Kipling turned back to look at him, the wind whipping his black hair. He'd lost his hat somewhere *en route*, and the skin of his face and nose were peeling from sunburn. Their unplanned two-day fishing stop had caused most of the damage to the writer's fair skin.

A stranger on the train had heard Kipling's comment that the sparkling Yellowstone River, below the train windows, probably hid some good trout. "Lay over at Yankee Jim's, if you want some good trout fishing," the stranger had said.

It only took a few minutes for the writer to find out who Yankee Jim was and to put the conductor on notice that he wanted to be dropped there. By then Thorne was growing used to such impromptu, headstrong decisions, and had his small grip in hand when the train ground to a halt. Their trunks would be delivered on to Livingston and transferred to the line going south from there. The two men would catch up later where the branch line ended near the park.

Even though Thorne was not a fisherman, he had taken his turn with the rod over the next two days, and had discovered the stranger's comment about good fishing had been an understatement. The men had paid their bed and board to Yankee Jim, a crusty character who had lived in a cabin on the river for nearly thirty years. The weathered, bearded Jim had a small income from the toll he charged for use of a twenty-mile wagon road he'd constructed single-handedly. The rent he got for guiding fishermen added to his income in summer. How a man could stand to live here in winter was beyond Thorne's imagination.

A windier individual Thorne had never heard as Yankee Jim had regaled them with tales of hunting, fighting Indians, and various other types of violence. A guest of Jim's that week was a man who owned a stock farm upriver and his beautiful, twenty-five-year-old wife. Thorne noticed how Kipling hardly took his eyes off her the whole time they sat by the fire the first night, drinks in hand, listening to Yankee Jim's stories.

Now, as the stage bowled along the dusty road, Thorne's thoughts turned to their stalkers. He hoped the unpredictable and sudden departure from the train had thrown off their pursuers. A walk-through of the train had revealed no one suspicious. It was a long chance he would have known their pursuers. Ann Gilcrease was so adept at disguises, she could have been in plain sight, but unrecognizable. As for Rudolph Blixter, alias California, Thorne could only assume he was the other stalker. Thorne had seen no one on the train that even resembled the big, bluff man.

Either the coach driver was trying to keep some sort of schedule, or was showing off his skill for the crowd of New England passengers. Thorne gripped the iron rail rimming the roof of the coach as the stage hit the bottom of a gully and bounded up the far slope.

"*Hyah! Hyah!*" The driver popped the lines over the backs of the straining team. Trace chains jingled and the lathered horses leaned into their breast straps. To take his mind off the danger of the swaying coach, Thorne raised his eyes to the forested slopes and distant peaks, still snow-capped in early July. He made a quick mental calculation and realized today was the 4th — Independence Day. No wonder many in the touring party were waving miniature American flags, and fastening them to the sides of the coach. Having no reason to reflect on the day of the month, he'd lost all track of time these past weeks. He and Kipling had traveled far and experienced much — not all of it pleasant — since they'd met aboard *The City of Peking*. He suspected there was much more to come.

The coach careened around a curve, leaning precariously. Thorne grabbed a trunk to brace himself. Feminine laughter squealed from the open windows below him. How long could the team run at this pace, pulling this load? The road dipped and curved, but was gradually climbing.

They passed other stages heading north, loaded with travelers who'd done their tour of the park. Shouted greetings whipped past, along with the red dust.

This section of the West still resembled wilderness, but was certainly getting crowded, Thorne reflected. He breathed deeply. The upland air was like a heady gas — clear, pure, and invigorating. No haze obscured distant objects. Mountains, appearing to be about ten miles away, were in reality more than six times that far. Perspective of distance was lost, and the deceived eye saw hillsides of giant conifers as low-growing ground cover.

The stage pitched and swayed. The driver seemed to delight in testing the outer limits of centrifugal force, holding the horses on the curves to a speed that barely kept the wheels adhering to the road. The way now ran along a ridge sixty feet above the Gardiner River. The spinning, steel-shod rims slipped to the outside with only inches to spare as the driver nonchalantly guided the team into a bend. Thorne lay flat on his stomach, gripping the low, iron rail, peering down over the edge of the roof, squinting through the fine dust at the whirling blur of spokes in the big wheels. Through his chest and belly, he felt every lurch and slip and bump of the heavy stage, and admired the unknown Yankee genius who'd designed the ungainly yet gracefully efficient Concord.

Down off the ridge they went, the horses now at a full gallop. All the weight of the overloaded coach hit the bottom of the dip — and something broke. The stage lurched to the left, flinging Kipling off as if shot from a cannon. Thorne was jammed against a heavy trunk, breaking the cord holding it, and both flew off the left side. He saw only a flash of rocks and grass. Then he tucked and rolled. His shoulder and back took the brunt of the fall, knocking the breath from him, and he tumbled over and over, feeling the brush and stones tearing at him, until he slid to a stop. Stunned, he lay for several seconds on his back, wondering how badly he was hurt. Then he heard a rending crash, the noise of splintering wood, followed by sudden silence.

The silence lasted only the space of one breath; then the air was filled with wailing, crying, screaming, cursing. Thorne sat up, his head reeling. Through a veil of dust, he saw the stage on its side about forty yards away. The team had broken loose and was running up the opposite slope of the draw.

He moved carefully to be sure nothing was broken. Where was Kipling? He'd seen the writer fly off the coach first, and looked back. Several yards away, the smaller man was crawling toward him on hands and knees, spectacles hanging by one bow from his right ear, blood leaking from his nose.

Thorne staggered to his feet, ignoring his cuts and bruises. "Are you all right?" He crouched next to Kipling, carefully removing the writer's spectacles. Noting they weren't broken, he slipped them into his own shirt pocket.

"What happened?" Kipling's eyes gave back a stunned, blank look.

"The stage wrecked. We got thrown off."

Kipling took a deep breath and slid to a sitting position. "I . . . think I'm OK." He felt his arms and legs. "Nothing broken that I can tell." His collarless white shirt was red with blood on top of the shoulder by his neck.

Thorne turned him and saw an oozing cut behind the ear. Pulling his own clean handkerchief from a vest pocket, he pressed it to the cut. "Hold that for a few minutes. You got a nasty gash on your head."

Kipling nodded and did as instructed. Thorne took the spectacles out of his pocket, wiped them as best he could on his shirt-tail, and hooked them behind the writer's ears. "That should help the world come back into focus. Sit still a minute and let me check on some of these other folks." He moved toward the wrecked stage at a walk, beginning to feel the soreness of his own bruises.

The driver appeared unhurt and was helping calm some of the women who had climbed from the overturned stage and were sitting on the grass, crying and moaning. One man was holding his arm and cursing softly while another fashioned a rude splint from a short piece of paneling from the shattered coach.

"I've taken a quick survey. All my party are accounted for," a big, bearded man said, coming up to the driver. "Thank God, nobody was killed. What the hell happened, anyway?" demanded the head of the touring party. "You were driving too damned fast!"

The lean driver slowly rose to his feet, his face darkening at the accusation. "That's the way I always drive this route. I felt something give way underneath as we hit the bottom of that wash." He ignored the irate tour guide and walked to the overturned stage. One rear wheel was still slowly turning. He bent down and carefully examined the undercarriage. Thorne followed and watched him run a hand over the axles and look at the hubs. The coach lay on its left side. Thorne tried to reconstruct those final seconds in his mind. The coach had lurched violently to the left, as if the left front wheel had fallen into a hole, ejecting the topside passengers.

130

"Felt like the left front wheel came off," he commented to the crouching driver.

"I know, but that wasn't it," the driver said.

Thorne acquiesced to the man's experience and said no more. Then he noted the driver examining what could be seen of the left front hub. The lean man had evidently seen something because he wormed his way between the wheels to inspect the leather thorough brace. "Huh!" he grunted, wiggling back out and standing up, anger and puzzlement on his dust-streaked face.

Just then the following coach came clattering over the rise. The driver had time to rein in the trotting team when he saw the devastation. He set the brake, looped the lines around the brake handle, and climbed down. The first driver approached him. "Thorough brace broke when we hit the bottom of the grade, Charley," he said, pointing. "Thank God, nobody killed. A few cuts and bruises. One man broke a wrist."

Thorne was standing a few feet from the two drivers. Tourists were swarming out of the second coach, talking excitedly. The lean driver noticed Thorne nearby, and turned his back on him to speak to the newly arrived coachman, but Thorne still overheard his next remark.

"Come, take a look at that thorough brace, Charley. It broke because somebody cut it nearly in two!"

A soft knock sounded on the door of a first-floor room in the Mammoth Hot Springs Hotel. The rap was followed by three distinct notes from a harmonica.

Ann Gilcrease took a quick look at herself in the small wall mirror, patted her hair into place, and tugged her bodice down slightly to reveal more of her ample breasts. Satisfied with the result, she turned to open the door.

A large, florid man entered quickly and closed the door behind him, twisting the key in the lock.

"I was beginning to wonder what had happened to you," she said, smiling at him.

He yanked off a voluminous white wig and tossed it on the bed. "Damnation! It's hot out there!" He seemed out of breath and out of sorts. The thinning red hair under the wig contrasted sharply with the white beard he wore. "And this beard itches like the very devil. You got something to drink?" He plopped down in one of two armchairs in the room, tugging at his necktie.

"You'll have to admit, no one recognized you on the train," she said, stooping to pull a flat silver flask from her valise on the floor. She handed it to him. "If there's one thing I'm good at, it's make-up and disguises."

"Yeah," he nodded grudgingly as he tilted the flask to his lips and took a long swallow. "*Whew!*" He handed the flask back to her.

Another sharp rap at the door made them both jump.

"Yes?" she answered. "Who is it?"

"Telegram for you, Miss Martin," came a voice.

"Just a moment." She fumbled in her reticule for a coin. Opening the door, she favored the young desk clerk with a winning smile. "Thank you so much."

"My pleasure," he replied, taking the quarter she pressed into his hand.

The big man moved out from behind the door as she closed it. "I think I like you better as Julie Ann Martin." He grinned.

She ignored him as she tore open the envelope and pulled out a small, folded sheet.

The brief message read:

The book can be completed.

There was no name, but she knew it came from their contact at Seaside Press in San Francisco. It was telling her they could stop harassing Rudyard Kipling and should now kill him. She tried to maintain a pokerface to hide her shock. She had almost begun to enjoy arranging "accidents" for the writer and outwitting her old nemesis, Alexander Thorne. It had become a game as they moved across the country.

"What is it?" the man asked.

She handed him the telegram without speaking.

He read the message. "Well, now I can stop running around pretending I'm a loud-mouthed fisherman called California," he said with obvious relief. "Or a white-headed old tourist. Time to revert to my best rôle as Rudolph Blixter, executioner."

She paced to the window and drew back the curtain. High mountain sunshine streamed through the glass, bathing her in welcome warmth, driving away an inner chill. During the war and for twenty years afterward, she couldn't seem to satisfy her craving for vengeance

133

against the Yankee invaders. But the fires had finally burned out. For the past four years she'd continued hiring herself out, through her many underground connections, to various criminals to seduce, stalk, entrap, and even murder. It was a business she would rather have given up. Yet most of her life, she had done nothing else and so, out of habit, continued to follow the same well-worn path. She had to admit that she would have found a legitimate job boring; she still reveled in the thrill of the chase, the danger of being caught or killed. But she wasn't far from fifty, and was sensing a need to rest, to find some safe haven, a sheltered harbor out of the storms. Alex Thorne had been right when he asked her what she would do when she became too old to attract men. That time had not yet come, and, before it did, she had one hole card to play.

Rudolph Blixter had a nefarious past just as she did. But, more to the point, he appeared to be in love with her. She'd purposely fostered this attraction since they began working together on this mission several weeks before. Blixter had been contacted in Japan and told to go aboard *The City of Peking* to make the life of one Rudyard Kipling very precarious. She had met Blixter in San Francisco when they were brought together by a hooded man with a connection to Seaside Press and given instructions to shadow the writer and make his life a living hell as he journeyed across America. They were ordered not to kill, but to discourage him from continuing, force him to cut short his trip and return to India. The only reason given was that Kipling needed to be forced back into the clutches of some unnamed, but powerful, Indian enemy. The mystery of it appealed to her sense of suspense and travel and danger. And it left them free to come up with their own ways of operating. They reported by coded telegram back to San Francisco. Kipling was good-looking, even though she would have preferred him without the cigar and glasses. She smiled at the idea of being attracted to a man half her age. The red-headed, barrel-chested Blixter was a more realistic prospect. He was about five years older than she, and very congenial to work with. By nature, he was not as devious as most of the men in this business. Both of them had well-stocked bank accounts under assumed names, and her intention from the beginning was to land this man for a husband. The very idea of being married seemed odd to her, after all the men who'd posed as her husbands, and all the lovers she'd had. The lure of stability after a rootless life drew her more than emotional or physical attraction to this balding, middle-aged assassin. But she'd take what she could get. It had always been her way.

"When those two dropped off the train to go trout fishing, we came near to losing them," she remarked, coming back to the present.

"Well, I was the one who had to stay behind and keep an eye on them," Blixter said. "Camping in the woods and stealing food for two days was no picnic," he grumbled.

"I had to kill two days at Cinnabar Station, waiting for the three of you to show up on the next train," she said. "While I was there, I found out that old man

Mosely usually drove the first stage in the procession, and always drove like a madman to impress the women tourists, so I slipped under the coach the last night and slit that thorough brace . . .”

“And without Thorne and Kipling being aware of it, I herded ’em toward that coach when all the passengers made a dash for the stages.” Blixter grinned at her. “What a team, you and me!”

“A deadly duo,” she agreed, returning his smile. “All we had to do was follow along in the third stage and watch the fun.”

“Yeah. That wreck just banged him up a bit. Too bad neither of us had a chance to play him a little mouth organ music at the Clackamas River when you shot him with that arrow, or after this morning’s wreck.”

“Too dangerous leaving our signature. But I’m sure Kipling knew it was us. If he didn’t, Alex Thorne surely did,” she said, turning back to look out the window at several plumes of steam rising from distant geysers. She had taken pains to stay out of sight when the passengers from the wrecked stage had been divided up among the following coaches and brought here to the Mammoth Hot Springs Hotel. The six-horse hitch, dragging the broken doubletree, had already shown up at their barn and the hostlers had taken them out of harness.

“All that cat-and-mouse stuff is over now,” Blixter said. “Our bosses have decided it’s time to finish off the Britisher.”

“Have you ever read any of his stories?” she asked, still staring out the window.

"No."

"I haven't either. I've heard he's a very good writer."

"Maybe so," Blixter said, splashing some water into the bowl on the nightstand. "Wonder what that weasel could've done to make such a mighty enemy in India?"

"I wonder what he's like as a man," she countered. "Were you ever curious about a man you were hired to kill?"

"Naw. It's strictly business with me."

"Someone would have to be rotten with hate to pay thousands in blood money," she mused, feeling reflective. "I can't imagine how a small fella like that Britisher could be a threat to anyone."

"Napoléon was a little man," he reminded her. "It's the size of the teeth, not the size of the dog." He was holding a wet handkerchief to his glued beard and attempting to peel it off.

"Don't do that!" she cried. "You must stay in disguise a little longer while we're here in Yellowstone."

He frowned at her, but turned away from the mirror. "Why?"

"You wouldn't want them to recognize you. The footing on the plank walkways around here is precarious. Wouldn't it be tragic if Mister Kipling were to trip and fall into one of the boiling hot basins of water?"

She saw the light dawning in his eyes. "Accidents have also been known to happen on these overlooks above the falls of the Yellowstone."

"The deadly possibilities are endless," she said. "We may not have to ride these dusty trains any farther

East." She rubbed up against him. "We've probably even got time for ourselves before preparing our last rendezvous with them," she said seductively.

Thirty minutes later, Blixter finished buttoning his shirt, then reached for the gray wig on the bedpost. "I need a beer. I'll meet you in the barroom in about an hour," he said.

She felt a sudden pang of disappointment and irritation that he would just jump up and run off with no conversation, no show of tenderness, after their lovemaking. But most men were like that, and he was even more so, she'd discovered, in their several trysts on the train.

He looked into the mirror to adjust the white hairpiece. "Let's not be getting any ideas about each other," he said bluntly. "As soon as this Kipling fella is disposed of, I've got places to go . . . alone." He turned around and faced her. "It's been good fun, but you and I are like oil and water . . . never meant to be together."

The slamming door left her with a bitterness she could almost taste.

CHAPTER
TEN

"I can't do it!" Kipling tore the sheet in half and threw the pieces on the floor beside his chair.

"What?" Thorne had been leaning against a post on the front porch of the Mammoth Hot Springs Hotel, watching the frustrated writer.

"I've written this letter twice, but I can't make it sound believable. My editor, and anyone at home who reads it, will think I've gone suddenly mad." He smoothed another blank sheet of paper in his folder. "Now, I'll start again, very solemnly and soberly for the third time, and see if I can describe places in this park in a way that readers who've not seen it will believe." After a slight hesitation, he began scratching his pen across the paper.

Thorne chuckled while packing rough-cut tobacco into his pipe. "You're only the latest to have that problem. More than eighty years ago, John Colter was one of the first white men to see this country. He wasn't near as literate as you are, and, when he tried to describe what he'd seen here, everyone thought he'd been alone in the wilderness too long and was a mite teched in the head."

Kipling paused. "All these hot springs and fantastic formations and geysers and colors. It's like . . . describing the surface of the moon or Mars. If my editor finds out I took a bang on the head when I fell off that stage, he'll know I've gone round the bend for sure."

"It's something you have to see to believe, that's certain," Thorne said, raking a wooden match across the rough railing and puffing his pipe to life.

Tourists strolled in and out the front door of the huge yellow hotel. Several coaches in the front driveway were taking on passengers for the daily tours. Kipling and Thorne had decided to wait a day to let Kipling's head have time to begin healing. Except for a minor soreness when he sat for long periods, the arrow wound was nearly well. Both men had arranged to pay for the extra luxury of hot, soaking baths provided by the hotel with water drawn from nearby thermal springs.

"I think it's a good idea to hire a buggy and driver to take us on a tour tomorrow," Thorne remarked, staring at a loaded coach pulling away. Not the least of his reasons was so he could be relieved from his constant vigilance against other passengers, never knowing where the next attempt on Kipling might come from.

"Just what I've seen within walking distance of the hotel is enough to discombobulate the most gullible person I know," Kipling said. "I'll have to add a postscript to these letters, stating that those who have doubts about what I'm saying will have to make a trip to America to see for themselves." He stared out at the landscape denuded by the heat and steam and chemicals. "It's as if we're sitting rather uneasily on a thin crust over a boiling, spouting hell. Even the ground around here rings as hollow as an empty kerosene tin. Someday soon the Mammoth Hotel, guests and all, will sink into the caverns below and be turned into a stalactite." He took a deep breath and went back to composing his letter.

Thorne puffed on his pipe, one foot propped on the low railing, both elbows leaning on his knee. "Did you get enough of the touring parties' 'patriotic exercises' last evening?" he asked. He'd begun to enjoy baiting the writer.

Kipling looked up at him. "Is that what they're called? I can think of several other names . . . wild advertisement, gas, bunkum, blow . . . call them anything you please beyond the bounds of common sense."

Thorne couldn't suppress a grin. To celebrate the 4th of July, the tourists had selected a clergyman from their number, placed him on the first-level landing, and crowded in the lobby below to hear him regale them with collective compliments. And he didn't disappoint, assuring the crowd that they were the greatest, freest, richest, most sublime, and chivalrous people on the face of the earth. He quoted the Declaration of Independence, led them in singing "The Star Spangled Banner", and "My Country 'Tis of Thee", to the tune of "God Save the Queen".

"And they didn't even stand up, except for the American national anthem!" Kipling noted. "I'm beginning to think the people in this country keep telling themselves they're the greatest, wealthiest, and most favored, only because they feel inferior and have to bolster their self-esteem in some fashion. All this hot air sounds absolutely ridiculous to a foreigner. At first I thought they were joking, but I've heard it so often, it's become silly babble."

"You know," Thorne said, "if I have to form a mental image of the abstract concept of liberty, I picture a great horned owl, rather than the bald eagle. Wise and stoic and all-seeing."

"Strange," Kipling replied. "I think of American liberty as a feisty bear cub on its hind legs, roaring defiant nationalism at the world. On the other hand, I think of the British lion as somewhat snaggle-toothed and sleepy, its best years behind it." He resumed his writing, often pausing to stare off into space, evidently trying to organize his thoughts and pick the precise wording for his Indian readers. Finally he stopped and closed his folder. "That's enough for today. I'm sure what I see in the next day or two will far exceed anything so far, and I can't use up all my adjectives at one whack."

"Ready for lunch?"

"Lead on."

"How's your head?"

"Hurts. But the cut is scabbed over and starting to heal. I just have to be careful when I comb my hair."

"Your head's harder than that rocky ground."

"One good thing about it, though," Kipling said as they selected a table in the hotel dining room.

"What's that?"

"I wasn't unconscious. And I didn't hear harmonica music this time, so that wreck was a pure accident."

Thorne scanned the menu in silence for several seconds as he tried to form his reply. "It was an accident, all right," he said, "but it was arranged."

"Huh?"

"The leather thorough brace was cut nearly in two and it broke under the strain."

Kipling looked blank. "What's a thorough brace?"

"It's like a thick leather spring. Basically a heavy strap that is doubled back and forth on itself until it's several inches thick. There's one on each side, running fore and aft . . . they cradle the coach body and allow it to rock and sway without taking the jolting directly from the road."

Kipling frowned. "Maybe it just wore out or rotted."

Thorne shook his head. "I heard the drivers talking. Our Mister Mosely inspected the undercarriage and saw it right away."

"There were a lot of others on that stage. How can you be sure it was meant for me?"

"There's no way to be certain, but, odds are, it was. It appears our stalkers aren't particular how many others they hurt or kill."

"But we didn't hear the mouth organ."

"I didn't hear it aboard ship, either. You know that arrow wound was no accident, and we didn't hear it then."

Kipling picked up his menu, shaking his head and looking bewildered. "If I only knew what this was all about, maybe I could do something to correct the situation."

"What'll it be, gentlemen?" asked a rosy-cheeked young waitress.

They both ordered fried ham, potatoes, biscuits, and coffee.

"I was so busy enjoying the scenery and the ride, I forgot to look for California," Kipling said after the waitress left.

"I scanned the crowd. Didn't see him or Ann Gilcrease. But they were very likely there, and I didn't recognize them."

"So it's a good bet they're here in the hotel with us," Kipling said, glancing over his shoulder.

"Wouldn't be surprised," Thorne said. He smiled grimly. "Hate to think we were being ignored or abandoned after all these weeks."

"It's hard for me to picture that fat, jovial, talkative Rudolph Blixter as anything but what he appeared to be," Kipling said.

"That's why I'm here," Thorne said. "You have the eyes and mind of a reporter. I've been trained to think deviously, to delve behind the obvious."

"Well, if someone has set out to ruin my American trip, they're succeeding," Kipling said, gingerly touching the gash behind his ear. "Remind me to buy another hat," he continued. "This high altitude sun will make my head throb even worse than it already does."

"Think you're up for a tour tomorrow?"

"You can bet on it. We young men snap back quickly." He grinned. "Good idea to hire a buggy and

144

driver so we can have our own itinerary, not have to fight the crowds, and be safe from those damned stalkers."

To their chagrin, the last available buggy had been hired by a middle-aged couple from Chicago. But the white-haired husband graciously offered to share the fragile-looking buggy with Kipling and Thorne.

Kipling silently gave his consent with a nod of his head, and Thorne shook hands with the older gentleman.

"Blake Slattery!" the old man said in a gruff voice. "And this is my wife Maggie."

Thorne completed the introductions, and the older couple gave no indication they'd ever heard of Rudyard Kipling. But Kipling seemed to have gotten used to the idea of not being known, as yet, in America, especially in what he called the "wild, unsettled West, where the people don't read". As he put it: "Most of them are too busy carving a living from the wilderness and patting themselves on the back. Maybe a hundred years hence, some degree of literacy beyond the columns of the local paper will manifest itself."

Their gregarious driver gave his name simply as Tom. The four passengers boarded the open phaeton that had two forward-facing upholstered seats. With a light tap from the driver, a team of sleek-muscled Morgans bounded away, hauling the trap and its human cargo as if the whole thing weighed nothing at all.

The rest of the day was a delight to the whole party. Even Thorne, who was subconsciously vigilant, knew they were safe for the time being and made up his mind to relax and enjoy the tour.

The only sand in the salve, as far as Thorne could see, was Maggie Slattery, who chewed gum constantly and kept up a running commentary on her ailments. Thorne ignored the aggravations of such people. But Kipling was much younger and less tolerant of fools.

Several years before, Thorne had visited this park, and the place still held a fascination for him that no amount of exposure could dull. Kipling's imagination added to the wonders, endowing them with nearly human character. The writer made only a few comments, spiced with hyperbole, but Thorne borrowed his notes that evening and was amazed at the passages.

> . . . I met a stream of iron-red hot water which ducked into a hole like a rabbit. Followed a gentle chuckle of laughter, and then a deep, exhausted sigh from nowhere in particular. Fifty feet above my head a jet of steam rose up and died out in the blue . . . The dirty white deposit gave place to lime whiter than snow; and I found a basin which . . . was made of frosted silver; it was filled with water as clear as the sky. I do not know the depth of that wonder. The eye looked down beyond grottoes and caves of beryl into an abyss that communicated directly with the central fires of earth. And the pool was in pain, so that it could not refrain from talking about it; muttering and chattering and moaning. From the lips of the

lime-ledges, forty feet under water, spurts of silver bubbles would fly up and break the peace of the crystal atop. Then the whole pool would shake and grow dim, and there were noises. I removed myself only to find other pools all equally unhappy, rifts in the ground, full of running, red-hot water, slippery sheets of deposit overlaid with greenish grey hot water, and here and there pit-holes dry as a rifled tomb in India, dusty and waterless . . .

Earlier in the day, while Tom drove the party through the sights, Maggie Slattery finally left off about the agonies of her allergies, her lumbago, her liver problems, and gazed, open-mouthed, at the geysers and the fire holes, uttering — "Good Lord!" — every thirty seconds or so.

"What *I* say," cried the old lady, waxing theological, "after having seen all this, is that the Lord has ordained a hell for such as disbelieve His gracious works. And if we find a thing so dreadful as all that steam and sulphur allowed on the face of the earth, mustn't we believe that there is something ten thousand times more terrible below prepared unto our destruction?"

"Dammit, Molly, keep your feet!" Tom cried as the near mare stumbled. Thorne caught a flicker from the corner of the driver's eye, and a slight hint of a smile.

Taking the bit in her teeth, Maggie plunged ahead. "*Now* I shall be able to say something to Anna Fincher about her way of living. Shan't I, Blake?" She turned to her husband.

"I guess so. But she's really a good girl," Blake said in weak defense.

"Huh! How can you say that about a girl who goes to dances?"

Feeling uncomfortable at witnessing this disagreement at close range, Thorne got out of the buggy when it stopped. Kipling joined him alongside Tom who had gotten down to examine the hoof of one of his Morgans. Satisfying himself there was no injury to the animal, Tom led the team up a steep hill, with Thorne and Kipling walking beside him. Tom glanced back at the older couple, still arguing.

"I drive lots of different kinds of folks through this place," he remarked. "Blamed curious. Seems a pity they should 'a' come so far just to liken Norris Basin to hell. By comparison, I reckon Chicago would 'a' served 'em just as well."

After a several-minute walk to stretch their legs and let the couple settle their differences, the three men climbed back into the buggy and Tom drove them into a quiet spruce forest, the wheels spinning almost noiselessly on the thick mold and dead needles. The old man and woman ignored each other and sat silent for the next hour. Thorne was grateful.

"That's the Firehole River you hear off to the right," Tom said presently. "It's fed by the run-off from hot springs and geysers. I'll stop soon so you can see the waterfall. Pretty river, but the water's too warm for fish to live in."

The sun was nearly at the treetops when Tom pulled up to a rough, wooden shanty where they were to eat and spend the night.

The proprietor already had steaks grilling on an open fire out front, and the aroma made Thorne's stomach growl.

"Bears, buffalo, deer . . . all kinds of wildlife in this park," Tom remarked when Maggie asked him about the dangers of being in the wilderness. "Nothing that will bother you here, though."

"Saw a beaver lodge a half mile below here on the Firehole River," Kipling remarked in a low voice to Thorne. "Think I'll slip down there and take a look."

"I'll join you."

While the Chicago couple engaged the driver in conversation, the two men walked away into the crisp, quiet evening. They located the beaver lodge, a pile of peeled branches resembling bleached white bones in a massive heap on the far side of the water. Some ways below, the beavers had built a dam, and a placid lake had spread out behind it.

"Reckon they'll come out?" Kipling asked in a hoarse whisper as the two men crouched behind some fallen timber on the shore.

"Stay real quiet," Thorne said. "If we're lucky, we'll see one before it gets too dark."

Less than a minute later, Kipling nudged Thorne and pointed. Three beavers were gliding downstream, soundlessly, hardly making ripples in the still water. One of the animals went down to inspect the dam while the other two came toward the hiding men and began to forage for supper. They made no sound at all until they paused to eat some beaver grass hardly ten yards away.

After a minute or two, Thorne motioned for them to creep a step closer to get a better view in the fading light.

Just then Maggie Slattery came clattering and sliding down the bank, umbrella in hand. "Beavers! Beavers! Young man, where are those beavers?" she shrilled.

They heard a loud *splat!* like the report of a misfiring pistol as the beaver smacked its tail on the water. The three animals disappeared.

"Good Lord! What was that? A shot?"

"Too bad it missed her," Kipling grated between his teeth as he stood up and glared at the old woman.

Maggie stared across the vacant water, then retrieved a few small stones and began heaving them awkwardly at the beaver lodge. "Perhaps if you rattle them up, they'll come out. I do so want to see a beaver."

The two men walked past her and went silently up the bank toward the shanty and supper.

As Maggie bent to get another stone, something small and shiny fell from the pocket of her dress. Thorne caught a glimpse of the silver object before she hastily snatched it up from the pine needles and tucked it out of sight. Even in the fading light, he could have sworn he'd seen a harmonica. He started to say something, but she went on tossing rocks without looking at him. *My imagination again,* he thought as he hurried to catch up with Kipling.

That night they turned in early and were grateful for the heavy blankets on their bunks.

The next morning, while sipping a steaming cup of coffee, Kipling said: "If the nights in July get this cold, the park must be an absolute frozen hell in winter." As he stepped outside to greet the morning sun, barely lighting the tops of the tall conifers, he shivered in the frosty air.

"The park's closed in winter, except for a maintenance crew." Thorne turned up the collar of his jacket. "The snow drifts so deep, the buffalo can find forage only near those hot springs."

Tom had the horses hitched and was eager to be off right after breakfast. The heady air was intoxicating as the sun rose and warmed them. Startled prairie dogs and chipmunks scampered away at their approach.

Two hours and several miles later, Tom drew the team to a halt at the edge of a geyser basin. Kipling and Thorne and the Chicago couple climbed out and ventured toward the venting steam and boiling spouts of water. Thorne squinted at the acres of dazzling white formations spread out before them.

"Looks like a frozen snow field," Kipling observed. "But it's warm underfoot."

Barely ten yards from the road, a roaring blast of steam every few seconds made them cringe. A small volcano spat hot liquid mud to the skies. Hot water rumbled underfoot, plunging through dead pines in steaming cataracts, finally to spread out and die on a

151

waste of white where gray-green, black, and yellow pools bubbled and hissed.

For once, Maggie Slattery was speechless.

"Dreadful waste of steam power," her husband Blake muttered into his beard.

The whole area stank of rotten eggs as if the pit of hell were just below the surface. Sulphur crystals crumbled underfoot as the party stepped carefully along the beaten path among the pools.

"How do you know this steam has enough vents for safety valves?" Blake Slattery asked Tom. "What's to keep it from suddenly blowing us all to kingdom come?"

"Faith," Tom replied with a straight face.

Kipling gingerly approached a pool of clear, hot water. The sides and bottom as far down as he could see were stained with red and yellow. Near the edge, his foot sank and water squirted up. He quickly shifted his weight and stepped even closer, testing for solid ground. Except for a slight movement on the surface, the water was as invisible as the air around him. Stretching forward to look into the depths of the pool, he asked Tom over his shoulder: "Can any kind of growth live in this?" Hot mud oozed up around the soles of his boots.

"Nothing that I know of," Tom replied. "You could drop a fish in there and it would be instantly poached."

Kipling heard a grunt behind him. Before he could turn, a heavy body slammed into him, knocking him forward. He flailed his arms, fighting to keep his balance, to prevent plunging headfirst into the boiling

152

water. But he was too far over. At the last instant, he thrust out a foot at an underwater rock to stop his momentum, and his left leg splashed, knee-deep into the edge of the pool.

"*Yeeow!*" He leapt backward, colliding for a second time with Blake Slattery, knocking the old man sideways. Thorne and the driver caught both men as they tumbled onto the path, preventing them from continuing into the steaming water on the other side.

"I'm scalded!" Kipling cried, grabbing his left leg.

Thorne pulled his jackknife and slit the writer's pants up past the knee. Kipling's tight, high, riding boot had prevented a worse burn, but the skin of the leg above the boot top was red.

"Did the water get down inside?"

"No!" Kipling gasped.

Tom had run to the buggy and was back with his canteen, pouring cool water over the reddened knee.

"I caught my foot and stumbled," Blake Slattery said, awkwardly heaving his bulk up from the ground. Dirty holes gaped in both knees of his gray trousers.

The driver scooped up handfuls of warm mud and cooled them with the canteen water before slathering them onto Kipling's scalded skin. Kipling cringed at his touch. "Maybe this will help for now," Tom said.

"*Ahhh!*" Kipling caught his breath, perspiration gleaming on his forehead.

Along with the boot, the fact that Kipling had jerked his leg out quickly had saved his lower leg from a bad scalding. "That's probably going to blister," Thorne said. "You'll lose a little hide around your knee. Painful, but not serious."

Kipling looked up with an anguished expression. "It's never serious when it's somebody else's burn," he moaned. "Can you take my boot off?"

The driver and Thorne assisted in carefully tugging off the boot. The writer's sock was damp near the top, but otherwise there was no damage. Kipling began to feel a little nauseous, so they let him sit on the ground with his head down for several minutes.

Thorne glanced at Blake Slattery. The older man was somewhat barrel-shaped — probably not too nimble, even in his youth. Thorne's suspicious nature saw this as another "arranged" accident. But his logical mind could find no reasons for his suspicions.

"I'm all right now," Kipling said, although he was still pale. "Help me on with this boot. I'm ready to go."

The voice interrupted Thorne's dark reverie, and he moved quickly to slide the boot on. The smooth, black leather still showed the twin scuffs of the rattlesnake fangs. These boots had been his salvation twice now. He lifted the smaller man to his feet so he could stamp his foot down into the boot. He was assisting Kipling toward the buggy when a cavalryman rode up.

"Saw you fall. Everyone OK here?"

Thorne briefed him on the accident.

"You'd be amazed how often this happens," he said. "One of the innkeepers down at Old Faithful is good at treating burns. If you're going that way, she can fix you up. In the meantime, cold water and wet moss will soothe it."

154

"You're not an American," Kipling said.

"That's right," the young man answered. "Recognized the accent, did ye? I'm a Scotsman by origin, but an American by adoption. Ex-Cape Mounted Rifles. There are a lot of us in the ranks."

The trooper wore a dark-blue shirt and light-blue trousers cut to fit over his boots. A cartridge belt holding a holstered single-action Army Colt circled his lean waist. Slung on the McClellan saddle was the standard issue single-shot Springfield carbine.

Kipling seemed to forget his burn and paused by the buggy to talk with this young man of similar age and background, who identified himself as Corporal Stanley Owens.

"Not near the discipline here as in the Queen's service," Owens said in reply to a query by Kipling. "We aren't particular about small things. I can wear any darn' thing I please. I wouldn't dare come on parade in the old country looking like this." He grinned, indicating the buttons missing on his open blouse and his unshaven face. "But they taught me here how to trust myself and my shooting irons. For example, I don't need fifty orders to move across the park and catch a poacher. Oh, yes, they have poachers here," he said in response to Kipling's surprised exclamation, "and they're bold ones who come in with an outfit and shoot bison. If you interfere, they shoot at you. We confiscate their guns and ponies," he said matter-of-factly, a grin splitting the wind-burned face under the shade of the gray hat. Without appearing to take any notice of his horse, he held the reins in one fist while his big mount backed and shivered and sidled and plunged. All the while, Owens kept one foot out of the hooded stirrup, one hand on the horse's sweating neck. "He's not used to the park, this brute, and he's a confirmed bolter on parade. But we understand each other."

Whoosh! A roar of steam blasted down the road. The horse spun, ready to bolt. Owens checked his mount's momentum and the animal reared up until he nearly fell back on the rider.

"Oh, no you don't!" The trooper brought him down, and steadied him. "We settled that little matter when I was breaking him." He looked at Kipling. "The amount of schooling that goes into one English troop horse would be enough for a whole squadron of these Montana horses."

"We'd best be on our way," Tom interrupted, climbing up and taking the reins. "We've got a lot to see before sundown."

But Kipling seemed to have forgotten his burn and wanted to continue the conversation. "So you like this cavalry better?" he asked.

"To my way o' thinking, most things are better here, sir," the young trooper said. "Freer, if ye know what I mean. The only thing is, since we've about run out of Indians to fight, we're assigned mostly to guard duty in the park . . . keeping tourists from chipping the colorful cones to pieces for souvenirs, dumping soft soap into the mouths of the geysers to see if they'll get indigestion . . . that sort of thing. Planting hedges and digging ditches is all right as a variation, but too much of that can ruin an army." He slipped his toe back into the stirrup. "I've got to patrol fifteen miles from here. Good luck to ye!" He wheeled his horse and plunged away.

The mud dulled the sting of Kipling's scalded leg for the rest of the day while Tom led them on another long tour. At one stop, they got out and walked up a valley, surrounded by plumes of steam, still pools of turquoise, stretches of blue cornflowers, lumps of lime, ridges of white and multi-colored boulders.

The old lady from Chicago poked her parasol at the pools as though they were a pack of wolves about to devour her. She'd hardly turned her back on one of them, when a twenty-foot column of water and steam shot up behind her. She shrieked and sprang away with the speed of a gazelle. Her husband turned aside, hiding a grin in his beard as he continued to chew his tobacco and mutter something about a waste of steam power.

Across a field, several hundred yards away, an iridescent plume of spun glass stood up against the sky.

"That's Old Faithful," Tom said. "It goes off every sixty-five minutes, plays for five minutes, then sends up a column of water a hundred and fifty feet high. By the time we've looked around at the other geysers, he'll be ready to play again."

"Except for the regularity of an Old Faithful, I wonder if there's any pattern to all these eruptions?" Kipling said.

"I suspect there probably is," Tom answered. "But nobody's really studied them to that extent. After the

Krakatoa eruption in 'Eighty-Three, all the geysers went mad together, spouting, spurting, and bellowing until we were afraid they'd rip up the whole field. So some mysterious sympathies exist among all of them, throughout the world. There's a big one called the Giantess, up there a ways. When she goes off, she shakes the entire hotel."

An hour later, they made their way back to Old Faithful and sat down with a group of other tourists on the benches a safe distance away to watch. They began to hear the water sobbing up and down the throat with the sound of waves in a cave. Then came several preliminary gushes, then a roar and a rush. The glittering column of diamonds rose, quivered, stood still for a minute. Then it broke, subsiding into a confused snarl of water no more than thirty feet high.

Several young ladies in a group remarked that it was pretty and elegant, then took their long hairpins and began scratching something into the bottoms of shallow pools nearby.

When they'd departed, Thorne and Kipling walked over and looked in. Kipling shook his head. "Americans don't deserve the wonders of this place," he said. "A hundred years from now visitors will know that 'Hattie' and 'Mamie' and 'Sadie' and 'Sophie' and a dozen others have been here."

" 'Fools' names, like fools' faces . . . ,' " Thorne began.

" '. . . always appear in public places,' " Kipling finished. "That saying must have originated in America. Disgusting!"

158

CHAPTER
ELEVEN

"Are you ready to do the Grand Cañon of the Yellowstone?" Thorne inquired, eyeing his companion who sat propped up on the bed in his hotel room.

"When do we leave?" Kipling asked.

"I was expecting a negative answer. You must be feeling good."

"I didn't travel all this way just to miss a show like that," Kipling said, laying aside the notebook he'd been writing in.

"Mabel O'Toole must have done a good job on your leg."

Kipling pulled back the pants leg that Thorne had slit to just above the knee. "Feels fine now," he said, displaying his gauze-wrapped upper leg and knee. "I'm sure it'll hurt like hell later, but that salve has taken care of the problem now."

"Did you ever think your trip to America would be like this?"

"I knew the West was a rough, frontier country, but I didn't anticipate getting so many small injuries. If I'd known that before, I might have skipped this country altogether." Then he paused. "No, I think not. I would have come anyway. It's been worth it."

"Hope you never regret that decision," Thorne said. "I'm beginning to believe that not only is some stalker out to do you harm, but that you're accident prone as well. They don't need a lot of help."

"Then you don't think getting knocked into that steaming pool was anything, more or less, than an accident?" Kipling asked, arching his eyebrows above his glasses.

"I don't see how it could have been anything else," Thorne replied thoughtfully. "That old man was just clumsy. And you saw what his wife was like. And, of course, there was no harmonica music, although I could have sworn I saw her drop a small harmonica out of her pocket when she came along and scared those beavers off."

"Did you take a real good look at that couple?" Kipling asked.

Thorne paused from cleaning his revolver he'd taken apart on the night stand. "What do you mean?"

"I mean could his running into me have been deliberate?"

"Not a chance." Then Thorne laughed. "Listen to us, would you. For weeks I've been trying to convince you that these were deliberate accidents, and you've resisted the idea. Now our roles are reversed." He shook his head and picked up the cylinder and inserted it into the frame of the gun. "They've got us going in circles, no doubt about it. I've made up my mind that the stalkers are Ann Gilcrease and California, so I'm telling myself that everything that doesn't fit their mold is really an accident. Not a good way for an ex-Secret Service man

160

to think." He slid the pin under the barrel, locking in the cylinder, then snapped the loading gate shut and wiped off the excess oil. "I think the touring party is forming up out front. Let's go."

Thorne did not see the old couple from Chicago in the group of some two dozen tourists. "Any party without the Slatterys has to be a good one," Kipling remarked *sotto voce* when Thorne pointed out their absence.

The sun was far down the western sky as the party made their way afoot toward the upper falls of the Yellowstone gorge not far from the hotel. Talking among themselves, the group walked down a path through the pine woods to the edge of the cañon. A roar of falling water precluded normal conversation when the men and women grouped themselves along various vantage points within the wooden railing enclosing the flat rock overlook.

Thorne was scanning the crowd more than the river, but saw no one who looked the least suspicious. Kipling took his eyes off the falls long enough to rest them on a pretty young woman who was evidently traveling with her parents. From their dialects, Thorne identified them as New Englanders. Thorne stood close to Kipling, resting one hand on the butt of his gun under the tail of his corduroy coat.

The falls was an impressive sight. The dark water came sliding around a bend, glassy and green. Then the whole thing abruptly disappeared from sight. Only a roar and a mist gave an indication of what was happening below. In the depths of the cañon, the river appeared again as a finger-wide trickle.

"See that gentle broth of ripples lapping the sides of the gorge below?" their driver, Tom, said, pointing.

Kipling nodded.

"Those are actually huge waves. Gives you an idea how deep that is."

The crowd was gasping and gawking and pointing, hardly believing their eyes.

"The water drops one hundred and ten feet here," Tom said.

Thorne barely heard him, so fascinated was he by the beauty of the afternoon sun lighting the sloping cañon walls in a blaze of yellow and other pastels.

After several minutes, the crowd grew restless and then, two and three at a time, began to drift back up the path through the pines. Kipling, Thorne, and Tom were the last to follow.

Less than a mile away was the lower falls of the Yellowstone.

"Wait till you see it," Tom said. "It's three times higher than the upper falls."

To reach the lower falls overlook, the group had to descend singly down a long, steep stairway built into the side of the gorge. The view was hidden by trees until the tourists reached the large flat rock of the overlook.

Suddenly, with no warning, they were gaping into a gulf seventeen hundred feet deep. Eagles and fish hawks circled far below. The staggered, serrated walls of the mighty gorge wore slashes of yellow, white, crimson, amber, green, and cobalt. And far down in the bottom, still relentlessly carving, ran the tiny jade-green strip of river.

Kipling shook his head in silent wonder. After two or three minutes, he leaned close to Thorne to make himself heard. "This cañon . . . it's burning like Troy. But it will burn forever. Thank goodness, no pen or brush could ever portray these splendors adequately."

"Actually it was a series of paintings, especially one of the lower falls and this very cañon by Thomas Moran that helped persuade Congress to make this place a national park seventeen years ago. Easterners couldn't conceive of its beauty."

"I can understand why," Kipling said. "I won't try to describe this cañon. It's my peculiar property . . . nobody else will share it with me."

They were catching part of a cooling mist. A continuous, earth-shaking roar enveloped their senses as tons of water slid over the edge and vanished from sight.

"Inspiration is fleeting!" Kipling cried above the noise. "Beauty is vain and the power of the mind for wonder is limited. There's too much here to absorb."

The touring group finally saturated themselves and began to drift away, climbing the steep steps, holding onto the railing, some of the elderly pausing now and then to catch their breath.

Kipling and Thorne continued to stare at this wilderness spectacle after the others were out of sight. Thorne discovered, by keeping his eyes on the glassy river as it swept toward the falls, that it gradually produced a dizzying, almost hypnotic effect. The solid green water, tiny flecks of froth dancing here and there, slid toward the falls and solidly went over. Standing on the flat rock just above the water made him feel as if the whole world was sliding in chrysolite from under his feet. The whole, smooth, continuous movement seemed to be drawing him toward the falls. Thorne realized the spellbinding effect and jerked his eyes away. But Kipling was equally enraptured. He leaned over the wooden railing as if the force of the flowing river was sucking him inexorably into the green water plunging into the abyss. Time and motion were pulling him headfirst into the vortex of the universe.

Before Thorne could say anything or reach for him, Kipling put his head down and sank to a sitting position on the edge of the flat rock. Still somewhat dizzy, Thorne went to his hands and knees and crawled over to Kipling. "You OK?"

"I will be in a minute. Strange effect that has on a person." He rubbed a hand across his closed eyes.

"How is your leg?"

"Fine."

"How about your head?"

"The cut's all right. I'll be ready to go in a minute."

Suddenly the notes of a harmonica sounded somewhere close, even overcoming the low roar of the falls. It was playing a lively jig, "The Irish Washerwoman".

Thorne sprang to a crouch, yanking his gun, his eyes scanning the thick timber above. Where was it coming from? More urgently, what did it portend?

Kipling's eyes went wide at the sound.

Thorne was frustrated. Should he run, or stay still? Was someone waiting for them on the steep steps that snaked up through the pine timber? He dashed toward the foot of the stairs, trying to get a glimpse of the mouth-organ player. But, as far as he could see, the steps were empty. Another half minute of the quick-time jig, then the sound gradually became fainter, and ceased. Thorne strained to hear over the roar of the falls as he sprang up several of the steps and paused, looking. Nothing. Then he realized he'd left Kipling unprotected and out of his sight several yards below. He bounded back down the steps. Kipling had gotten to his feet and was walking gingerly, as if his leg were paining him.

"Quick! We need to get out of here," Thorne said, grabbing him by the arm. "I don't know which way it's coming from, but we've just heard the fire bell." He led the way to the stairs that was their only way out.

They'd taken no more than a half dozen steps up the steep ascent when a rumble, like thunder, overrode the roar of the falls below. They halted, breathing heavily. The rumble grew louder, then changed to banging, crashing as if the whole forested hillside were collapsing on them.

Thorne stood rigid and wide-eyed. He shoved his gun into its holster. Whatever it was, a pistol would be no defense against it. From out of the dusky shadows, a light-colored boulder, bigger than an overstuffed chair, came hurtling down on them, crushing everything in its path. A rockslide of smaller stones ripped and bounced through the foliage like hundreds of deadly missiles.

Thorne's heart leaped. Instinct took over. Grabbing the smaller man around the waist, he hurled him over the railing and dove after him. They rolled into the partial shelter of a huge ponderosa pine and flattened themselves against the thick bole. The pale boulder flashed by, crushing a section of stairway and railings, bounded high off a landing, then struck the stone platform at the overlook, exploding into splinters of rock, before disappearing with a huge splash into the river. A hail of rocks bounced and ricocheted off the surrounding trees and hillside for another ten seconds, before rattling to a stop. An eerie silence settled in.

"Stay quiet," Thorne whispered. His own heart was pounding so hard, his voice shook. "Somebody might be coming to check on his handiwork." He pulled his gun again and they waited. But the muted roar of the falls was the only sound. If anyone above was moving, the noise of the river masked the sounds. It was growing too dark under the trees to see anything. Thorne took a deep breath to steady himself. His pulse slowed.

"Are you hurt?" he asked over his shoulder.

"No. Just a little more bruised from being slung over that rail. But it saved my life. Thanks."

"That's what I'm here for," Thorne said. "To protect you when I can, to tend your wounds when I can't." He thought for a moment. "Let's stay here until it gets good and dark."

"Some of those other tourists might come looking for us," Kipling said, still sounding breathless.

"Then we'll show ourselves. But if we wait, whoever rolled that boulder down on us might think they did us in, and then leave. We can fool them into thinking we're dead. Not likely anyone will discover the damage to those stairs and the overlook until the next tour group comes tomorrow."

"I'd like to pack up and leave tonight," Kipling said. "I'm convinced now. And I don't mind admitting I'm scared."

"Leaving in the middle of the night is a good idea, except that no coaches run at night, unless we can find Tom and convince him, with a hefty bribe, to take us. Even though he knows this park, he might not want to attempt the roads in the dark. Besides, we'd probably wind up at Cinnabar Station or Livingston with a bunch of other tourists waiting for tomorrow's train. Our stalkers might be there, too. So we won't gain anything by leaving before daylight. We'd be better off lying low for a few days and give them an opportunity to be gone ahead of us."

"We can't avoid people altogether," Kipling said, sounding calmer. "And we don't even know what these stalkers look like."

Thorne chewed on that thought for a few moments as they both settled into a sitting position, backs against the thick tree trunk.

"I guess you're right," Thorne said. "We'll start back to the hotel in about a half hour. Let on like nothing happened. Anybody asks, we took advantage of the full moon to climb down to the river for a little fishing. That way, when this damage is discovered, we can say we know nothing about it. Rock slides in this park are common. The geography of the area has been constantly changing for thousands of years."

"If we hadn't heard that harmonica music, I'd be inclined to think this was actually an accident," Kipling said.

"The harmonica is meant to paralyze us with fear, to make us lose our heads and panic. It seems to me, Blixter is strong enough to dislodge a boulder that size if it wasn't too firmly imbedded." The more Thorne thought about this latest attempt on their lives, the more his mood began to change from frustration and fear to anger. If only he were able to confront their pursuers! If Ann Gilcrease was behind this, he knew he was up against one of the cleverest and most devious criminals he'd ever encountered. It would be sheer luck if he caught her in the act. She had had many years to practice her craft, and, if she didn't want to be recognized or caught, then she wouldn't. It was as simple as that. He didn't know how adept Blixter was — if, in fact, he was her partner. He gritted his teeth. This was like flailing away in the fog. While Kipling was relatively intact, Thorne considered trying to convince him to cut short his trip and get safely out of the country. At the beginning of this sojourn, aboard ship, and then in San Francisco, he would never have entertained such a thought. It was tantamount to giving up. But now, weeks later, he was no closer to solving this mystery than he had been then. Should he

168

stubbornly continue trying to protect Kipling? Where did pride stop and good sense begin? He was obviously overmatched against these ghosts. How would he feel if, on the next try, they were successful in killing Kipling? The idea that he might be killed as well, he dismissed as unimportant. He had lived with the near occasion of death for years. But he felt the weight of responsibility for the safety of this foreign traveler. An artist with words might be cut down; the world would never know what might have been.

A full moon rose, shafts of light penetrating the overhead branches and silvering irregular patches of pine needles around them.

"Let's go," Thorne said, getting up.

Kipling had been on his feet for several minutes, flexing his legs and muttering about stiffened muscles and bruises. "I could use a good hot buttered rum in the hotel bar to get the chill out of my bones," he said as they began their ascent through the trees.

Without benefit of the stairs, they pulled themselves up the slick bank by grabbing the branches of small evergreens. Often Thorne had to scrabble his way up a few feet, then lie down and reach back for Kipling's hand to pull him up. The writer's burned and bandaged knee was often sliding on the ground. "Can't hurt much worse than it already does," he groaned.

They eventually reached a portion of the stairway that wasn't badly damaged and made their way toward it. From there, the last 150 feet to the top was relatively easy. Walking back to the hotel in the bright moonlight, they went quietly to their room and washed up before going to the hotel bar. Kipling relaxed after the first drink, but Thorne kept eyeing everyone who came into the room, wondering if their stalkers could have been watching from the inky shadows as the two men returned in the bright moonlight. He snuffed the candle on the table to give himself better vision in the dim room, and to make them less visible in case someone was lining them up in a rifle sight through a window. He had no idea what was coming next, but so far the "accidents" had been rather inventive. He didn't expect to be shot in a public place. Only once before had gunfire been used on them, and that was deep underground in the Chinese opium den in San Francisco. Trying to anticipate what these stalkers might do was impossible. Even though he drank little and looked much, he saw no one who even remotely resembled Ann Gilcrease or Rudolph Blixter.

The two men retired to their room, Thorne taking the bunk nearest the window and hanging his gun belt on the head post within easy reach.

But no further problems were encountered that night. The next morning Kipling had the innkeeper change the bandage on his burned knee before they left the park by coach and returned to the train at Cinnabar Station to go on to Livingston, Montana.

CHAPTER
TWELVE

"I could sure use a cigar," Kipling said, licking his lips.

"Don't tell me a young man like you is a slave to the noxious root," Thorne said with a slight smile. He would never admit it, but he would have welcomed a pipeful of Cavendish, maybe with a slight mixture of Latakia.

"At this point I'd be a slave to anything that would take my mind off this . . ." Kipling gestured at their surroundings, both inside and outside the narrow gauge train car.

"This train has no smoking accommodations, so you'll just have to put up with our conversation," the uniformed conductor said. His gray mustache looked incongruous on his smooth, boyish face. "Nothing but glare, desert, and alkali dust," he added. "Guess I've gotten used to it, I've made this run so many times." He went to a window outside the spacious lavatory where they were sitting and raised it as far as it would go. "Can't tell if it's hotter with dirty air, or no air at all."

The narrow gauge spur line they were riding had descended into the valley of the Great Salt Lake. Sweat beaded on Kipling's forehead and trickled down his nose. He loosened one more button on his grimy shirt and pushed his sleeves above his elbows. "The run between Delhi and Ahmedabad on a May day would be bliss to this torture," he said.

Thorne and the conductor looked blankly at each other. The comparison was lost on them.

"What's that?" Kipling jerked his head around. "Looked like somebody just threw a big bundle of rags onto the train."

Harrington, the conductor, chuckled. "Just an Indian jumping on," he said. "We don't stop for them, but we're generally going slow enough so they can leap on and off with no trouble. Even the squaws. Thirty years ago, those Paiutes were tough fighters, but no more. Once the country got settled up good and the trains came, the railroad companies let 'em ride free of charge. But they can't come inside . . . they have to stand on the platforms between cars."

Thorne was intrigued. His gaze followed the conductor's pointing finger. He could see three Indians through the window of the door at the end of the car.

"Yeah, they just jump off and on anywhere, like the cable-car riders in San Francisco," the conductor said. "All I know is those Indians were dirt poor before the whites came, and they haven't improved their lot one iota, since . . . except maybe for these free rides."

As the train rounded a curve, a squaw leaped off, staggered, but found her feet before she fell.

"Where's she going?" Kipling asked. "There's not a blessed thing out there . . . just an arid plain."

"Beats me," the conductor said. "I've seen 'em just walk off toward the horizon like they knew where they were going. Never figured it out."

Kipling took off his glasses and mopped his brow with a damp shirt sleeve. "And this is the valley that the efforts of the Mormons caused to blossom like the rose," he said.

"You'll see the orchards and the grass and the fields once we get a little farther on where the irrigation starts," Harrington said.

The train had come south, along the eastern edge of Idaho, traversed a high desert of endless shrubs, and finally descended through the red rock pass into the valley over the approximate route that had been taken by Brigham Young and his followers a generation earlier.

"You've come at a bad time to see the irrigation ditches shining with water and everything green and fresh," Harrington said. "We're in the middle of one of the worst droughts in years."

A brilliant reflection caught Kipling's eye.

"That's the Great Salt Lake over yonder," Harrington said. "Even its level has dropped." He moved over and slid into a window seat. "See the flat terraces, like steps, up the sides of the valley?" He pointed. "You can make out the general shape o' the landscape under the trees. Well, I'm told those are former lake levels from centuries past when this was really an inland sea."

In spite of the dry spell, the valley in and around the orderly streets of the city was green with vegetation.

"I'm sure this valley wasn't near as lush when the Mormons first looked down from that pass, and Brigham Young said, 'This is the place.' "

"More likely he said, 'This is the end o' the road. We ain't runnin' no farther,' " Kipling said, in his best American accent.

"They sure enough weren't welcome back East," Harrington said. "On the other hand, this valley ain't too Gentile-friendly yet, but it's a heap better now than it was. At least the Saints and the Gentiles can work alongside each other without much trouble. Time is changin' things pretty quick. The hills around about here are stuffed with gold and silver and lead, and all hell atop the Mormon church can't keep the Gentile from flocking in when that's the case. At Ogden, thirty miles from Salt Lake, the Gentile vote swamped the Mormon vote in the municipal elections this year. Ogden is only one-third Gentile, but most o' them are grown men, capable of voting, whereas the Mormons are all cluttered up with children."

"I'd say there's probably some erosion going on, too," Thorne said, staring out the window at the approaching city. "When these young folks are rubbin' up more and more against their kind among the easier-going ways of the Gentile . . . well, it's bound to happen, as it does with any strict religion."

In regard to most habits and beliefs of his fellow man, Thorne had always been a live-and-let-live sort of person. As long as he wasn't being pushed or hurt by what someone else held fast to, he was inclined to let them be. In his opinion, it was a colossal invasion of

174

privacy for the U.S. government to pass laws and try to pressure the members of the Latter-day Saints to discontinue their practice of polygamy, as long as it was their belief and voluntary among members of the church.

"They think if it was OK with God in Old Testament days, there's nothing wrong with it now," Harrington said, when the subject came up among them. "And I can't argue with their logic."

"If they all looked like those long-legged beauties I saw in San Francisco, it would be great, at least for a while," Kipling said. "But I doubt that's the case. And can you imagine all the caterwauling and back-biting that would be going on among those women about who was the favorite and who was doing more than her share of the work, and so forth."

"You *know* a lot of that goes on among themselves, even though, from all appearances, wives seem subservient to their husbands," Harrington said.

"Not my cup o' tea," Thorne said. "Besides, I can't even afford one wife at this stage."

Thanks to a bridge repair, the train was twelve hours late, and it deposited Thorne and Kipling at the Salt Lake City depot just after suppertime on a Saturday evening. They walked into the center of town in the breathless heat, noting the dry water ditches, and the limp, dusty leaves of the trees that lined the thoroughfares.

The late Brigham Young had his picture for sale in every bookstore they ducked into. Kipling bought a copy of the Book of Mormon and glanced through it as they walked. The bookstore clerk had directed them to the temple, and the two men arrived after the workmen had departed for the day. They sat on a granite block and gazed at this physical tribute to Mormonism.

"Thirty years a-building and three million dollars sunk into it, so far, the clerk told me," Kipling remarked, eyeing the building. "About a hundred feet high, wouldn't you say? With walls every bit of ten feet thick. When it's finished, the towers are to be two hundred feet tall."

They silently contemplated the massive structure in the long evening twilight.

"What are you going to tell your paper about this place?" Thorne finally asked.

"I'll have a few choice words to describe it," Kipling answered. "But the long and short of it is this . . . it looks like they voted a child to be the architect."

" 'Unless you become as a little child, you shall not enter the Kingdom of Heaven,' " quoted Thorne.

"I don't think that's what they had in mind," Kipling said. "The flatness and meanness of the thing almost makes me weep when I look at the magnificent granite blocks strewn around here and think of the art that three million dollars might have called in to the aid of the church."

He moved a few feet and sat down on a wheelbarrow and opened the Book of Mormon, and didn't stop reading until it was too dark to see the print.

Then they hunted up a hotel, ate some supper, and Kipling read late into the night.

"Well, did you learn anything?" Thorne asked the next morning at breakfast, noting Kipling's weary look.

"I was at it pretty late," he conceded. "The two quarts of coffee I ordered earlier from that Gentile in the kitchen kept my eyes open. The Book of Mormon is a sure cure for insomnia. I wasn't too enlightened. It seems a considerable mish-mash. Divided into the books of Nephi, Jackob, Enos, Jarom, Omni, Mormon, Mosiah, the Record of Seniff, the book of Alma, Helaman, the third of Nephi, the book of Ether, and the final book of Moroni. Six hundred pages of small print. An amazing effort from the brothers Joseph and Hyrum Smith. I'll have to admit, I had to scan parts of it in order to finish."

"I thought they simply translated all that from some golden plates an angel left for them to find. What happened to those plates?" Thorne asked. "The same thing that happened to the stone tablets with the Ten Commandments in the Ark of the Covenant?"

Kipling shrugged. "There are eight men who swear they've seen the physical golden plates, and three men swear that the angel appeared to them. If you're a Mormon, I guess you have to take them at their word. The whole thing rests on that. The Mormon Bible begins at the days of Zedekiah, King of Judah, and ends in a wild and weltering quagmire of tribal fights, bits of revelation, and wholesale cribs from the Bible." He stabbed the last bite of pancake with his fork and popped it into his mouth, wiping his mustache with a napkin. "I admire the brothers Smith for their inspiration." He smiled. "As a humble fellow worker in the field of fiction, I know how hard it is to get good names for one's characters. But Joseph and Hyrum were bolder men than I have ever been. They created Teancum and Coriantumy, Pahoran, Kishkumen, and Gadianton, and several other priceless names I've already forgotten. But they were smart enough to steer clear of geography. They were astutely vague as to the locality of places because they were by no means certain what lay in the next country. They marched and countermarched bloodthirsty armies across their pages, and added new and amazing chapters to the records of the New Testament, and reorganized the heavens and the earth, as it is always lawful to do in print. But they lacked style. It was almost as if, when they grew weary, they slipped out of some grandiose Bible verse into prose that might have come from a penny dreadful!"

Thorne laughed, almost choking on a swallow of water. "So, I take it, you won't be a convert any time soon."

"Seriously there are the makings of a very fine creed. It seems rather stricter than the Church of Rome . . . for example they prohibit coffee, tea, chocolate, alcohol, or stimulants of any kind. They adhere to plain dress, hard work, and enforced tithing. Drop the polygamy plank in the platform, but on the other hand deal lightly with certain other forms of excess. Keep the quality of the recruits down to a low mental level and see that the best of the agricultural science available is in the hands of the elders, and you have a first-class engine for pioneer work."

"So you're looking at it from a practical angle."

Kipling nodded. "The tawdry mysticism and the borrowings from Freemasonry serve the low-caste Swede and the Dane, the Welshman and the Cornish cotter, just as well as a highly organized heaven."

Thorne shook his head with a wry smile. "Remind me never to tell you what I believe in. You'd tear it to shreds."

The next two hours they spent walking the streets and looking at the orderly houses, the fenced yards, and the sober, industrious people. Main Street was full of countryfolk who'd come in to trade with the Zion Mercantile Co-operative Institute.

The two men hired a local man to give them a short tour of the city in his buggy. "There's only one thing missing here that I can see," Kipling said as the buggy started down the street. "Joy. I haven't seen anybody but a few Gentile storekeepers laugh or smile since we've been here."

"Salvation is serious business," Thorne replied. "Besides, if you were as plain and homely as some of these women, had to dress in homemade clothes, and were one of several hardworking wives, what would you have to smile about?"

"Some of these hulking, board-faced men are no prize, either, except maybe as providers," Kipling countered.

Their driver, a bearded man who seemed to relish his job, stopped in front of every fourth house to say something like: "That's where Elder Johnson kept Amelia Bathershins, his fifth wife . . . no, his third.

Amelia, she was took on after Keziah, but Keziah was the Elder's pet and he didn't dare let Amelia come across Keziah for fear of her spilin' Keziah's beauty."

Thorne's neutrality to this religion began to tilt as they heard the domestic details of polygamy. Human nature could not be legislated out of existence.

Finally tiring of this sort of recitation, they paid off the guide and let him go, preferring instead to look at the vine-covered houses along the empty streets and listen to the pleasant music of wind among the trees bringing the smell of summer flowers and hay.

"Well, it's nearly noon and hot as blazes," Thorne said. "I think we should catch one of those trams I've seen running and go swimming in Salt Lake. Bound to be a few folks a little happier on the beach."

They bought two sleeveless, short-legged bathing outfits, and rode the open-top rail cars some dozen miles to the edge of the great, glaring lake.

"The sun off this water and these salt flats could blind a man," Kipling said, squinting around at the several hundred people scattered up and down the beach. Except in the distant hills, there was not a bit of greenery anywhere to relieve the eye. Piers and bathhouses and refreshment stalls dotted the long gray-white shoreline. They changed in one of the small bathhouses and hopped quickly over the heated ground to the water. Kipling gestured at the buildings. "These man-made things only accentuate the utter barrenness of the place. Americans don't mix with their scenery as yet."

180

"Hard to blend into anything here," Thorne said, wading into the tepid water. "I've been in this lake once before. Be ready for a surprise."

"Wow! This is strange!" Kipling cried, struggling toward deeper water.

"Have faith," Thorne said. "Walk!"

Kipling walked, waist deep, then chest deep. "Oh, Lord!" he cried. "My legs are flying up. Feels like I'm struggling in a high wind."

Thorne laughed. He'd experienced this inability to sink. Both of them rode head and shoulders out of the water. The other hundred or more bathers were in the same condition.

Kipling struck off to swim, but pulled up after a few strokes. "I can't get a grip on the water," he said, wiping the salty water from his face with one hand.

Thorne closed his eyes against the glare of sky and floated on his back. The watery couch gave him a sensation of near weightlessness.

An hour later, when the two men waded ashore and dried off with two small towels they'd bought, they were even more sunburned than they'd been before in Yellowstone. Their arms, legs, and faces would eventually be peeling. Kipling had taken the precaution of thickly layering ointment on his burned leg and wrapping it in gauze he carried in his trunk before going into the stinging salt. "Felt all right when I was in that warm, sticky brine," Kipling said. "Now we dry off quick in this heat, and we're streaked with white from head to toe."

"Try wiping off once you're dry," Thorne said. "Those salt crystals make it feel like you're rubbing your sunburned skin with sand. We'll rinse off back at the hotel."

The open rail car they rode back to town contained about a hundred joking, laughing young men and women. Kipling observed it all until they were nearly at the station.

"There's the gaiety you said was lacking," Thorne said as the two men followed a stream of passengers off the train.

"I still sense an underlying current of melancholy," the writer replied.

"The Church of Jesus Christ of Latter-day Saints doesn't promise a heaven on earth, or that life is going to be a lark. They're all about helping each other struggle through the hardships to their reward at the end. When you think about it, that's what a lot of other religions teach as well."

"Maybe so," Kipling replied, "but there's no law against keeping things a bit lighter as you go."

Ann Gilcrease sat alone in the double seat of the day coach, sweltering in the July heat as the train rolled east out of the deserts of Utah into the grassy plains of Colorado. She would have been even hotter if she hadn't disposed of her gray wig, extra padding around her bust and hips, and her spectacles of clear glass, then washed her face of all make-up. No longer could she pass for Maggie Slattery, elderly, gabby, bossy wife of a white-bearded Chicago gentleman.

182

In spite of her depressed mood, she had to smile with pleasure at the superb acting job. She and Blixter had traveled around Yellowstone Park with Thorne and Kipling all that time, and neither man had suspected them. It was probably the best performance of her long career. True, Blixter had bungled his job of knocking Kipling into that pool that would have instantly boiled him. Ann could have forgiven her partner for that blunder if he had been kind to her. His blunt rejection of her as a long-term partner had stung her more deeply than she liked to admit. He had taken her one last time and dumped her. Most of her life, since she'd been a raven-haired teen, she'd been accustomed to men falling over each other to be with her, to be attentive to her, to bed her. And she had manipulated this power to her advantage. But now, when she had substantially lowered her standards to consider Blixter as a possible husband, he had flatly and rudely rejected her. She was furious; her pride was bruised. Even so, they might have finished their job together of disposing of the Anglo-Indian writer, but they had vehemently disagreed on their next move. It was his idea to dislodge the boulder and start the slide that he was sure would crush Thorne and Kipling like two pesky ants. She felt there was too much risk of being caught, with the touring party close by. But he had insisted, so, to avoid an open rift, she'd given him reluctant help. She had not waited to see if the boulder had done its work. They'd find out in the morning when an uproar ensued. She'd fled back to the hotel. Later that evening, Thorne and Kipling had been spotted in the hotel bar, none the worse for their experience. Since there was no stirring of officialdom, she and Blixter concluded the men had not even reported the incident to the hotel manager or the troops camped not far from the inn.

When Blixter was asleep that night, she'd slipped out with her small grip and hired a buggy to take her to the railroad in Livingston, where she'd caught a train at daybreak the next morning, and headed south and east to Denver.

She and Blixter had received half their pay in advance for the job — $5,000 each, in gold, with the rest to be paid on the successful completion of their grisly mission. At the moment, she was caught in a dilemma. Should she go ahead and finish the job on her own and collect the remainder of her pay, leaving Blixter to stew about it? Or should she warn the two men and leave Blixter equally frustrated? True, she would have only the $5,000 advance and no more, plus incurring the wrath of their mysterious boss at Seaside Press in San Francisco. But, what of it? Five thousand was plenty. She'd certainly earned that much so far. Except what she had saved out for travel expenses, the money was safe in a St. Louis bank, and she could disappear and assume a new identity. It was enough to live on for a few years. She might even take a cruise. Anything to distract her mind and get her safely out of the country. She had to admit she was growing too old for this kind of life. In payment for his having used her and dumped her, she even considered arranging a fatal "accident" for Blixter. She was somewhat fearful of the man; he had a vengeful streak in him.

Both she and Blixter knew the itinerary of Thorne and Kipling from the intercepted letters to the writer's newspaper. Of course, their route could change since they knew they were being followed and harassed. There was also a chance Blixter might continue on his own and try to kill the writer in Salt Lake or Denver or Omaha. Coming from Salt Lake, she was ahead of them now. She would wait for them to show up at the Denver depot, then keep them in sight to Omaha, all the while watching for Blixter to turn up. She would somehow make sure he didn't harm Kipling. That was *her* job, and she would accomplish it alone. She touched the nickel-plated, five-shot .32-caliber Smith & Wesson with the four-inch tip-up barrel she carried in the pocket of her traveling skirt. If Thorne and Kipling were not bothered in Utah or Colorado or Nebraska, they would very likely begin to suspect their pursuers had given up, and begin to let down their guard. Even though it was not on their known itinerary, she had a strong hunch where they would go from Omaha. Kipling would not pass up an opportunity to visit Mark Twain's Hannibal.

She closed her eyes and rested her head against the seat back as she dozed in the stifling heat, perspiration dampening her bare neck.

Sometime later she awoke to the pounding of a hundred drums and a rush of intensely cold air blowing in the open window. The train had ground to a stop; the plains all about them were covered a foot deep in hailstones as large as the top of a sherry glass. She breathed deeply of the cold, fresh air. She'd been dealing with sudden changes all her life, and this one she welcomed.

CHAPTER
THIRTEEN

"America is a strange country," Kipling said, dropping onto the dark-green velvet of the day coach seat beside Thorne.

"So I've heard you say," Thorne replied absently, glancing up from his newspaper.

They were a week away from Salt Lake City, having made a one-day stop in Denver and a two-day stop in Omaha where Kipling had found only a few things to interest him. On their way east across Iowa toward Chicago, Kipling had decided he wanted to visit Mark Twain's home town. So they'd changed trains in Dubuque, and were now traveling south along the Mississippi River.

Thorne waited for his friend to continue with his observation.

"Just met a woman in the common car, up forward, who wanted to tell someone her story."

"And that someone was you."

"Of course. I find people fascinating . . . all kinds of people. She was muzzy with beer, and teary-eyed because she was nearly broke and the conductor hadn't returned with change from her last five-dollar bill. But that was the least of her problems. To reduce our

187

two-hour conversation to the bare essentials, she was the husband-abandoned actress of a fourth-rate, stranded, broken down manager-bereft company. She lamented the fact that she'd originally come from a farm in far-off New Jersey, had been wooed and won by a traveling actor named Alf who her pa never liked. She told me how she and Alf had risked their meager capital on the word of a faithless manager who had disbanded his company of actors a hundred miles from nowhere, leaving her and Alf stranded, how they had walked the railway tracks, begging from farmhouses, stealing to live. Alf had taken to whiskey. But they later hooked up with another company of traveling players, barn-stormed, taken insults from low-life audiences, and been involved in shooting scrapes. Alf finally took up with another woman and left. As a stranded, out-of-work actress, she was now taking the train to Saint Louis to beg help from a distant cousin who'd once been kind to her."

"Pretty wild story. Wonder how much of it was invented to get your sympathy?"

"If she imagined it, she was a good storyteller. I'm sure if I wrote up something like it for my paper, the editor would reject it as melodrama." Kipling grinned. "I did give her a few dollars, and the conductor showed up with her change. Between us, we restored her faith in human nature."

"I'll bet."

"Then she fell asleep across the seat, full of gratitude and beer, her blonde hair all tangled. That face, in repose, was actually beautiful, and I had a fleeting notion to kiss her."

"You never met a woman you weren't attracted to," Thorne said.

"Not many, I'll admit. American women especially."

Thorne jerked upright in his seat. "My God, that could have been Ann Gilcrease!" He leaped up and dashed toward the forward end of the car.

"No! She was too young for —"

The door slammed behind Thorne, cutting off the rest of the sentence.

Thorne arrived, breathless, in the common lounge, two cars forward. One man was seated by a window, smoking a cigar and reading the paper. "Did you see a blonde woman in here a bit ago?" Thorne shot the question at a white-coated Negro porter who was cleaning up empty beer glasses from a low table.

"I just come on duty, suh."

The stout passenger looked up from his newspaper. "There was a woman like that in here a while ago," he said. "Appeared she'd had a bit too much to drink. A gent came in and helped her up. They left together."

"A big, burly man with thinning red hair?"

"Don't recollect. Wasn't paying much attention."

Thorne blew out his breath through clenched teeth. Ann Gilcrease and Rudolph Blixter — he'd lay money on it. Ann could make herself look as young or as old as she wished. She'd been toying with Kipling. He turned back toward his car.

"Nobody there," Thorne said in answer to Kipling's question. He dropped into his seat. "Just in case, better

189

make sure I'm with you next time you strike up a conversation with any strangers . . . male or female."

Thorne tried vainly to see out into the darkness beyond the window. "We're moving again."

"Very slowly," Kipling replied. "The conductor said the rails had spread, but we were lucky to have a section crew flag down the engineer until they could lever the rails back into some approximation of the correct gauge. Those tracks should be spiked firmly into place, but nine out of ten fatal railway accidents I've read about have some sort of cheerful statement like . . . 'The accident is supposed to have been due to the rails spreading.' What do you think would cause that so often . . . soft ground, or heat, or heavy train traffic? I think most of the trains that get through do it because of sheer luck, or nerve, or reckless daring. That's just the way it is. We could just as well have gone off the rails, upset, caught fire, and been roasted alive."

"You seem overly concerned with wrecks and burning to death," Thorne said mildly.

"Happens often to those overloaded, poorly maintained trains in India. I suppose I'm just more conscious of it than you are, even though I've read that it's fairly frequent in this country as well. After traversing the Black Cañon of the Gunnison, the high snow sheds, and burning our brakes down that grade toward Denver, how can you be so calm? We've just about used up all our luck this trip."

"Save you the cost of a traditional funeral," Thorne said to needle the excitable Kipling.

190

"Maybe being burned up would be better than the *traditional* American funeral."

"Oh, you're referring to your conversation with that mortician in Omaha."

Kipling grimaced at the memory. "I shouldn't have offered to buy him a drink. I learned more than I ever wanted to know about his business when he took me next door to his funeral parlor. That was the most ghoulish thing I've ever seen. And the man bragged that he was providing a great service and being artistic into the bargain."

"Story material," Thorne said.

"I told him how corpses are burnt in India. He said . . . 'Oh, we're vastly superior. We embalm our dead.' Then he produced the horrible weapons of his trade and showed me how he held a man back from the corruption that's every man's birthright. 'I wish I could live a few generations to see how my people keep,' says he. 'But I'm sure it's all right. Nothing can touch 'em after I've embalmed 'em.' "

Thorne wondered how he might change the subject.

"Can you imagine," Kipling continued, waving his hands, "the fraud of funerals, where there are no shoes, no backs or bottoms to the suits or dresses . . . only a loose black cloth. The head and chest are fixed up to show through the window of the casket. Your poor body has been drained and shot full of some preserving chemicals the undertaker guarantees will ward off decomposition for a thousand years. Can you imagine anything more awful than to take your last rest as much of a dead fraud as ever you were a living lie . . . to go into the darkness one half of you shaved, trimmed, and dressed for an evening party, while the other half . . . the half that your friends cannot see . . . is wrapped in a flapping black sheet? I know a little of burial customs in other parts of the world, and I tried to make that undertaker comprehend the heathen, grotesque, giggling horror of it all. But he couldn't see it."

Kipling paused to get his breath, his eyes blazing at the folly of it. His voice had been rising as he ranted, and several other passengers were looking curiously at him.

"Bury me cased in canvas like a fishing rod in the deep sea . . . burn me on a backwater of the Hugli with damp wood and no oil . . . pin me under a Pullman car and let the lighted stove do its worst . . . sizzle me with a fallen electric wire or whelm me in the sludge of a broken river dam. But may I never go down to the pit, grinning out of a plate-glass window, in a backless dress coat, even if I were held against the ravages of the grave forever and ever!"

"We're passing some lights out there," Thorne interrupted. "I think we're going through Keokuk. I'm going to catch a nap. At the rate we're stopping and starting, we won't be in Hannibal before daylight."

When Ann Gilcrease stepped off the train at the Hannibal depot, she could have been mistaken for a member of one of several sects that flourished in Iowa, Indiana, or Missouri. She wore a large sunbonnet that effectively hid her face from anyone who wasn't looking directly at her from the front. Her gray dress was of a severe cut, plain, full-skirted, with a high neck. Not the most comfortable garb for the steamy heat of late July in this river town. But it was the last outfit she carried that was any sort of disguise. Besides underclothes and a few personal items, the only thing she had left in her small grip was a tan blouse and a divided riding skirt that reached mid-calf. She had a plan for its use.

Two cars down, Thorne and Kipling alighted, carrying their small bags. The men headed for the baggage car to collect their steamer trunks.

Picking up her small grip, she moved away toward the downtown section of the village, stepping aside from the cloud of dust stirred up by a passing horse and buggy. The dirt streets were dry and churned inches deep by the continuing drought that was plaguing the whole region. At one of the cross streets, she glanced longingly at the broad, shining surface of the Mississippi a block away. A whisper of cooling breeze found its way to her face inside the big, hooded sunbonnet. The train, with many stops and delays because of the faulty roadbed, was ten hours late, and it was already past nine-thirty in the morning. She found a place to eat a late breakfast and took a table by the front window where she could watch the street. Before long the two men she'd shadowed since Denver would come along this main street, either on foot or in a hack. They would likely check their trunks into a hotel, then begin touring the town. If there was one thing on which she'd been briefed about Kipling, it was that he admired Mark Twain as the best writer America had produced, with Bret Harte a close second. Thorne and

Kipling would walk around town, probably stop for a meal, see Mark Twain's boyhood home, maybe climb the big hill at the upper end of town. As she sipped her coffee and stared out at the sparse mid-morning foot and horse traffic, she pondered one thing — a point crucial to her plan. Would the two men visit Glasscock's Island on the Mississippi River? This island, called Jackson's Island in Twain's books, was one of the places the author had frequented and made world famous in his writings. If they did, she had to be ready. It was a perfect place for an ambush — isolated, a couple of miles below the town, heavily wooded. All the other places she and Blixter had arranged for accidents had been rather public. But they'd received the telegram telling them the big man in India had decided he didn't want Kipling's life made miserable — he wanted him dead. So she'd been on the look-out for an opportunity to catch the pair alone and far enough from other people so the job could be neatly and quickly done. When she thought of killing Kipling, and especially her old nemesis, Alex Thorne, her heart beat faster and she grew excited, almost as excited as just before lovemaking. Intrigue and deception had been her life, killing and sex had been her thrill. But she must never be caught in a crime. The gallows or, more likely, a long prison term were anathema to her. She couldn't abide the vision of herself in coarse prison garb, ordered about by mannish armed matrons, working in some steamy prison laundry or doing some other drab work the rest of her days among the dregs of female society.

Her reflections were interrupted by the sight of Thorne and Kipling strolling along the street. She paid for her food and went outside, keeping them in sight as they turned a corner more than a block ahead. For the next hour she followed them, mingling with the foot traffic, pretending to window shop. She would have to be really careless to lose them in this little burg. Once they stopped a stranger to ask directions. She saw him pointing and explaining.

In front of the white, frame house where Sam Clemens had lived as a boy, a crippled Negro sat on a low stool, strumming a banjo and singing spirituals in a pleasant bass voice. She smiled at the thought of pulling out her harmonica and joining him. A crowd had gathered, and Ann was able to get within three feet of Thorne and Kipling who had also stopped to listen.

The Negro finished one song to scattered applause. Two people dropped coins into the straw hat that lay at the musician's feet. He flashed a toothy grin, then flowed into "Swing Low, Sweet Chariot".

The men talked in low tones as she edged closer, slipping the ties on her sunbonnet to uncover her ears.

". . . to Cardiff Hill . . . nearly lunch time," Thorne was saying, consulting his watch.

"Got to see Jackson's Island," Kipling said. "We'll go after we eat."

"We'll have to hire someone to take us over."

"Saw a sign by the waterfront where we can rent a boat."

Ann slid out of the crowd and walked quickly away. She'd heard all she needed to hear.

She stopped at the café where she'd eaten and ordered a picnic lunch of fried chicken, cornbread, and cold yams. The cook slipped in a tiny jar of greens at no charge and tied up the bundle in a red-checked napkin. It was just noon when she stopped at a saloon near the boat landing and ordered a bottle of red wine to take with her. She quickly slipped out the side door to placate the nervous bartender who didn't want a woman being served in his saloon seen. She put the food and the wine into the small grip with her spare clothing.

"You gonna take it out on the river yourself, ma'am?" the skeptical fisherman asked. He was a tall, gawky man with a prominent Adam's apple. "I don't generally rent out my spare boat. There's a fella down yonder who rents, though."

"I'd rather rent from you," she said, giving him her best smile. "Oh, I'm just going to meet some friends over on the island for a picnic. Be back by dark. Here, I'll give you two gold dollars. That should more than pay for it."

The fisherman gulped, his Adam's apple bobbing up and down. "Sure will," he said. "But . . ."

"Oh, I'm up to it, I assure you. See the calluses on those hands? Anybody from a Shaker community is used to hard work. Don't worry, I'll be fine. And I'll take care of your boat."

Finally convinced, he shipped the oars in the oarlocks and placed a folded towel on the middle thwart for her to sit on.

She stepped in, took her place, and stowed her grip under the rear thwart. The fisherman untied the bow and gave her a shove off. She rowed out toward the middle of the deserted river, the current carrying her steadily downstream. It was easy enough to stroke smoothly toward the opposite shore, allowing the drift to carry her down toward the head of three-mile-long Glasscock's Island. The river was low due to the drought, and the current was running only about three miles per hour. She was facing back toward the town as she rowed and keeping a careful eye on the landing for her quarry.

It was good to be out in the fresh air and sunshine, getting some needed exercise, stretching her muscles that had been too long cramped up in a train. She put off her sunbonnet to get the sun and breeze on her face, then unbuttoned the high neck of the dress, and pushed her sleeves above the elbows.

Ten minutes later, she rested on her oars and drifted past the big sandbar at the head of the island, surprised at how close the island lay to the Illinois shore. Only a narrow chute of some thirty yards divided the two. Less than halfway down the island she found a level spot about five feet above water, and drove the boat in among the bushes that overhung the shoreline. Climbing out, she tied up, making sure the craft was concealed in the brush. Then she took her grip and trudged up the bank to a shady spot scoured clear of undergrowth by past floods. The gray soil was soft and sandy, with a few creepers climbing over a dead log. She put down her bag and stretched. Except for a few chirping birds and the soft swish of the current around a snag, the silence was profound. It was a peace that would not last.

Making sure she was not within sight of any passing riverboats or fishermen, she opened her bag and changed into the cooler, divided riding skirt and the tan blouse. She continued to wear the high-top shoes since she had no others. The gray dress she folded and put in the grip after removing the food and wine. The color of her clothing blended into her woodland surroundings. She found a sheltered spot where she could see toward town, sat down on the log, and ate her lunch, savoring the quiet of the river as it whispered along.

Just when she was finishing, an upbound steamboat came thrashing by. She heard and saw it coming in plenty of time to hide in the dense woods and watch it through the leaves. It carried mostly cargo; only a few people were about the decks. Trains were rapidly making steamboat travel a thing of the past.

She was daydreaming, watching the steamboat churn away upstream, when she looked back and saw a small boat moving out from the town, heading toward the island. By the time she saw it coming out from behind the steamer, it was halfway across.

Her heart rate went up as she squatted by her grip and took out the Smith & Wesson .32 and checked to be sure it had all five chambers loaded. The small pistol was in perfect working order, its action clean, smooth, and well oiled. She slipped the gun into the side pocket of the heavy riding skirt. Into the other pocket she placed the shiny, German-made harmonica, along with a slim wooden box containing a folded straight razor. A sheathed camping knife on her belt completed her preparations.

Although still at least a mile away, the boat was noticeably clearer. The oars were dipping and flashing in the sunlight, moving the boat toward the head of the island. She could barely make out the outlines of two men in it.

Time to go. It would take her a good fifteen minutes to reach the head of the island through the woods. She straightened her skirt, then took a deep breath and reached into her grip, pulling out the half-empty wine bottle. Uncorking and tipping it up, she took three healthy swallows of the dry, red vintage. It produced a warm glow as it went down. There were only a couple of swallows left. "What the hell!" She drained the bottle and tossed it aside. There was an excitement building within her, but not from fear. She was about to experience one of the greatest thrills of her life. Without a backward glance, she strode away through grass and wildflowers, then plunged into the heavier growth, past drooping vines and over rotten, moss-covered logs.

CHAPTER
FOURTEEN

She had spent a good portion of her time the past few years in wilderness places and had come to know the habits of many wild animals. Most were not harmful to humans unless surprised or cornered or protecting young. Yet, she could never quite quell her uneasiness around poisonous snakes, scorpions, centipedes, and spiders of various kinds — creatures she was more likely to encounter by surprise in dark, hidden places. Thus, she took her time, treading carefully, while she trekked toward the north end of the island.

Stepping over a decaying log, she froze at a rustling in the leaves and grass. Her heart was pounding when she spotted a four-foot timber rattler slithering away to disappear in the undergrowth. For a minute she remained still to let her racing pulse calm a little, then made a wide detour. To her, it was entirely appropriate for the devil to be depicted as a reptile in the Bible. Blixter had been the one who caught the rattler in the rocks near the depot and turned it loose in Kipling's train compartment; she would not come near the snake.

Perhaps the going would be more open along the river's edge. But two huge trees on the western

200

shoreline had been toppled by water and wind, their gnarled roots thrusting up to form a barrier ten feet high. She changed course again to the interior of the island and a few minutes later saw a break in the trees ahead. Creeping behind the trunk of a giant sycamore, she gazed out on the sparkling waters of the giant river lapping gently at the edges of a long sandbar. She squinted against the glare of the white sand at a rowboat grounding on the shoals a few feet off the end of the bar.

Thorne shipped the oars and the two men climbed out to pull the bow up high on the beach. They were talking, but breeze and distance carried the words away. Ann moved back into the heavier timber to her right. Many past floods had deposited tons of sand, allowing only a few weeds to grow. The sand had drifted and formed a depression, like snow, around the bole of a giant oak. She slid to a sitting position in this depression, hidden by the trunk and a mass of tangled vegetation, sloping toward the flat bar.

The men would most certainly come into the woods and explore the island. Yet, for a good fifteen minutes, they talked and gestured and wandered around the sandbar, within her sight, but not her hearing. Then, to her alarm, they went back to the boat and began to climb in. Maybe they were going back, or were just going to drift along the edge of the island and view it from the river.

She took out her harmonica, wiped it off, licked her lips, and began playing the first song that came to mind, "Tenting Tonight On the Old Camp Ground".

It stopped the two men like a shot of electricity. They stared toward the woods, but she was completely hidden from view. She stopped playing for several seconds. When they didn't move, she began "Sweet Betsy From Pike", playing as loudly as she could.

Thorne yanked his pistol and sprinted toward the woods. She dropped the harmonica in her pocket and drew the Smith & Wesson, cocking it. He would run straight into her ambush. She needn't fear Kipling, who was lagging behind and almost certainly wasn't armed. Thorne was the danger now, like a grizzly defending a cub. If she could bring him down, she could deal with Kipling at her leisure.

"A good, clean shot," she murmured, rising to her feet and raising her gun hand alongside the tree. His vision would be suddenly impaired as he rushed out of the glare into the dim woods. She'd put a bullet into him before he saw her.

Thorne dashed across the packed sand, leaped a half-buried log of driftwood — and plunged knee-deep into a depression of boggy sand and mud. The mucky sinkhole stopped him so suddenly he was flung forward on his face, the gun flying out of his hand.

She heard him swearing from ten yards distant as he struggled to pull up one leg and then the other. But he only sank deeper, while the quicksand closed around his thighs like wet cement.

For several seconds Ann watched his useless flailing. Only when assured he could not escape his trap did she step across the soft sand and walk out of her cover, around the tangled brush down to the bar. She held the small Smith & Wesson cocked and pointed at him.

He stopped struggling, a grim look on his face. Then, like a snake striking, he threw himself forward and grabbed his Remington that was half submerged. She saw him swing it up, thumbing back the hammer. She fired. The bullet splatted into the muck beside him, and she held her breath to be struck herself. But the hammer of his pistol was caught halfway to full cock, jammed by the sand and mud. Now she had him, and she knew it. She smiled calmly, although an exquisite thrill was pulsing through her.

"You bitch!" he yelled hoarsely, frustration sounding in his voice. "Why are you trying to kill us?"

She knew he was shouting only to stall off her second shot. She couldn't believe she'd missed him by six inches from a distance of ten yards. Nerves had caused her to jerk the trigger; she wasn't used to someone trying to shoot back at her from only thirty feet away. She breathed deeply, cocking the hammer once more. Her .32 had a spur trigger, but a strong pull, so it wasn't likely to go off accidentally.

Her eyes flicked between Thorne and Kipling as she backed around to keep them both in sight. She gave herself a few seconds to make sure she had the upper hand, and to settle the tendency of her voice to shake before she spoke. "Nothing personal, Alex. We were hired to take care of Mister Kipling." Her gun barrel swung between the two men. Kipling had not made a move. He stood frozen, staring at her from several yards away. He was wearing gray canvas pants and white shirt. His knee-high boots were soaked, and perspiration trickled down his sunburned forehead and nose.

"We?" said Thorne. "Where's Blixter?"

"Oh, so you know about him, too. I pegged you as a smart man when we first met in Tombstone, Alex. My judgment wasn't wrong. Yes, Rudolph and I are partners. We were hired to make this little man's life miserable, but just recently we got word that the cat-and-mouse game was over and he was to be killed."

"Who's paying you to do this? I know you don't work for free."

"You're correct." She backed up a few steps. "Move over there," she said to Kipling, indicating he was to get closer to the mired Thorne.

The writer obeyed without a word.

"I think a man should know why he's being killed. At least you can go out with a satisfied mind. Rudolph and I were hired to cause a few 'accidents' that could not be traced to anyone."

"And who is your employer?" Thorne asked.

"Actually, I'm not sure. Someone in India is all I know. A very rich and powerful person . . . a man to whom Mister Kipling has given unforgivable pain and insult."

"I can't imagine . . ." Kipling began.

"Shut up!" she snapped. "The way you talk about Americans, I'm surprised hundreds of them aren't bidding to kill you."

"How do you know that?"

"We've intercepted and read your letters to your newspaper. Oh, don't worry, they were always resealed and mailed on," she added.

"Just out of curiosity, how much were you paid?" Thorne asked, twisting around to look directly at her. The movement caused him to sink nearly to his belt.

"We got our orders from someone at Seaside Publishing Company."

"Seaside Press!" Kipling cried. "Those are the dogs who are stealing my work and printing it in this country without paying me."

Ann nodded. "Well, don't ask me why they're killing the goose with the golden eggs, but I presume the high Indian muckety-muck is footing the bill, and making up for any future losses they might incur." She grinned at them. The slight breeze off the river dispersed the heat waves that rose from the sand. She was feeling a little fuzzy from the bottle of wine she'd consumed and the effect of the hot sun on her bare head. "Oh, remember your traveling companions in Yellowstone . . . the old couple from Chicago?"

They stared at her.

"Oh, young man, stir up those beavers!" Her voice went to a higher pitch, mimicking Maggie Slattery. "I do so want to see a beaver!" She laughed at the astonished look on Kipling's face. Her laugh came out as a giggle. The wine was going to her head.

"Damn!" Thorne exploded. "It's a good thing I retired. I'm getting really bad at undercover work."

"Or, I'm getting better," she said.

"Where *is* Blixter?"

"He and I had a parting of the ways after Yellowstone. Since I got to you first, I'll collect the second half of the prize for finishing the job. I don't know where he is, but I can guess he's probably trying to head you off at some point where you planned to be on your trip . . . maybe Chicago. But, if I know Rudolph, he'll probably head for Hartford."

"Hartford?" Kipling asked.

"Of course. He knows you'd never leave this country without paying a visit to the American you most admire . . . Mark Twain. He has a beautiful home in Hartford, I'm told. And I knew you'd come to Hannibal for the same reason . . . to see Twain's home town and the places he wrote about." She giggled again, feeling light-headed. "But Rudolph will be chasing after a dead man because you're not leaving this island." She couldn't resist the urge to boast a little. "I have nothing against you, Alex . . . always liked you, in fact. But you dealt yourself into this. I won't kill you . . . that sinkhole you jumped into will do that soon enough. I'll just shoot Kipling." She waved the barrel in his direction. "In order for me to collect, his body must be found and identified. The man you rented that boat from will come looking for it when you don't show up by tomorrow. He'll find Kipling, and you, too, Alex, if you still have your head above the surface, which doesn't seem likely. With any luck, they'll think you got into a fight and killed each other. All very neatly done, don't you think?" She'd better finish this before she completely lost her edge. "This will be quick." She raised her gun and pointed it at Kipling only a few feet away.

A sudden roar blasted her ears and a stinging pain slammed her hand. Her gun went skidding across the sand.

Thorne had both thumbs on the hammer, trying to draw it back for a second shot. Kipling was running to pick up a stick of driftwood for a weapon.

Suddenly panicked, she turned and ran for cover among the trees — her hand numb. She bounded into the woods, fear at her heels. No second shot came as the trees covered her. But she didn't slow. Long before she covered the mile to her boat, feeling trickled back into her hand, and she saw blood spattered on her clothes. What a fool she was! She should have made him throw the gun away. He must have been quietly wiping it off as she bragged, half drunk, telling them the whole story.

The wine, the fear, the adrenaline gave wings to her feet at first. But her false energy crashed just before she reached her picnic site, and she staggered the last hundred yards, gasping, completely spent. Leaning over, she labored to catch her breath. Excruciating pain shot through her right hand. Blood was dripping from the ragged wound. On wobbly legs, she went to the water's edge to wash and assess the damage. The bullet had torn through the flesh between her right thumb and forefinger, but missed the bones. She gritted her teeth at the pain as she pulled out a clean handkerchief and awkwardly tied it around the hand. It didn't seem to stem the flow, but it would eventually. She had to get medical attention. She pitched her small grip into the rented boat, and climbed in after it.

Alex Thorne surely wasn't such a good marksman that he could knock the gun out of someone's hand. It must have been a lucky shot; he'd probably been aiming to kill her, but, in his haste, had jerked the barrel a fraction to the right.

Taking up an oar in her left hand, she prodded the bank. The boat was still tied. Cursing, she drew her sheath knife and cut the rope. The boat drifted backward as the sluggish current took it. She knew she couldn't return to Hannibal; she had to row downstream. But now she couldn't row; she couldn't grip the oar. She began to feel clammy and nauseous, the shock from the wound, along with the alcohol and sudden exertion of her mile sprint. She retched over the side of the boat. The glare of the sun on the water, the heat, made everything look bright. Then she knew nothing.

"No!" Thorne shouted. "Don't go after her. That's what she wants . . . to ambush you in those woods with a knife or a razor. Even wounded, she's dangerous."

Kipling hesitated, glancing toward the heavy timber, then back. "Give me your gun . . . she's getting away."

"Forget it. The gun's jammed again. That's why I didn't get a second shot. Here!" He awkwardly flung the Remington toward Kipling. "Wash this off in the river. Get all the grit out of it. Be careful. It's got five rounds in it."

Thorne was still scanning the edge of the empty woods when Kipling returned with the clean gun, wiping it on his shirt tail.

"Now I need your help to get me out of here."

Kipling found and extricated from a pile of brush a pole about eight feet long, bleached almost white by exposure.

But the effort was in vain. Each man grabbed one end. Thorne tried to lean forward and help himself while Kipling threw his weight backward, digging in his heels and hauling with all his strength. Nothing moved except his boot heels which slid in the sand.

"It's no use," Thorne panted. "We need a rope and something to anchor it to. Maybe several ropes and several men." The twisting, lunging effort had only caused him to sink deeper, the muddy water creeping over his belt. "Take the boat and row back to town for help."

Kipling came to the edge of the sinkhole, frowning. He tossed the clean Remington to Thorne who checked the mechanism, then eased the hammer down.

"This is getting damned uncomfortable, but I'll be all right for a couple of hours. And my gun's working, in case she comes back. Just lay this pole across here so it's on firm ground on both sides. I'll hang onto it until you get back."

Thorne hung both arms over the stout pole and tried to lever himself up out of the clinging muck. But the river had formed its trap well. He wondered how many deer or raccoon had gone down in this sinkhole or others like it. His lower body felt as if it were being squeezed by wet cement.

Just over an hour later, Thorne was dragged out by three men with ropes. The two brawny whites and a massive Negro had been recruited hastily from a waterfront warehouse by Kipling, and hired for five dollars each to come to the rescue.

"You didn't tell them what really happened here, did you?" Thorne asked, washing off in the river's edge and eyeing the three men rowing away.

"Of course not. We'd have been answering questions for days."

"Good. Let's get back to town."

"As long as we're here, I want to explore the rest of this island," Kipling said. "I know it's fiction, but Tom and Huck and Joe Harper and Nigger Jim are all real people to me."

As they started toward the edge of the timber, Kipling stooped to pick up something gleaming in the sand. It was Ann Gilcrease's small nickel-plated Smith & Wesson.

Thorne saw where his bullet had smashed the pearl grips. "Keep it as a souvenir of this day," Thorne said.

"It's still workable," Kipling said, after a quick examination. "I'll get that handle fixed." He slipped it into his side pocket. "You think she's still on the island?" he asked as they entered the deep woods.

"My instinct says no." He looked carefully around in the green gloom. "But I've underestimated her before."

★ ★ ★

Thirty-seven miles downriver the stern-wheel steamer, *J. P. Slade*, was just approaching the upper end of Eagle Island. Ann Gilcrease, dressed again in her gray, high-necked dress, was watching the red sky of the fading sunset from the hurricane deck, her hand wrapped in a clean, white bandage. In a few minutes, she would retire to her tiny stateroom and have a good stiff drink to help her sleep. There was no laudanum aboard the young purser had told her while he poured carbolic acid over her hand and prepared to take a few stitches in it.

"I'm not real skilled at this, ma'am," he said, looking at her with concern as she sat with her hand over a porcelain basin. "Take a pull at this jug to dull the pain. I'll be as quick and gentle as I can." He handed her a small crock jug. "You look a little pale. Maybe you oughta lie down while I work on this."

"Actually, I'd rather wait till I get to Saint Louis and have a real doctor treat this, or sew it up," she said, tipping up the jug and taking a healthy swallow. "If you'll just wrap it tight in a clean bandage, I think I can stand it until then."

He nodded, seeming relieved to be dismissed from his surgical duties. He bandaged it as requested.

While he cut and tied the bandage, she reflected on how lucky she had been. The pilot had seen her drifting, bloody and unconscious, in the bottom of her skiff about five miles downstream from Glasscock's Island. He'd slowed the steamboat long enough to have the yawl put over and the skiff pulled in and secured alongside.

When she was revived with smelling salts and food, she had related to the captain that she had been out on a picnic and had accidentally ripped her hand with a hunting knife while trying to cut some willows. She'd tried to go for help, but became faint.

The captain had raised his bushy, gray eyebrows when she told him there was no one she wanted to be notified, that she had a sister in St. Louis who would look after her. She knew her story seemed a little thin, and she also knew the captain would send a telegram to the Hannibal constable at the first opportunity, since she'd been found closest to that town. She'd paid her passage to St. Louis with gold, which seemed to placate the captain, then was given a tiny stateroom and the purser was instructed to look after her needs. She had changed into her other outfit from the small grip, and had turned over her bloody riding skirt and blouse to the purser to be washed.

If her less-than-plausible story would hold up until she could leave the boat in St. Louis, she'd find a doctor, then close out her bank account. With her money, she planned to book passage to Rio de Janeiro, via New Orleans. She would at last retire from this dangerous life, and start anew in another country.

As the red sky faded to dusk, she went back inside her stateroom and closed the door. Where was that purser with the whiskey she'd ordered? It would dull the pain in her throbbing hand and offset the slight hangover from the wine. She lay back on the pillow and held the bandaged hand over her head. Pain was only temporary; it could be endured. It was simply a matter of focusing on something else. She wondered if Rudolph Blixter would catch up with Kipling and Thorne. Her only regret was that she wouldn't be around to find out the end of the story.

CHAPTER
FIFTEEN

"Don't misunderstand," Kipling said, striking a match to his cigar and puffing it to life. "I love these Americans."

Thorne cocked an eyebrow. "You could have fooled me."

It was three days later and the two men were aboard a southbound steamboat on their way to Cairo, Illinois, and then up the Ohio River to Louisville, Kentucky. Thorne had convinced Kipling it wouldn't be wise for them to take on the city of Chicago right now, for two reasons — by departing from their itinerary, they might throw Blixter off their trail; second, it would give Kipling more time to let his various contusions heal while he experienced part of the mid-Southern portion of America.

Kipling welcomed the chance to travel by boat, rather than train, for a time. He wanted to see more of "Twain's river", as he called it, to compare his own views of it to descriptions in *Life on the Mississippi*, published five years earlier. Kipling had bought a copy of the book in a Hannibal shop.

They booked passage on the *Lilly B.*, a small stern-wheeler, geared more to passengers than to freight. Reclining in wooden chairs in the shade of the boiler deck, their feet propped on the railing, they smoked and watched the shoreline slide by, heavy with the leaves of summer.

Thorne knew if he encouraged Kipling to expound on his remark about loving Americans, he was letting himself in for an extended lecture. But he had nothing else to do at the moment. "So you've changed your mind about Americans?" he asked.

"If there's any contemptuous criticism to be done, I'll do it myself. But . . . my heart has gone out to them beyond all other people. And, for the life of me, I can't tell why. They're raw at the edges, almost more conceited than the British, vulgar and cocksure and lawless. But I love them, and I realized it when I met an Englishman in Yellowstone who laughed at them, thinking they were beneath the consideration of a true Briton. Of course, this young man was wearing a starched collar and traveling with a valet and acting as if he dared not touch anything without his white gloves on, for fear of contaminating himself. He was a ridiculous spectacle."

"So, what do you like about us Americans?" Thorne asked, trying to bring him down to specifics.

But Kipling was not to be hurried. "I admit everything," he said. "Your government's provisional . . . your law's the notion of the moment . . . your railways are made of hairpins and matchsticks . . . and most of your good luck lives in your woods and mines and rivers, and not in your brains. But for all that, Americans may be the biggest, finest, and best people on the surface of the globe!" He started to cross his legs, winced at the still sore burned patch on his knee, and decided just to stretch out his legs in front of him. "Just you wait a hundred years and see how they'll behave when they've had the screw put on them and have forgotten a few of the patriarchal teachings of the late Mister George Washington. Wait till the Anglo-American-German-Jew . . . the man of the future . . . is properly equipped. He'll have just the least little kink in his hair now and again . . . he'll carry the English lungs above the Teuton feet that can walk forever. And he will have long, thin, bony Yankee hands with the big blue veins on the wrist, from one end of the earth to the other. He'll be the finest writer, poet, dramatist . . . especially dramatist . . . the world has ever seen. He'll be a musician and a painter, too. At present there is too much balcony and too little Romeo in the life-plays of his fellow citizens. Later on, when the proportion is adjusted and he sees the possibilities of his land, he'll produce things that will make the effete East stare. He'll also be a complex and highly composite administrator. There is nothing known to man that he will not be, and his country will sway the world with one foot just as a man tilts a see-saw plank."

Kipling paused to puff on his cigar, and Thorne said: "I believe you've gotten a little carried away."

"I sincerely believe what I say," Kipling continued. "The potential to be a great people is there. Sixty million people, chiefly of English instincts, trained from youth to believe that nothing is impossible. They won't slink through the centuries like Russian peasantry. They are bound to leave their mark somewhere . . . and don't you forget it." He got up and stretched, then flipped his half-smoked cigar over the railing into the river. "Too bad we won't live to see it. A hundred years from now India and America will be worth observing. At present, the one is burned out while the other is just stoking up."

The July sun reflected off the sheen of river and Thorne was sweating in the humidity. "Let's go see what they've cooked up for lunch." It was clear that Kipling was not going to give him anything specific. Although the writer could be very reticent at times, he also liked to hear himself expound on all things American, and many of his monologues were too general for Thorne to get a grip on. Thorne preferred the concrete to the hypothetical.

Kipling continued to make observations and notes about everything and everyone he saw on the boat. He engaged strangers in conversation and spent considerable time in his cabin writing up notes and composing letters to his newspaper in India. The letters would be posted in Louisville.

At half past nine that night, a thunderstorm rolled up from the west. Lightning revealed thunderheads in the distance. Then wind began to blow and the rain came slashing down, sweeping across the boat. The pilot had taken the precaution of running in and tying up for the night at a landing on the Illinois side of the river at dusk when he saw the storm approaching. Darkness and high winds were not conducive to safe piloting.

If Kipling was nervous on trains, Thorne was that way aboard steamboats. He reflected that his life was, to a great degree, dependent on mechanical things. If he hadn't been able to clean enough of the grit out of his Remington surreptitiously, while distracting Ann Gilcrease with conversation, he and Kipling likely would have been dead and buried by now. While he undressed for bed, he wondered about his old nemesis. Was she lying dead in the underbrush on that island or on the Illinois shore, being eaten by buzzards and coyotes? He hoped not. Any human — even a mortal enemy — deserved a better fate than that. Kipling had marveled at the accuracy of the shot that had struck her gun hand. Thorne hadn't let on it'd been strictly luck. Once the hammer had been freed up so it could be drawn back to full cock, he had only one chance. Thank God the barrel wasn't plugged. If he'd missed, he would not have gotten off another shot. She had missed him with the small pocket pistol when she first came out of the woods. He should not have been so eager and rash as to go running toward the sound of the harmonica. The music had been bait for the trap. But he couldn't have known that. Always before, the music had come just before or just after some deliberate accident. It had never been used as a lure. If each event had not played out exactly as it had, the outcome could have been very different.

Neither he nor Kipling had let on to anyone in Hannibal that his being mired in quicksand was anything but an accident. From the comments of the three warehouse workers who'd rescued him, this was not an uncommon occurrence on the river. Although they'd spent the next two days sightseeing in the town, they'd seen no trace of Ann Gilcrease. They questioned the man at the waterfront they'd rented their boat from. Had he seen anything of a middle-aged woman who might have rented a boat or hired a river man to take her across to the island?

"Nope. But a fisherman I know . . . Harold Wilkins is his name . . . told me he rented his spare skiff to a woman the other day, and he ain't seen hide nor skirt of her since."

"Really?"

"Yeah. Said she paid him good for the rent, but she took off with his boat. My guess is she upset and drowned. Old women don't have no business out on that river alone. His boat'll turn up snagged on sumpin' a few miles downriver. Her body will never be found."

Thorne slid into his upper bunk and pulled the sheet to his waist. He was tired and the rain beating down outside would make for good sleeping. When he closed his eyes, Kipling was still sitting by the light of the coal-oil lamp, writing in his journal.

Probably because Ann Gilcrease was the last thing on his mind before he went to sleep, he dreamed about her. He was mired in the heavy quicksand, sinking deeper and deeper while she aimed her pistol at him and fired shot after shot, just nicking the tops of his ears. Kipling tried to run to his rescue, but couldn't move. Thorne felt his legs being squeezed by the sand and mud, cutting off circulation. He cried out for help.

Suddenly he awoke to find his right foot jammed between the mattress and the sideboard of the bunk. He freed himself and sat up. The light was still on.

"Are you all right?" Kipling asked, lamplight reflecting from his glasses. "You yelled out in your sleep."

"Just a bad dream. I was stuck in that sinkhole again." He took a deep breath to clear his head of the vision.

"Once was quite enough of that," Kipling said, turning back to his writing.

"What time is it, anyway?"

Kipling pulled his watch from a vest pocket. "Eleven-forty."

Thorne had been asleep only an hour. The rain still played a long, steady drum roll on the roof and deck outside. The air had cooled, and no mosquitoes penetrated the louvered door into the cabin. He wanted to put his mind on something else before going back to sleep. "I don't know about you, but I think Ann Gilcrease did us a favor."

"How's that?"

"It relieved my mind when she told us why she and Blixter are after you."

"I thought it might be something like that." Kipling nodded. "The two of them have been sneaky and devious. But they were only following orders of my enemy in India. Americans acting on their own are more straight up. If someone from this country had wanted me dead, he would have just walked up and shot me . . . no stealth, no subterfuge, no trying to

220

make it look like an accident. That's the way Americans settle their disputes. That's one of the things I admire about them, although I don't agree with everyone going armed and settling the most trifling differences with deadly weapons, instead of words or fists."

"Do you know this man who wants you so bad?"

"I met him once at a reception given in his honor. We don't travel in the same circles. He's very rich and very powerful."

"So I gather, if he could reach halfway around the world and pay that kind of money just to have you permanently silenced. What did you do to incur that kind of wrath?"

"He comes from a very wealthy family who own manufacturing plants, not only in India, but in other parts of the world. Having no need to work for a living, he dabbles in politics. Satisfies his need for adulation. But he has a vile temper . . . cannot stand the slightest criticism. I wrote a series of articles for my paper and exposed him as a fraud, embezzler, and low-down cheat. He was publicly disgraced and dismissed from the high government post he held. Only by his family's influence was he able to avoid a prison term. He privately threatened he'd get me, but I ignored him. Idle threats."

"Evidently not so idle."

"That was the main reason my paper sent me off on a world tour . . . to get me out of India and defuse the tension." He smiled. "I couldn't have planned it any better . . . a free trip and all I had to do was report my impressions of what I saw."

"Looks like you're paying a high price for this 'free' trip."

"If you mean these few cuts and bruises and burns, they're nothing."

"The trip isn't over. Have you given any thought to cutting your tour short and leaving the country? You could go straight on down to New Orleans and get a ship."

"I've come this far, and enjoyed myself immensely. Why should I quit now?"

"Maybe so you'll live to be twenty-five," Thorne said, sitting up and dangling his legs over the edge of the bunk.

"If he can reach me here, he can reach me anywhere." Kipling shrugged. "I'll write an exposé of this. Even without solid proof I could take to court, maybe it would be enough to put the law onto him again. Or his relatives might do something to squash his homicidal tendencies. He's ruining their family name."

"An exposé might have the opposite effect . . . you might so enrage him he'll send someone after you at your newspaper."

"And maybe we'll have another New Madrid earthquake tonight that will wreck this boat and kill us. I'm a fatalist when it comes to 'what might happen'."

Next day the *Lilly B.* nosed up to the long St. Louis waterfront to discharge and load passengers and freight. An urchin hawking the *St. Louis Chronicle* along the cobblestone landing caught Thorne's ear, and he bought a copy, then rocked back in a shaded deck chair to read. Most of the news was probably bad, but scanning the paper would distract his mind from the steamy heat that smothered the waterfront.

Buried on page ten was a one-column item that caused the front legs of the tilted chair to come crashing to the deck. His heart began to beat faster as he read:

INJURED WOMAN
PLUCKED FROM RIVER,
DISAPPEARS

His eyes flicked down the lines of print, quickly picking out the essentials of the story. A woman, calling herself Ann Davis, had been rescued, bleeding and unconscious, from a drifting skiff four days earlier by the crew of a downbound riverboat. Suffering from a severely lacerated hand, she refused any but the most basic treatment until she could get to St. Louis where, she stated, a relative was waiting to help her. She told the captain of the *J. P. Slade* she had accidentally cut herself while on a picnic. Suspicious of her story, and suspecting foul play, Captain John Anderson attempted to detain her until he could send a telegram to Hannibal to see if the constable there knew anything about her or about a missing skiff.

But she eluded the *J. P. Slade*'s purser and vanished ashore in our city. At present, nothing further is known of her real story,

the article concluded.

223

"Damn!" Thorne breathed. "Of all the fantastic luck! She has powers of survival that border on the supernatural." He rose on unsteady legs to go wake Kipling from his nap.

When they docked at Louisville two days later, their first order of business was to find a gunsmith.

"Ah, an old model number two," the gunsmith said, turning the weapon over and holding it to the light of his shop window. "Fancy. Mostly carried by women and gamblers."

"I'm the latter," Kipling muttered just loud enough for Thorne to hear.

"I never throw anything away," the gunsmith continued. "I'm sure I have a set of ivory grips back here somewhere that'll fit this."

It was only a matter of five minutes before the grips were found, cleaned, and installed. "Haven't seen one of these for a while," the smith said, carefully testing the action. He opened the gun and removed the cylinder, cleaned the chambers, ran an oily patch down the barrel, lubricated the mechanism, and tested it. "Seems to be in perfect shape."

"You got any Thirty-Two rimfire cartridges for it?" Thorne asked.

"Sure. How many?"

"Two boxes should be enough."

Kipling paid the gunsmith, and they left to find a hotel.

After their steamer trunks were installed in a hotel two blocks from the waterfront, Thorne asked: "Can I trust you not to get killed while I make a short visit to my sister and her family?"

"Now that I'm carrying a pistol, I feel like an American. I can deal with anything."

"Just don't get cocky," Thorne said. "She lives thirty miles south of here on a farm. I'll just be gone overnight."

"I'll manage to stay alive that long."

"I'd invite you along, but you'd be bored with us talking family stuff. Sorry to say, you're not yet famous enough so they've heard of you."

"I may take my new gun out in the countryside and get familiar with it."

"I'll meet you back here around six tomorrow evening, then," Thorne said, picking up his small grip.

Thirty-six hours later, the two men were eating breakfast aboard a boat bound upriver to Cincinnati.

"I'm becoming more American every day," Kipling said, setting down his coffee cup.

"Oh?"

"The hotel clerk directed me to an isolated place on the riverbank a few miles from town and I rented a buggy, went out there, and did some shooting. I can't quite hit a gnat's eyebrow at twenty paces, but I found out I have a natural talent for shooting. And this little pistol doesn't have enough recoil to bother me. Even in one practice session, I've become a fairly decent pistol shot."

"Good. Add that to your list of accomplishments. Now I can depend on you to help protect yourself if we run into Blixter."

"Then you think he hasn't given up."

"If he's gone to all this trouble for a five thousand dollar advance, why wouldn't he want to finish the job for another five thousand?"

"We have that information only from the mouth of Ann Gilcrease. Is the truth in her?"

"That's the question of the summer," Thorne replied, taking a bite of bacon and toast.

He noticed Kipling squirming and scratching his legs. "What's the matter? Those wool pants itching? It's midsummer in mid-America. You need some lighter clothes."

"You're right. I'll go change. Anybody who can stand the summers in India, shouldn't be bothered by the heat here. But it feels like heat rash."

Thirty minutes later, Kipling slid off his trousers in their stateroom. "Oh, Lord, look at this!" he wailed. The insides of his legs, from ankles to thighs, were a mass of red welts. "I never saw prickly heat like this. It's up around my waist and even on my scrotum. The itch is maddening. I feel like I could take a wire brush to it."

Thorne looked at the hundreds of tiny red dots that blended into one magnificent rash. "Did you wade through any tall grass yesterday?"

"Yes. And, early in the day, it was wet with dew. I got soaked walking back and forth to set up my targets of bottles and cans on a log by the river."

Thorne nodded, grinning. "To have missed this is to have missed one of the most exquisite tortures America has to offer. It's an experience never to be forgotten. You, my friend, have a classic case of chiggers!"

CHAPTER
SIXTEEN

"That'll be four bits for the shave and haircut and a dollar for the lotion," the Cincinnati barber said, shaking out the drape as Kipling climbed down from the chair.

Kipling paid the bald, mustachioed man, adding a twenty-cent tip.

"If that stuff don't do the trick, I'll give your money back," the barber added, pointing at the small, square bottle containing a thick, dark liquid. The label read: *Twitchell-Champlin Co. Portland, Maine* on one side. On the other, molded into the glass, were the words: *Neuralgic Anodyne.*

"Just what the hell are chiggers, anyway?" Kipling asked, scratching his thigh. "In Kentucky, I ate Southern grits, and I acquired Southern chiggers. I prefer the former."

"I'm very familiar with those little critters," the barber said. "Sometimes called red bugs. Damn' near need a strong magnifying glass to even see 'em." He turned and rang open the cash register drawer and deposited the money. "Chiggers are the larva of mites . . . bloodsuckers who chew on humans for lunch." He

228

grinned under the handlebar mustache. "If no humans are handy, they go for animals."

"Worse than the parasites in Africa," Kipling said.

"I've read chiggers are in Africa, too," Thorne volunteered.

"Western Americans are rapidly exterminating the buffalo," Kipling said. "What's taking them so long to make the chigger extinct?"

"No meat on a chigger," the barber said. "Kill the buffalo, you get rid of the Indians who depend on them."

Kipling pulled the cork and sniffed the bottle. "Whew! The devil's own mixture."

"Soothes the nerve endings," the barber assured him as the two men departed.

"How did the 'neuralgic anodyne' work?" Thorne asked as they rolled north across the Ohio countryside the next morning, bound for Chicago.

Kipling looked up from his notebook. "Made me forget the itch, all right. A legion of fallen angels couldn't have set me on fire like that did. Damn' near had to bathe in lotion to cool down. But, I'll have to admit, they're better today."

"Then I suppose it's fortunate we stopped in the Queen City of the West."

"The what?"

"That's what Cincinnati was called in earlier years."

"Now every burg west of the Mississippi has adopted the title."

Kipling had enjoyed their brief stay in the river town — the wagons rumbling up and down the hilly, brick-paved streets, the fine old buildings overlooking the broad Ohio River, the quaint taverns where they enjoyed good German beer and hearty sandwiches.

But the heat of summer had settled in, and Kipling thought a cooler climate near the Great Lakes would help the itch.

"I've spent a little time in Chicago, now and then, over the years," Thorne said. "Can't say it's one of my favorite places. I'm surprised you want to go there."

"Any traveler to America has to see that city," Kipling replied. "Good or bad, I need to experience it, record my impressions for the newspaper back home. It's not just my preferences . . . my readers need to know."

"Then I won't prejudice your view by giving my opinion."

After several more stops, the train reached Chicago just after dark that evening. The two men took a hack from the depot to the Palmer House in the heart of downtown.

Kipling looked around as they entered the hotel. "Do you think they're still following us? That woman was rescued by the riverboat."

"I think she's had enough," Thorne said, more hopeful than confident. "It's Blixter we need to look out for."

"Surely we're safe in a big city with crowds of people around," Kipling continued, as if trying to convince himself.

"We can't let our guard down anywhere," Thorne replied, thrusting the key into the lock of their hotel room.

Next day they hired a cab to take them on a tour of the city. Kipling said little as the cab driver pointed out the various sights with pride. Their cab blended into a stream of traffic passing over a canal bridge. The liquid beneath was black as ink.

"What abominations are in that water?" Kipling muttered under his breath.

"There are more than a million people in this city," the driver was saying, turning onto a street that was wide and flat and seemed to go on forever, strung with a tangle of overhead wires.

"Except for London, I've never seen so many white people together in one place," Kipling said.

The street was alive with signs and advertisements of every size and description, and it seemed to Thorne that each door had a vendor hawking his wares to the pedestrians on the sidewalk.

The writer turned to Thorne. "Every one of them must be howling . . . 'For the sake of money, employ or buy from me and me only!' "

Thorne nodded.

"It reminds me of famine-relief distribution in India, with men leaping up and stretching out their arms above the crowd in hopes of being seen, while the women slap the stomachs of their hungry children and whimper. I understand that and would rather see it than this scene of what white men call 'legitimate competition'."

The cab driver, oblivious to the Englishman's comments, was droning on about how many millions of dollars of certain goods were produced at a certain factory, and how many people were employed there, how this or that mansion was worth over a million dollars.

After two hours of this, they wearily directed their guide to return them to the Palmer House. The driver seemed disappointed the men were unimpressed by the statistics he had been quoting.

Their hotel was a bustling place as well, with people hurrying in and out on urgent business, clutching papers and telegrams. The two men escaped the mirrored and marbled lobby by wandering into the hotel bar. There, a big man wearing a watch chain across his massive girth, leaned unsteadily on the bar. He set down his empty glass and declared to them: "This Palmer House is the finest hotel in the finest city on God Almighty's earth!"

Before Kipling could make some caustic remark, Thorne hurried him past to a table where they ordered two beers, and Thorne thrust a copy of the *Chicago Tribune* into his hands to distract him. It was a mistake. All things Chicago grated on him.

For several minutes they drank their foamy mugs in silence while Kipling perused the newspaper. Finally he laid it aside. "It's a good thing I'm writing to an Indian audience," he said, signaling for another beer. "Otherwise, people in Britain would expect me to fall into ecstasies over the marvelous progress of Chicago since the days of the great fire, the raising of the entire city so many feet above the level of Lake Michigan, and generally grovel before the golden calf. But my readers, most of whom are desperately poor, don't judge themselves by these standards." He accepted and paid the bartender for the two mugs of beer. "This paper just reflects, in slang, what everyone here says and does, shows the level of intelligence of the Pullman car porter, and the accuracy of the excited fishwife. Am I to believe these newspapers educate the public?"

After weeks of hearing similar diatribes, Thorne was listening with only half an ear. Thank God they had only one more day in this city. To Thorne's disgust, Kipling wanted to see the famous stockyards and the slaughterhouses. "When the wind is right, you'll get all of the stockyards you want," Thorne assured him.

Suddenly he caught his breath. A woman with her arm in a sling and a bandaged hand had just walked past the open door. He sprang to his feet, sloshing beer out of their glasses, and sprang to the door. For several seconds he stared at the woman who was talking to the desk clerk. Then he exhaled a sigh of relief and turned back to the barroom. Even Ann Gilcrease could not have transformed herself into this very slight female who was less than five feet tall. He would have to get his nerves under better control.

"What was all that about?" Kipling asked.

"Thought I saw an old friend, but I was mistaken."

★   ★   ★

Thanks to the famous Chicago stockyards, Thorne had lost his appetite. By the time they settled into their Pullman the next night, bound for Cleveland and points east, he knew he wouldn't eat for another day and could easily lose the five extra pounds he'd put on since the beginning of their trip.

The two had gone first to the stockyards, about six miles from the city, to view the vast maze of pens, half filled with cattle. When they couldn't stay upwind, Thorne had held his breath as much as possible. Then they'd toured a slaughterhouse. Given his more than twenty years in the Secret Service, Thorne had seen his share of gruesome and bloody things and didn't consider himself particularly squeamish. But this was nearly too much for his sensibilities. The blurred images he was now trying to force from his memory consisted of masses of blood and flesh and offal, sweltering, stinking heat, the sight of dumb beasts being led to the killing floor in continuous streams. It was enough to make him become a vegetarian.

When they emerged into fresh air and rode a hack back to their hotel, he could hardly get the stench out of his nostrils and his clothes. Kipling rode beside him in the hack, quickly scribbling all the sordid details into his notebook before they escaped his memory.

Even now, many hours later as they pulled out of the city, the sunset streaking red through the dirty air behind them, Thorne wasn't hungry. He had eaten nothing all day and even felt queasy when Kipling suggested supper. For security, Thorne accompanied him to the dining car. To distract himself from the sickening smell of cooking food while Kipling ate, Thorne borrowed several newly written letters the writer had composed for transmittal to his paper. He picked up the hand-written sheets and leaned back in his chair. Under the swaying overhead lamps, he read:

> ... the great American nation ... very seldom attempts to put back anything that it has taken from Nature's shelves. It grabs all it can and moves on. But the moving-on is nearly finished and the grabbing must stop, and then the federal Government will have to establish a Woods and Forests Department the like of which was never seen in the world before. And all the people who have been accustomed to hack, mangle, and burn timber as they please will object, with shots and protestations, to this infringement of their rights. The nigger will breed bounteously, and he will have to be reckoned with; and the manufacturer will have to be contented with smaller profits, and he will have to be reckoned with; and the railways will no longer rule the countries through which they run, and they will have to be reckoned with. And nobody will approve of it in the least.
>
> Yes; it will be a spectacle for all the world to watch, this big, slashing colt of a nation that has got off with a flying start on a freshly littered course, being pulled back to the ruck by that very mutton-fisted jockey, Necessity. There will be excitement in America when they discover ... the rapidly diminishing bounty of Nature ...

Thorne lowered the sheets. "Amazing!" he breathed softly.

"What's that?" Kipling asked, looking up from cutting his steak.

"You seem to have the gift of prophecy when it comes to America's natural resources."

"A stranger's foresight, maybe . . . not prophecy. It takes no supernatural powers to see the water, timber, land, and all the rest of it are being used up as if there were no tomorrow. The same thing happened long ago in Europe and India. There are no trees left in Ireland, for example. It's one thing to be proud of one's country, but another to conserve its resources. See what I wrote on that next page there." He gestured with his fork.

Thorne shuffled the papers and read:

But the men and women set *us* an example in patriotism. They believe in their land and its future, and its honor, and its glory, and they are not ashamed to say so. From the largest to the least runs this same proud, passionate conviction to which I take off my hat and for which I love them. An average English householder seems to regard his country as an abstraction to supply him with policemen and fire-brigades. The cockney cad cannot understand what the word means . . .

"Ah, so you were serious when you said you love Americans in spite of all the nasty things you've had to write about them."

236

"I guess you could say it's a love-hate relationship, like some rocky courtships."

"I see." Thorne shuffled the pages together and replaced them in the folder on the table. This man was nothing if not brilliant and complex. An excellent observer and reporter. A little too opinionated, maybe. But he was young yet. With time, he would learn to excuse some of the foibles of his fellow man. He was cutting his way to fame, and it wouldn't be many years before the world would know him as a great writer of fiction — provided his powerful enemy in India did not get to him first.

"I'm taking this country in big gulps, five-hundred-mile jumps," Kipling said between bites. "Is there anything in Cleveland you want to see?"

Thorne shook his head. "I've been there, and can just as easily pass it by."

"Good. We've got our tickets through to Buffalo. Then it's on to Elmira."

"Elmira, New York?"

"Yes. I'm told Twain and his family spend the summers there at his sister-in-law's place where he's done most of his writing for the last twenty years."

"Is he expecting you?"

"No. But I'm sure he's beleaguered by strangers all the time for everything . . . from his autograph to free endorsements for cigars. I just want to catch him there, introduce myself, and at least shake his hand."

Two days later they detrained in Elmira, New York after dark, and took a hack to a rather run-down hotel near the center of town. Maybe if Blixter wasn't following too closely, he wouldn't look for them here.

"Clemens?" the clerk said in reply to their inquiry next morning. "Not sure where he is. He has a brother-in-law here he comes to visit this time of year."

"Sam Clemens is gone to Europe for the summer," declared a fat drummer, passing through the lobby when he heard their exchange.

"Oh, no!" Kipling cried. "I've missed him."

"Don't take that for gospel," the clerk said mildly as the drummer went out the front door, lugging his sample case. "Clemens has spent more than nineteen summers here, but to some of these Elmira folk, he's still a new arrival."

Thorne laughed. "Well, let's go chase him down."

Elmira was criss-crossed with railroad tracks. A town of 30,000, the clerk had said. Considerable manufacturing of door sashes and window frames. Surrounded by rolling hills and farms, it was a pleasant-looking place this summer morning, but in no way distinguished except for the possible presence of a world-famous author.

They walked toward the railroad depot, keeping an eye out for a hack. A blue-uniformed policeman, strolling his beat, offered the information that he'd seen Twain, or someone very much like him, driving a buggy the day before. "He lives out yonder at East Hill," the policeman continued. "Three miles from here."

Within a block they flagged down an empty hack. As they stepped in, Kipling remarked in awe: "Fancy living in a town where you could see the author of *Tom*

Sawyer jolting over the pavement in a buggy! He's got to be close by."

The hack went up a long hill, passing sunflowers blossoming by the roadside. Summer crops waved and cows grazed quietly in knee-deep clover.

"He's likely bedeviled by outsiders all the time to have fled up this hill for refuge," Thorne said.

The driver stopped at a little, white, wooden shanty to ask directions. A woman, seated in the yard, sketching the view of the Chemuny River far below said: "It's a pretty Gothic house on the left-hand side, a little farther on."

Shortly the driver pulled up to an ivy-covered house fronted by a shady porch. As they climbed down, a lady came out. "You're looking for Mister Clemens, I take it."

"Yes, ma'am," Thorne replied.

"Sorry to disappoint, but two days ago he returned to Hartford to take care of some business with his publisher."

Kipling looked suddenly deflated.

"If you go straight to his house there, you'll probably catch him. He's not due back here for a week."

They thanked her and had the driver return them to the hotel, then on to the depot. They caught the early afternoon train, and twenty-six hours later were in Hartford.

By the time they'd reached Hartford, stored their steamer trunks at the depot, and hired a hack to Mark Twain's home, it was mid-afternoon.

"Lord, would you look at that mansion!" Kipling marveled as they alighted and paid off the driver. They stood for a few moments and gazed at the size and shape of the huge structure — three-stories high with gables and cupolas; four, tall, ornate chimneys; outer walls of patterned red brick. It must have been very costly to build, even eighteen years before.

Then it was up the driveway and onto the porch. They rang the bell.

"Don't see anyone about. Reckon he's home?" Thorne said.

Footsteps sounded in the foyer and the door opened. Mark Twain stood looking at them expectantly from under bushy white brows. Since Kipling seemed to have lost his tongue, Thorne introduced himself as a retired Secret Service agent. Then: ". . . and I'm traveling with this gentleman . . . an excellent young English author, Rudyard Kipling. He's come all the way from India to meet you."

"I've always admired your work," Kipling blurted out. "Your writing has inspired my own."

Twain gripped the young man's hand, and said in a very calm, slow voice: "Well, you think you owe me something and you've come to tell me so. That's what I call squaring a debt handsomely. Rudyard Kipling . . . ? That name rings a bell. I believe my neighbor, Mister Warner, mentioned having read some of your work."

They shook hands all around. Thorne noted Twain's hands were slim and strong.

"Won't you come in?" Twain said, moving aside. "All the servants are gone since my family's in Elmira for

240

the summer," he said as they stepped into the dim coolness of the tile-paved entrance hall.

Twain's mane of white hair gave the initial impression that he was an old man. But the face and manner belied this. He was not yet fifty-five.

"You caught me at a good time," Twain said. "I was about to fix myself some tea, but, now that I have company, I have an excuse for a whiskey, instead. What can I get you?"

"Whiskey is fine," Kipling said.

"Same for me," Thorne echoed.

Twain disappeared into the dining room, and returned carrying a tray with a pitcher of water, a cut-glass decanter of whiskey, and three glasses. "It's a mighty warm day. Why don't we sit out on the porch," he suggested.

They followed him back outside where he set the tray on a tiny table in front of a padded armchair. Thorne and Kipling occupied two wicker chairs opposite the author, who draped himself across the armchair. He was dressed in a light, tropical suit and string tie, appearing comfortable in the sultry August afternoon. The heat was somewhat relieved by a steady breeze. It stirred the leaves of the tall sycamores near the house with a sound like rushing water.

"Sorry I don't have anything but branch water to cut this with," he said.

"That's just the way I like it," Kipling said.

"Good!" Twain said. "Cigar?" He proffered a humidor that stood on the table.

Kipling selected one, but Thorne declined with thanks.

Twain reached into his side coat pocket and pulled out a corncob pipe and began packing it from a worn, cloth pouch. He struck a stick match to Kipling's cigar, and then lit his own pipe.

"If you're an author, then you've had experience with copyright," Twain said, throwing a leg over the arm of the chair and puffing contentedly.

"It does me no good in this country, because the law doesn't cover me," Kipling said, his face darkening at the subject. "I've even seen pirated editions of my work in China. The worst offender in America is Seaside Publishing Company. You'd think if a man had any honor at all, he'd offer to pay for foreign works, even if they're not strictly obliged to by law."

Thorne hoped Kipling didn't mention Seaside's connection with hiring assassins to stalk him. This wasn't the time or the place for all that.

But Twain was off and running on the subject of copyright. "Copyright?" he said, raising his eyebrows. "Some men have morals, and some men have . . . other things. I presume a publisher is a man. He is not born . . . he is created . . . by circumstances. My publishers have morals. They pay me for the English productions of my books. When you hear men talking about my books and Bret Harte's works being pirated, ask them if they're sure of their facts. I think they'll find they're paid for.

"I remember a publisher . . . I think he's dead now, although I didn't kill him . . . who used to take short

242

stories of mine, one at a time, and made separate books of them. If I wrote an essay on dentistry or theology or any little thing of that kind . . . just an essay that long . . ." — he held up a thumb and forefinger to indicate a half inch — "any sort of essay . . . that publisher would amend and improve my essay. He would get another man to pad it or cut it, exactly as his needs required. Then he would publish a book called "Dentistry by Mark Twain", with that little essay and some other things added that were not mine. Theology would make another book, and so on. I don't consider that fair . . . in fact, it's an insult."

Kipling murmured his agreement and took a sip of whiskey.

"There is a great deal of nonsense talked about international copyright," Twain continued. "The proper way to treat a copyright is to make it exactly like real estate in every way. It will settle itself under these conditions. If Congress were to bring in a law that a man's life was not to extend over a hundred and sixty years, everyone would laugh. That law wouldn't concern anybody. The man would be out of the jurisdiction of the court. A term of years in copyright comes to exactly the same thing. No law can make a book live or cause it to die before the appointed time."

"I see what you mean," Kipling said, awed by this literary sage.

"A man, whether his name be William Shakespeare or Bill Smith, should have as complete control over his copyright as he would over his real estate. Let him gamble it away, drink it away, or give it to the church.

Let his heirs and assigns treat it in the same manner." He held the corncob pipe in one hand and casually stroked his square chin with the other. His eyes seemed to twinkle under the bushy brows. "Every now and again I go down to Washington, sitting on a board to drive that sort of view into Congress. I put the real estate view of the case before one of the senators. He said . . . 'Suppose a man has written a book that will live forever?' I said . . . 'Neither you nor I will ever live to see that man, but we'll assume it. What then?' He said . . . 'I want to protect the world against that man's heirs and assigns, working under your theory.' I said . . . 'You think that all the world has no commercial sense. The book that will live forever can't be artificially kept up at inflated prices. There will always be very expensive editions of it and cheap ones issuing side-by-side.'

"Take the case of Sir Walter Scott's novels," Twain said, jabbing the stem of his pipe at Kipling. "When the copyright notes protected them, I bought editions as expensive as I could afford, because I liked them. At the same time that very firm was selling editions that a cat might buy. They had their real estate and, not being fools, recognized that one portion of the plot could be worked as a gold mine, another as a vegetable garden, and another as a marble quarry. Do you see?"

"It boils down to the fact that a man should have as much right to the work of his brains as to the work of his hands," Kipling said, drawing on his cigar.

Thorne sat back in his chair, sipping his whiskey and enjoying the conversation amid the pleasant summer

244

breeze in the shade of the long porch. Many don't recognize a high point in their lives until it's past. At this moment, with these two men, Thorne knew he was in the presence of greatness. He could tell that Kipling, after worshipping his literary hero from afar, was not at all disillusioned by the actual flesh-and-blood author. The young writer hung on every sentence uttered in that long, slow surge of a drawl that Twain's climb to Hartford society had not erased. From Kipling's face, it was evident that the landing of a twelve-pound salmon was nothing compared to this.

The whiskey glasses were recharged and a dash of water added.

With a glance at Thorne, as if he were daring too much, Kipling asked: "Did Tom Sawyer ever marry Judge Thatcher's daughter, Becky? And are we ever going to hear of Tom Sawyer as a man?"

"I haven't decided," Twain replied, getting up and refilling his pipe as he paced slowly up and down the porch. "I have a notion of writing the sequel to *Tom Sawyer* in two ways. In one I would make him rise to great honor and go to Congress, and in the other I would hang him. Then the friends and enemies of the book could take their choice."

"Oh, don't do that!" Kipling cried. "Tom Sawyer is real, to me at least. And I suspect he's real to a few hundred thousand other folk as well."

"Oh, he *is* real," Twain said. "He's all the boy that I have known or recollect . . . but that would be a good way of ending the book." He turned from the porch railing to face Kipling. "Because when you come to think of it, neither religion, training, nor education avails anything against the force of circumstances that drive a man. Suppose we took the next four-and-twenty years of Tom Sawyer's life, and gave a little joggle to the circumstances that controlled him. He would, logically and according to the joggle, turn out a rip or an angel."

"Do you believe that, then?"

"I think so. Isn't it what you call Kismet?"

"Yes, but don't give him two joggles and show the result, because he isn't your property any more. He belongs to us," Kipling pleaded.

Twain laughed heartily, then came back and draped himself in the chair once more.

"A good deal of your *Life on the Mississippi* is autobiographical, isn't it?" Kipling asked.

"As near as it can be . . . when a man is writing a book about himself. But in genuine autobiography, I believe it is impossible for a man to tell the truth about himself, or to avoid impressing the reader with the truth about himself. It is not in human nature to write the truth about itself."

"Do you ever intend to write an autobiography?"

"If I do, it will be as others have done . . . to make myself out better than I am in every way. But I'll fail, like everyone else, because readers can read between the lines and get a general impression of the writer beyond the words, whether he intends it or not."

Then Twain expounded on his theory of training a conscience. "Your conscience is a nuisance," he stated flatly. "A conscience is like a child. If you pet it and play with it and let it have everything that it wants, it becomes spoiled and intrudes on all your amusements and most of your griefs. Treat your conscience as you would treat anything else. When it is rebellious, spank it . . . be severe with it, argue with it, prevent it from coming in to play with you at all hours, and you will secure a good conscience . . . that is to say, a properly trained one. A spoiled one simply destroys all the pleasure in life." He sat back with a satisfied look, and took a puff on his pipe. "I think I have reduced mine to order. At least, I haven't heard from it for some time. Perhaps I've killed it from over-severity. It's wrong to kill a child, but, in spite of all I have said, a conscience differs from a child in many ways. Perhaps it's best when it's dead."

Thorne could hardly suppress a grin at this dollop of tongue-in-cheek humor Twain was famous for in a hundred lecture halls. But a glance at Kipling told him the young man was swallowing all of it with equal gravity.

The conversation drifted to Twain's early life and his days as a boy growing up in Hannibal. He spoke of his parents with great respect and how they'd influenced him for good.

Whatever subject he was discussing, he spoke with his eyes as much as his voice and was constantly animated, up and down out of his chair, pacing, gesturing.

On books and writing, the two men spoke as author to author, the old lion and the young cub. At one point, Twain went inside and came back with a book to show Kipling. Shortly thereafter, Kipling read aloud from some notes he'd been taking on his trip, and Twain howled with delight at the biting sarcasm of Kipling's observations.

Before Thorne was even aware of it, the afternoon had waned and long shadows were stretching away from the trees in the yard. Kipling finally realized how late it was, and reluctantly tossed off the last swallow of his drink and ground out the butt of his cigar in an ashtray. "We've taken up way more of your time than any escaped lunatic from India has a right to do," he said, rising from his chair. "We'd best be going."

"If the cook were here, I'd invite you to supper," Twain said. "And I'm not much of a hand in the kitchen. Have you got a place to stay the night?"

"Not yet. We came directly here from the depot."

"Then you'll be my guests tonight!" Twain declared. "This house is used to many overnight guests, and it seems like an empty cavern with just myself here."

"We couldn't impose on your hospitality like that," Kipling demurred, although Thorne saw he could hardly contain his eagerness.

"Nonsense! I've got all these empty bedrooms. I'd love the chance to continue our conversation."

"Well . . ."

"We'd be happy to stay," Thorne interjected. "We'll just go into town and have some supper and let you get back to whatever work you were doing," Thorne said.

"Would half past seven be all right?" Kipling asked.

"Perfect. I'll be finished looking over a contract by then . . . along with a little pick and shovel work on some galleys."

* * *

Kipling and Thorne walked off the porch, down the driveway, and turned toward town several blocks away. By common consent they walked to enjoy the beautiful weather.

"I wish I'd had the nerve to ask for that cob pipe he was smoking," Kipling said. "A pipe like that, new, costs five cents, but that one would be gold to me. I understand why certain savage tribes desire the liver of brave men slain in combat. That pipe would have given me, perhaps, a hint of his keen insight into the souls of men." He heaved a great sigh. "But he never laid it aside within stealing reach."

Thorne laughed.

"Did you see him put his hand on my shoulder? It was an investiture of the Star of India, blue silk, trumpets and studded jewel, all complete. If somewhere down the years, I should chance to fall to ruin, I'll tell the superintendent of the workhouse that Mark Twain once put his hand on my shoulder. Then the superintendent will give me a room to myself and a double allowance of paupers' tobacco."

Twenty minutes later they wedged themselves into a crowded restaurant and snatched two places at a table that was just being vacated. Outside the front window the rush of homebound traffic streamed past — pedestrians, buggies, and loaded trolleys.

Before a waiter could even find them, a big man pushed out of the throng and sat down quickly at their table. They turned back from the window to find themselves staring into the face of Rudolph Blixter!

Thorne reached instinctively for the Remington on his hip.

"Don't do it," Blixter said quietly. "I have a Derringer pointed at your belly under the table."

Thorne pulled his hand away.

"Hands on the table where I can see 'em . . . both of you!" he snapped.

They complied. Thorne's heart was pounding.

"I think you've probably figured out what's going on by now, so I'll get right to the point."

"Ann Gilcrease told us," Thorne said, tight-lipped.

"That bitch took off and left me to finish the job myself," he snarled. "No matter. I'll go her one better. I have a proposition for you," he said, looking at Kipling who had gone pale under his sunburn. "Ann and I were promised ten thousand each to make your life miserable, and then kill you. So far, we've each been paid a five thousand advance, with the other half payable upon completion of the job. Apparently she's run off with her half. But here's the deal . . . you pay me the five thousand I was going to get for killing you, and I'll quit dogging you and disappear. You're a nice fella, as far as I can see," Blixter said. "And a lot of fun to fish with, even if I was playing that buffoon named California. I don't see any reason to kill you. I have nothing against you. It's strictly business. I work for pay. I don't care where the payment comes from. You pay me, I let you live . . . it's that simple. That way, I get my money, you get your life, and I won't take a chance of being caught and prosecuted for murder."

250

"What about your employer?" Thorne asked, getting his emotions under control.

"That's my worry," he snapped. "If Ann can get away with her advance without finishing the job, so can I."

Thorne swallowed hard, wondering if Kipling was going to buy this assassin off. Thorne had not pegged the small man as possessing a great amount of physical courage — but he was wrong.

"First of all," Kipling said, looking the big, reddish-haired man directly in the eyes, "if I had five thousand dollars . . . which I don't . . . I certainly wouldn't waste it buying off a fat, bald toad like you."

Blixter's ears began to redden with the insult.

"Secondly, if I pay you off, what's to prevent your killing me anyway, and collecting again from your boss?"

"You'll just have to trust me on that," the big man growled.

"I'd as soon trust that rattlesnake you threw into my Pullman."

"You could borrow the money or wire your paper for it," Blixter said in a last-ditch effort.

"Get out of here before I start shouting for help and dare you to shoot me in this crowd," Kipling said.

"That's your final word on the matter, then?" Blixter said, straightening up from hunching over the table. Thorne saw the flash of the tiny gun in his massive fist. "When you're gutshot, it'll be too late to change your mind," he said, pushing back his chair. "You'll never see another sunrise." Then he was up and gone quickly, fading into the crowd near the front door.

Thorne jumped to his feet and went after him, but the killer was out of sight before Thorne could force his way to the street. Just as well, he thought, going back inside. Blixter would never have submitted to arrest, and a gunfight in this crowd was out of the question.

"Come on," he said to Kipling. "I've lost my appetite. Let's get out of here and see if we can shake him before we go back to Twain's place . . . although I'm sure he already knows where we're headed."

CHAPTER
SEVENTEEN

Alex Thorne was angry and disgusted — mostly with himself. He took pride in his ability to keep a cool head and work under the most extreme conditions. He knew Rudolph Blixter was stalking them yet, somehow, had let his guard down since their clash with Ann Gilcrease — as if she posed the only threat. Nothing had happened since Hannibal, and, unconsciously, his vigil had relaxed. He'd actually begun to enjoy this trip, like some carefree tourist, instead of the professional lawman he considered himself to be.

As they returned to Mark Twain's mansion, Thorne felt sorrier for Kipling than for himself. Real or not, Blixter's threat could very well ruin Kipling's evening with his famous host.

Twain greeted them at the door in his shirt sleeves and vest. "Come in. Hope you had a good supper."

The two men exchanged glances, and Thorne said: "Well . . . we decided not to eat."

"I can't speak to the quality of the eating houses hereabouts," Twain said, noting their reluctance. "About the only time I eat out in Hartford is when I get invited to some formal dinner. And, of course, the fare is usually better then." He ushered them into the dining room. It was lighted by a gas chandelier. "Why don't you let me fix you a sandwich? And I've got some good pale ale to wash them down." He started toward the kitchen door.

"We couldn't impose," Thorne said.

"No trouble a-tall. I have all the fixin's laid out to make myself a liverwurst and cheese on rye. Or, I can slice some smoked ham."

Thorne's appetite was returning. "Thanks, that would be good."

"Make mine liverwurst," Kipling said.

The long summer evening was fading from dusk to darkness when they carried their sandwiches and beer into the library off the dining room.

"Livy doesn't like me to eat in the library, especially when the maid isn't home to clean up after me. But, hell, we're here alone and it's my house . . ."

Each man took an upholstered chair, Twain choosing a low, padded rocker. They balanced the plates on their laps and set their beer bottles on the bare floor. The polished hardwood floor was partially covered with an Oriental rug. Chest-high bookshelves stood against every wall of the irregularly shaped room. A glassed-in conservatory, festooned with growing plants, jutted outward from the back of the library. It was a comfortable setting. Thorne could imagine how cozy it would be in the winter with the aroma of oak and hickory blazing in the fireplace and snow swirling down outside the windows. Samuel Clemens had come a long way from the poor river town he had mined for literary gold.

254

Kipling had evidently forgotten all about Blixter and his threats. The young writer was in his element, talking and laughing at Twain's humor.

"Personally I don't care for fiction and don't read novels," Twain was saying, "except when people plague me to know what I think of the latest book everyone is reading. But I read them for the grace and beauty of the style . . . not for the story. Some I liked and they amused me for a time. But what I prefer to read are facts and statistics of any kind. If they are only facts about raising radishes, they interest me. A little while ago, for instance, before you came in" — he pointed to an encyclopedia on one of the bookshelves — "I'd finished my work and was reading an article about mathematics. My own knowledge of math stops at twelve times twelve, but I enjoyed that article immensely. I didn't understand a word of it . . . but facts, or what a man believes to be facts, are always delightful. That mathematical fellow believed in his facts. So do I. Get your facts first and . . ." — his voice died away to a low drone — "then you can distort 'em as much as you please."

Kipling laughed. "Speaking of distorting the facts, some of the boys who are still at the *San Francisco Call* were telling me about your method of writing stories when you were a reporter there nearly a quarter century ago . . . how you'd procrastinate until the last minute, and then write a piece that had no relation to the facts, and had your editor pulling his hair. But you got the public clamoring for more."

255

Twain took a swallow of his beer, and smiled. "You can't believe everything you hear. I think my writing habits have changed a good deal since then. For example, I can do very little work here in Hartford. I go to my sister-in-law's place in Elmira, where you stopped on the way here. I stay there three months and work four or five hours a day in a study down the garden of that little house on the hill. Of course, I don't object to two or three interruptions. When a man is in the full swing of his work, these little things don't affect him.

"But eight or ten or twenty interruptions retard composition. And that's what happens here where I spend nine months of the year. I've long ago satisfied myself there's no hope of doing much work during those nine months. People come in and call. They call at all hours about everything in the world. One day, I started to keep a list of the interruptions. It began with a man who would see no one but me. He was an agent for photogravure reproductions of salon pictures. My books don't use them. After that, another man, who refused to see anyone but Mister Clemens, came to make me write to Washington about something. Then a third man came, then a fourth. By this time it was noon, and I'd grown tired of keeping the list. The fifth man sent up his card. It was Ben Koontz. Now here was someone I was glad to see . . . an old schoolmate of mine from Hannibal. I rushed downstairs to the front door and went to greet him with both hands extended in love and friendship. But it was a big, fat man who looked nothing like the Ben Koontz I remembered.

Turns out Ben had given his card to this traveling lightning-rod drummer."

"What happened then?" Kipling asked, leaning forward.

"I shut the door," Twain said simply. "I'd been bearded by a lightning-rod man in my own house."

As the men talked and ate, it grew completely dark outside the windows. Twain took their plates to the kitchen and opened three more beers. Kipling lit up a cigar while Thorne and Twain opted for pipefuls of aromatic tobacco.

Thorne sat with his back to one of the bookcases where he could see both windows and the conservatory. Gauzy white curtains were pulled back and tied to each side of the tall windows. There were no drapes that could be drawn. The sills of these windows were more than head-high above the ground outside, but a person could be watching them through the conservatory windows at that moment and still be screened from view by the leafy plants.

Blixter had vowed Kipling would not see another sunrise. Was it meant to paralyze the small man with fear, like a cobra mesmerizing a rodent? It didn't seem to be having that effect. Kipling was making the most of his time with Twain. Thorne was concerned about the two of them spending the night here. If Blixter was serious, he was probably watching the place right now and would bide his time until late, when the house was dark and quiet. Should they bring Twain into their confidence, or should the two of them make up some excuse to leave? Twain had seen the rough side of life during his time as a river pilot, then in the Nevada mining camps and San Francisco, so there was no reason to think he would be afraid of someone like Blixter. But Thorne couldn't take the chance on Twain being hurt or his beautiful home damaged. Indecision gnawed at him while the light conversation went on for another hour.

Finally Twain stood up and stretched. "I'm a mite older than you fellas, and it's been a long day." He laid his cold pipe aside and consulted his watch. "My bedroom's on the second floor. You should be comfortable in the guest bedroom right here, off the library. It even has a bathtub."

Thorne looked at Kipling. "Let's tell him."

Kipling nodded.

"Tell me what?" Twain looked from one to the other.

"Better sit down a minute." Then Thorne proceeded to relate the whole story, leaving out much of the detail.

Twain sat, entranced by the tale, his expressive eyes sparkling with excitement.

"So," Thorne concluded, "I think we'd best take our leave, in case he decides to strike tonight."

"What? Leave the protection of my house? I wouldn't hear of it. I'd never forgive myself if you went away from here and something bad happened to you. No, no. We'll just have to be ready." He thought for a moment. "I could put you upstairs in one of the other bedrooms. Then we'd probably have some warning if he broke in . . ." He stroked his chin, looking around the room.

Thorne stepped through the doorway into the guest room. "This room will be fine. Does that door lead out onto the porch?"

"Yes."

"Then there's a small window we might have to defend. If he came crashing through the conservatory, we'd hear the glass break. And with this door locked, he'd make noise enough to alert us if he picked the lock or tried to force the door."

"I see you're armed," Twain commented, gesturing at Thorne's holstered Remington.

Kipling silently pulled the .32 Smith & Wesson out of his side pocket.

"Ah, this will make three of us," Twain said. "Just a minute . . ." He went through the dining room, into the kitchen, and returned with a short-barreled revolver in his hand. "My cook keeps this in a drawer in case of burglars. Glad he left it here. It's a Thirty-Eight Colt . . . made right here in the Hartford factory," he added irrelevantly.

"I feel really bad about you getting involved in this," Thorne said.

"I haven't had this much adventure in years," Twain said. "You're the professional. Just tell me what you want me to do."

"I think you should go to your bed upstairs, and just keep your gun handy. We'll use this guest room. That way two floors will be covered. I'll try to be ready for anything. Hope those two beers don't make me so relaxed I'll get drowsy."

"I'll keep watch," Kipling said. "I'm not sleepy."

"It's urgent we both stay alert," Thorne said. He had dealt with men like Blixter before.

"I'll turn down the gas," Twain said. "If you need a light, there's a candle and matches on the nightstand."

"If you hear a commotion in the night, just crawl under your bed and keep your pistol with you," Thorne told Twain. "Don't come running down here to check on us."

"I can't be cowering in my own house if it's under attack," Twain said, but his eyes were aglow with merriment and excitement.

The men parted, and Twain drew down the gas until the frosted globes of the library chandelier were barely glowing.

Thorne and Kipling went into the dark bedroom. Thorne struck a match to the candle and set it on the wooden edge of the bathtub where it couldn't be seen from the window and the light wouldn't be in their eyes.

"I hope for everyone's sake he doesn't come tonight," Thorne said, checking his Remington. He made sure all six chambers were loaded. In a fast, furious, up-close fight, that's all he'd probably need or have time for, even though his belt loops were full of cartridges. He went to the window and pulled the curtain aside a few inches. "Blow out that candle."

Kipling complied. Thorne's night vision gradually returned and he could see the silvered grass and the black shadows sharply etched by a nearly full moon. A steady southwest wind was stirring the trees and bushes, so any unnatural movement would not be readily noticeable. "Wish I'd thought to ask Twain if his driver was at home." He looked across the open space of the back yard to the combination stable and house where Twain's Irish chauffeur lived with his wife and children. "I don't see any lights on. They either aren't home or they're in bed."

"Mister Twain told me they'd all gone on holiday to visit relatives while Twain and his family were in Elmira," Kipling said.

"Good." He dropped the curtain after scanning the yard. "Now all we can do is wait. Blixter has the advantage of knowing when. We have the advantage of knowing where . . . that is where in this huge house we are located. We could be in a third floor room and he wouldn't know it."

"Maybe we should be," Kipling said. "Then he'd have to go banging through a dark house and probably give us some warning."

Thorne shook his head. "If we were here alone, I'd agree with that, but we have one of the world's most beloved men to think about."

"You're right," Kipling said. He stretched out on the big bed, fully clothed. Through the windowpane the moonlight glinted dully on the nickel-plated Smith & Wesson resting across his buttoned vest. "If you were in Blixter's place, what would you do?" Kipling asked, breaking the silence.

"I'd wait outside the house behind a bush or tree, maybe with a rifle, and put a bullet in you as soon as you showed your head outside in the morning."

"Then he'd take a chance on being seen and heard by the neighbors. Harriet Beecher Stowe lives right across the yard behind this house. And, of course, Blixter would have no idea if I meant to exit by any one of several doors in this house, or if I would come out at six in the morning or wait until ten. The whole idea is for him to get me and get away. He'd have a much better chance in the dark."

"You're absolutely right. If he comes, he'll have to come in the dark, then make his escape to the depot, or on horseback, before anyone discovers what's happened here."

Thorne heard a shuffling and slid out his Remington, noticing the gas lights slightly brighter in the adjoining library.

"It's just me," came Twain's familiar voice. "Don't shoot."

"Whew! You scared me," Thorne said, holstering his weapon.

Twain came padding in, wearing his slippers and robe. "I couldn't sleep. Thought I'd make us a nightcap . . . a pot of coffee." He smiled.

"Good," Kipling said. "I could use some."

"Need some help?"

"No. I can manage." Twain headed through the formal dining room toward the kitchen.

Thorne let out a deep breath. He was wound tighter than a watch spring.

The three men sat in the dim bedroom and drank coffee by candlelight, conversing quietly. Thorne's ears were tuned to hear the slightest sound from outside in the windy, moonlit darkness. The thrashing of the leafy branches against the side of the house might have disguised any furtive sounds.

Finally, when the distant mantel clock struck two, Twain said good night for a second time, leaving the pot of coffee on the night stand. "Yell if you need me," he said, lifting his hand from the pocket of his robe to show the .38 Colt. He again dimmed the gas chandelier as he left the library.

The two men stretched out on the big bed, side-by-side, on top of the quilt.

Thorne thought he'd banished all thought of sleep, but suddenly opened his eyes. The candle was guttering. He had slept without knowing it. Kipling's regular breathing told him the writer was asleep.

Thorne got up, pulled the curtain aside, and looked out. The moon was at a different angle, but still silvered the wide yard. Everything looked tranquil. The wind had died down, but a light, steady breeze was still blowing. He started to drop the edge of the curtain and turn away when a slight movement caught his eye. He strained to see. There — at the corner of the stable — the well-trimmed bushes moved. It was not the wind. Several large pines with low-hanging limbs stood between the house and the stable, perfect cover for anyone approaching from the back. He was startled by the musical chiming of a mantel clock in another room. It struck four.

He looked again. Maybe he'd imagined it. Could it have been a stray dog or some nocturnal animal? There it was again, an unnatural movement of the lower limbs on that pine. Being careful not to wake Kipling, he sat down on the edge of the bed and tugged off his boots. Then, Remington in hand, he stole softly in his stockinged feet into the library and through the dining room toward the parlor and the front hall. He hoped there was an inside latch on the front door. If he could get outside through the front door into the black shadows of the porch, he could head off anyone who might be stealing up on the back of the house. If he were mistaken, no harm done. He'd crouch in the darkness and keep watch until dawn, only an hour or so away.

Moonlight filtered from the upstairs windows onto the polished banister of the front hall stairs. He turned toward the front door — and let out a yelp! Blixter stood, not a dozen feet away, eyes glaring in the moonlight. The assassin's pistol came up. Thorne desperately threw himself to the left, rolling on the tile floor, his gun arm out in front of him as he thumbed back the hammer. Both weapons roared simultaneously. *BOOM! BOOM! BOOM!* Yellow tongues of flame lashed out in the darkness as a furious cannonade reverberated off the walls of the entrance hall and echoed through the house. He heard glass smash but felt no agony of slugs tearing into him.

With a yell, Blixter threw up his hands, eyes staring in the wreathing powder smoke. Then he slumped back against the newel post. Thorne scrambled to his feet, firing point-blank at the blur of white shirt. The big man fell forward onto the tile floor, and Thorne saw blood between Blixter's shoulders. Thorne's nostrils stung from the smell of spent powder. His ears were ringing.

He was suddenly aware that Mark Twain was standing on the landing above, the .38 in his hand. Powder smoke curled from the barrel in a shaft of moonlight.

"Damn! He was in the house!" Thorne said, trying to catch his breath. "How . . . ?"

"I left the front door open in case he might try it," Twain said, coming down the steps. "I got him in the back just as both of you let go. I think you hit him in the front, too," he added, rolling the man over with his foot.

Thorne was suddenly aware of Kipling, standing at his elbow.

"I was awake," Twain continued, "watching from an upstairs window in the billiard room. Saw him moving toward the house, and figured he'd try the doors first. I was just coming down the stairs when he entered the foyer. Then he saw you and all hell broke loose."

Twain turned up the gaslight, and the fixture atop the newel post lit up the entrance hall.

"He didn't have a chance," Kipling said, looking down at the florid face that was beginning to pale. The shirt front was a mass of blood.

"Boys, I've got to sit down. My knees are shaking," Twain said, moving unsteadily toward the bottom stairs.

Thorne felt almost giddy with relief and the shock that was beginning to set in. "I'm afraid we've splintered some of your woodwork and put some holes in that patterned Tiffany ceiling," he said. "I'll pay to get it fixed."

"Like hell you will!" Twain said. "You've just made this house the biggest tourist attraction in Connecticut. I'll have to charge admission to keep the crowds down."

Thorne holstered his Remington and put a hand on Kipling's shoulder as the young writer stared, wide-eyed, at the bloody corpse on the tile floor. "It's over. You can finish your trip in peace."

"I think I need a drink," Kipling said, taking a deep breath.

"We'd better contact the police before we move that body," Thorne said.

"There's likely a desk sergeant on duty all night," Twain said. "If that damned telephone contraption is working, we can ring him up." He got to his feet and slipped the Colt into the pocket of his robe. He wavered a little as he walked widely around the body to the telephone on the wall near the front door. "While I'm doing this, get us three glasses. The decanter is on the sideboard in there."

CHAPTER
EIGHTEEN

"I'll treasure this!" Kipling said, holding up the worn corncob pipe.

"Just a little memento of your visit," Twain said. "Wish I could give you something better than a used pipe."

"You did . . . an inscribed copy of *The Adventures of Tom Sawyer*."

Kipling was like a schoolboy who'd just won a spelling bee.

They were interrupted by the *clanging* of a locomotive that braked near them in a hiss of steam.

It was a week later and all the formal legalities had been cleared up. Blixter's body had been claimed by his sister and a former wife in California. They had him buried in Hartford.

The police had taken sworn statements from the three witnesses, and the trio had testified at the inquest. The shooting was ruled a justifiable homicide.

News of the shooting in Mark Twain's home had caused a sensation. "I suppose I'll have to write up my version of this for the newspapers, and send a story to Howells at *Harper's Weekly*," Twain said. "Otherwise, I'll have no end of folks wanting to hear the tale from my own lips . . . and I might be tempted to distort the facts a little in my favor. All this excitement will follow me back to Elmira, and I won't get any work done for the rest of the summer." His eyes twinkled under the bushy brows.

A standing reward of $1,000 for Blixter had been paid by the Pinkerton Detective Agency to Thorne. The "blood money" had been angrily refused by Blixter's sister and former wife, so Thorne and Kipling split it. Twain refused any payment. "No amount of money could equal what you did for my reputation," he'd declared. "Jesse James is the most notorious gunman from Missouri. I'm second."

"Well, I can't say it's been a dull summer," Thorne remarked, gripping Kipling's hand. "Enjoy your trip to Pennsylvania, and then back to England. Next time I see you, maybe we'll have a more peaceful time together . . . without having to look over our shoulders."

"I'll never enjoy harmonica music again," Kipling said with a rueful smile. He turned to Twain. "I'll send you a collection of my stories when I get home. And it won't be a pirated edition."

"I'd like nothing better!" Twain declared. "We'll meet again. You can bet on it!"

EPILOGUE

The year following Kipling's visit, Mark Twain read Kipling's book, *Plain Tales from the Hills*. Charles Dudley Warner, Twain's neighbor and sometime collaborator, predicted Kipling would become famous.

In 1892 Kipling married an American woman he had met in England, and they moved to her home state of Vermont where they lived for four years while he continued to enhance his fame as an author. Twain was in Europe most of this time, but visited Kipling on return trips in April, 1893 and January, 1894. Twain became a great admirer of Kipling's work and often read his stories aloud to his own family. He mentioned Kipling several times in his book, *Following the Equator*, the account of his lecture tour around the globe that included numerous stops in India. Despite a thirty-year age difference, the two men became good friends and remained so the rest of their lives.

In 1907, Kipling won the Nobel Prize for Literature. That year, both Twain and Kipling were awarded honorary degrees from Oxford at the same ceremony. In a newspaper photo of the ceremonial procession, Kipling, walking just behind Twain, is looking at his watch as if he were in a hurry. It was typical of the high-strung, quick-witted, gregarious man who suffered from stomach trouble much of his life. He died of a bleeding ulcer in 1936 in London, almost twenty-six years after his good friend, Mark Twain, had succumbed to heart disease at his home in Redding, Connecticut.

Kipling did make a West-to-East journey across America in 1889. His Indian newspaper had sent him on the world trip to get him away from the trouble he'd caused by writing several disparaging articles, lampooning high government officials in India. No one stalked him or tried to kill him. He visited Twain in Elmira, New York, not in Hartford. And Twain was not actually involved in a shoot-out. However, in September, 1908, two burglars broke into Stormfield, his last home in Redding, Connecticut. They were driven off by Twain's butler who fired shots at them. The sheriff arrested the burglars a short time later. Twain was delighted with the excitement and even posed for a photograph, aiming the butler's gun. He said he was going to buy a couple of bulldogs, and hoped the burglars would call again.

Kipling's letters to his newspaper were collected into a book two years after his trip. When Americans read it, they were outraged at what he'd said about them. Editorials appeared calling him, among other things, "that impudent runt", and indicating he had little regard for the truth.

I've used his collected letters extensively in writing this novel and have transferred many of his written comments to verbal ones in my story, condensing and rearranging others for clarity and brevity. Also, much of Mark Twain's dialogue is used just as Kipling recorded it.

In this book, I've tried to capture the flavor of a brash, young, well-read Rudyard Kipling, who was seeing America for the first time at a period when the Western frontier was coming to a close.

Of Kipling, Twain once said: "Between us, we cover all knowledge. He knows all that can be known, and I know the rest."

About the Author

Tim Champlin, born John Michael Champlin in Fargo, North Dakota, was graduated from Middle Tennessee State University and earned a Master's degree from Peabody College in Nashville, Tennessee. Beginning his career as an author of the Western story with *Summer of the Sioux* in 1982, the American West represents for him "a huge, ever-changing block of space and time in which an individual had more freedom than the average person has today. For those brave, and sometimes desperate souls who ventured West looking for a better life, it must have been an exciting time to be alive." Champlin has achieved a notable stature in being able to capture that time in complex, often exciting, and historically accurate fictional narratives. He is the author of two series of Western novels, one concerned with Matt Tierney who comes of age in *Summer of the Sioux* and who begins his professional career as a reporter for the Chicago *Times-Herald* covering an expeditionary force venturing into the Big Horn country and the Yellowstone, and one with Jay McGraw, a callow youth who is plunged into outlawry at the beginning of *Colt Lightning*. There are six books in the Matt Tierney series and with *Deadly Season* a fifth featuring Jay McGraw. In *The Last Campaign*, Champlin provides a compelling narrative of Gerónimo's last days as a renegade leader.

Swift Thunder is an exciting and compelling story of the Pony Express. *Wayfaring Strangers* is an extraordinary story of the California Gold Rush. In all of Champlin's stories there are always unconventional plot ingredients, striking historical details, vivid characterizations of the multitude of ethnic and cultural diversity found on the frontier, and narratives rich and original and surprising. His exuberant tapestries include lumber schooners sailing the West Coast, early-day wet-plate photography, daredevils who thrill crowds with gas balloons and the first parachutes, Tong wars in San Francisco's Chinatown, Basque sheepherders, and the *Penitentes* of the Southwest, and are always highly entertaining. He also wrote *Territorial Rough Rider*.